Journey to the Dark Tower

Morgan and Merlin's Excellent Adventures: Book Two

By
MALORY

MALORY

CONTENTS

This one's for Lucy

CHAPTER 1 - IN WHICH JOHN MCTIERNAN PRETTY MUCH GETS A WRITING CREDIT

They'd lost Cutha this morning. And Fordræd the night before.

Well, not 'lost' exactly. They knew precisely where those two were. Or where their bodies were, anyway.

Most of the bits, certainly.

But Hroðulf was not going to panic. If there was one thing he'd learned over the last few days, it was that the ones who lost their heads in this sort of situation were those who ... lost their heads.

He raised a fist, and the remaining members of the war party took a weary knee. They'd been running flat out for some time now, and the woods were starting to take on a certain lovely, dark and deep quality. Discovering that Cutha had become the latest of them to fall prey to the demonic hunter they were all calling the 'hidden decapitator' had made them all lose their minds a touch.

It was time, Hroðulf thought, to bring back an element of decorum to proceedings.

"That must be far enough. Let's take a beat. Keep an eye on the trees but get some water down you. Wemba, my old friend, it's time to make yourself useful. Do you have any idea where we are?"

The slow, fat man stared blankly back at him before shaking his shaggy head. There was a time when they all joked about their rotund tracker's complete and utter uselessness, but somehow, those jokes didn't quite seem so funny anymore. "This ain't a part of the world I've been to before, boss. Your guess is as good as mine."

Hroðulf privately suspected he had a far better notion of where they were than Wemba, but – in the interest of the war band's morale – chose not to share that view. Instead, he blew out his cheeks and tried his hardest to devise a plan, any plan, that ended with them getting back, preferably alive, to Saxon territory.

He wasn't entirely sure when he'd assumed command of this little band of miscreants who had been left behind after the debacle at the walls of Tintagel. Needs must and all that. Although was it truly 'command' when all that meant was you were the one who got to yell 'run!' each time something grim happened to one or other of them?

"Okay, mate. No drama. Don't worry about it. We've been turned around a few times, so it's not your fault." Several of the others grumbled that a tracker who couldn't track probably shouldn't have his full ration of ale that night, but Hroðulf hushed that sort of talk down fast. The only way out of this mess was to ensure they sang from the same scroll. Besides, the fat man provided substantial cover should the situation demand it. "Look, this fucking country isn't that big, guys. We should easily be able to figure out the way home from here."

Several pairs of sceptical eyes regarded him. He guessed all the violent deaths of their fellows were putting a few doubts in the men's minds. "Look, if no one has any better ideas," there was an echoing silence, "well, then I say we just keep following the river northward and see where that takes us."

"That's the best you got? Follow the fucking river?"

Hroðulf was not interested in any of Carlet's backchat. "Look, fuck-face, Tintagel was by the sea, wasn't it? So, it stands to reason that we can just go upstream and this little beauty will take us all the way back home. Basic geography, innit? And, if we're lucky, we might link up with some of the others on the way. And Belion is your mother's brother."

Ten pairs of eyes stared deadly back at him. He was finding it all a touch dispiriting. "Come on, guys. We've been in tighter spots than this and come out the other side!"

His words sounded hollow even to himself.

He understood it wasn't just the fear of impending death that was grinding them down. It wasn't even the constant running battles with an unseen foe. And, surprising as it might seem, it wasn't even the succession of headless corpses that awaited them each morning.

No, it was the unnecessarily flippant commentary about their impending, bloody demises from the woods, which was getting so deeply under their skins.

As if on cue, there was a low rumble from their extreme left, and that fucking voice that had been tormenting them for five days was heard again. "There's something out here waiting for you, and it ain't no man. You're all gonna die."

At that sound, Hroðulf's men threw their javelins wildly into the undergrowth. He did his best to bring them back under control, but it was already too late. "Stop it, you morons! We're nearly out of those. Hold on to them until you actually see something worth attacking!"

There was a pause, and then one of the javelins was returned to them. With some significant interest. It took Beorhtric in the pit of his stomach and rocketed him backwards, pinning him to a tree like the world's ugliest butterfly exhibit.

Hroðulf didn't know what caused him the most despair—the loss of yet another of his men or the certainty of the subsequent quip from the woods.

When it came, he wondered if the speaker was wholly insane or just profoundly sadistic.

"Stick around."

***

Bors pulled a stray javelin from my thigh and winced at the spurt of blood that shot into the air. "You're sure you can heal through that? It looks nasty."

"I ain't got time to bleed."

I sense you are doing a 'bit' here, my dear. Speaking for Sir Bors, I am happy to say we're both finding it extremely charming, especially all the accents. Well done on those, particularly. However, and I do hesitate to bring it up when we're all having such fun, do you think we could hurry things up a touch? This is not the only war band King Uther has charged us with putting down, and we need to move our way through the list with a touch more alacrity.

I quickly cycled some Qi to my wound and was pleased when my femoral artery reknitted in seconds. I wasn't going to let on in my present company, but I was a bit unnerved by how close that one random throw had been to doing me some severe damage.

After all, if it bleeds, they can kill it.

It had been over a month now since Uther reluctantly sanctioned some of us to take to the countryside and harry the remnants of the Saxon army who hadn't taken the hint from the debagging in front of Tintagel's walls to speedily run for home.

Initially, his instinct had been to keep what remained of Arthur's Marghekyon close to Tintagel. Still, there were increasing reports of some pretty gnarly shit going down with the local population, so he'd let some of us loose to reign it in.

We'd been tracking this particular group for just under a week since stumbling across the aftermath of their activities at a smoking farmhouse.

It was fair to say that, having done my best to heal a couple of newly orphaned girls, I was not feeling especially charitable towards them. Indeed, if, after all they had done, the worst these men had to complain about was my attempt at an Austrian accent, I figured they were getting away pretty lightly.

But Merlin was right. The longer I indulged in Predator cosplay with this sorry group of Saxons, the more time the rest of the fuckers lingering around Dumnonia had to create yet more traumatised kids.

***

Seeing the grim expression cross Morgan's face, Bors hefted his giant axe onto his shoulder and nodded to Peredur to begin gearing up to move out. "Let's finish this."

***

The absurdity of just three attackers was the first thing to strike Hroðulf. Of course, as the next thing was a massive axe to the chest, he didn't have too long to mither about it.

Priorities, you see.

***

Bors tore through the lefthand side of the Saxons, each swing lopping off heads and limbs as he went. Peredur's sword work was far more elegant but no less deadly. In seconds, the war band was pretty much done.

That just left little old me.

The thing was, since Tintagel, I'd been feeling a little left out when it came to mixing it up in the melee. After much discussion, Drynwyn had agreed to stay back at Tintagel and keep trying to woo Arthur to pick him up again.

I make that sound less like I'd finally given up arguing with my enchanted sword and his obsession with fangirling over the Once and Future King than was the case. There was the slightest chance my epic bloodletting on these missions was more about me salving my wounded pride at feeling rejected by a piece of metal than anything the Saxons had gotten up to.

But that would be batshit crazy. Wouldn't it?

Anyhow . . .

As well as the sword clearly preferring Arthur's manly embrace, Merlin had pointed out that I'd become a little too reliant on the sword's ability to rain flaming

9

napalm death on all and sundry. Apparently, I needed to work on developing my Qi offensive capabilities.

Also, despite the amusing linguistic flexibility of the word 'fuck', it does get a touch old.

Besides Drynwyn's backstabbing, I recognised that Merlin was making a valid, broader point. The techniques I'd picked up thus far had been a touch random, and while [Personal Space Invader] had come through clutch more than once, both [Can of Whoopass] and [We want our Ent-Wives back] were pretty situational.

And weird.

Creating those three skills had been easy, but conceptualising new ones was much more challenging.

I did explain, my dear. You were bound to hit a reasonably brutal progression wall at some stage. Your development towards **Harry** *thus far has been astonishing.*

"I know. I know. I just feel I've clicked up to Pro in Fifa and been slaughtered by Accrington Stanley." There was a pause. "Merlin, mate, I need you to say, 'Accrington Stanley, who are they?'"

Why? I know who they are.

"It's for a joke."

We're in the middle of a battle, my dear. Why don't we focus on the matter at hand?

So, ignoring the cries of the slaughter occurring all around me, I focused on one particularly fat Saxon and considered the possibilities I had to bring his life to a screaming halt.

To be honest, I was pretty happy with my options in close combat. It wasn't long ago that I'd ripped the head off a dragon with [Can of Whoopass], and I'd yet to come across a swordfight Drynwyn couldn't handle for me: when he wasn't trying to wheedle his way into the Pendragon's grip, anyway.

I felt, though, that I was obviously lacking a touch of oomph when the enemy was at a longer range. That javelin through the leg was still bothering me some. It'd be nice to have something to reciprocate. "Any thoughts, Big M?"

Many. Would you like to be specific?

"I'm looking for a ranged attack that doesn't suck. Just once in a while, it would be nice to take care of business without needing a shower and a change of clothes afterwards."

Certainly.

My vision was suddenly overwhelmed by a flickering screen of ranged Qi techniques. They were blasting past so quickly that I could not understand what they did, much less how they worked.

"Mate, that's too many. You're going to need to thin things out for me a little. Can't you, I don't know, pre-select me some suitable options?"

I am unsure at what stage I became your personal shopper in our relationship.

"Ah, you love it."

I can assure you I do not. Not so long ago, I could command the heavens to obey my will. Now

...

"Now you're getting to play Yoda. So, please, do you think there should be less whining and more of a menu of cool ranged attack techniques? Chop, chop. There's a good force ghost mentor."

The flickering screen slowed down until there were just three options.

"That's more like it. So, what do we have here?"

Oh, so I have to explain them to you too, do I? Please let me know if breathing becomes too much of an imposition. I'll be sure to pick up the slack. The first of these choices relies on your connection to Drynwyn and familiarity with Fire Qi. It's a basic fireball casting that won't tax your channels too much but will -

"Nope. Not interested in anything basic. Next?"

Again, I should stress that there are noticeable gaps in your foundation, and your desire to constantly skip over the fundamentals because they're not 'fun' is likely to have significant long-term consequences for your development as a cultivator. I know of no cultivators who successfully achieved **Harry** *who did not have at least one fireball spell.*

"Sure, Jan. Next shiny, please."

There then followed a lot of sighing for someone with no body. *The second option is more complex, but you have sufficient affinity to Earth Qi to use it. This technique allows you to open a giant fissure in the ground to ...*

"Nope."

Nope?

"Nope."

Is there any particular reason, or are you being deliberately cussed now?

"It's hard enough being a girl in this cultivation business without inviting comment as to how many men my crack can swallow up."

I ... I don't know how to respond to that.

"Come on, third time's the charm."

Okay. Well, the third option is the most complex casting of the three. As of yet, you have not been able to make much connection with Metal Qi. However, I can see no reason you would eventually be unable to do so. Thus, should you master this technique, you will be able to use ambient iron as projectiles.

"Sold."

As I say, my dear, I cannot imagine you will easily be able to manifest this technique. Perhaps it would be better to . . .

His words were drowned out as the discarded swords and spears of the fallen Saxons rose into the air and spun themselves into a cyclone. The speed at which this technique burned through my Qi was quite astonishing, and I had to tap into the stored energy in my mana stone earrings to be able to maintain it. As soon as the hurricane of metal stabilised, I directed it towards the fat Saxon.

Well.

"Yes."

That was pretty conclusive.

"Indeed."

Apparently, you can access Metal Qi after all.

"Seems that way."

Subtle.

"That's my middle name."

"Fuck me, Celt. What did you do?" Bors had been standing too close to the impact zone of my technique and was now wiping pieces of diced Saxon off his face.

"Oh, you know. Just a cultivator doing cultivator things."

With a sense of crushing inevitability, can I please request you refrain from yet another pithy title for this spell?

"Too late."

[Get to da Choppa] technique named.

Sigh. Of course.

CHAPTER 2 - IN WHICH DO I HEAR THE WORDS 'REDEMPTION ARC' ...

Quickly checking there was no one about, Arthur rested his forehead against the cold, stone wall of Tintagel's keep.

The sensation eased the crushing weight of his headache for a moment, but only for a few seconds, and then it came crashing back down.

With interest.

And it was not just his head.

Everything hurt.

Since his return from that disastrous excursion to Isca Dumnoniorum, he had done his best to keep up a brave front. He was Prince Arthur, after all: the life and soul of every party and the hero that would unite his people beneath the strength of his sword and the justice of his rule.

After Isca and the slaughter of his Marghekyon, it was doubly important that he was seen not to have changed. Everyone knew the story of his appalling burns and subsequent wonderous healing at the hands of the new Court Mage. It was a great tavern tale - it should be, he's paid enough to that fucking bard - but no one wanted to be reminded of how close Briton had come to disaster should he have succumbed to his injuries.

While everyone made jokes about his hair, which had resolutely refused to grow back, it was clear that was as far as what had happened was ever to be discussed again.

From the kingdom's perspective, for sure Prince Arthur had suffered a reversal. But it was a minor one, and it would not do to be too worried about it. To sell that vision, everyone needed to see him back to his carousing, whoring, and fighting self.

But everything hurt.

And it didn't seem that anyone cared.

No, that was not entirely fair. Arthur sensed Morgan would be open to discussing things further. She'd been there for all of it, after all. If anyone could understand why he felt . . . changed by the experience, it was the red-haired Celt.

But she was out with Bors, wasn't she? Doing the sort of work his father made abundantly and repeatedly clear should have been his duty. He'd even suited up to lead a raid or two to show his willingness. But the very idea of initiating that sort of slaughter again . . .

He felt vomit surge up his throat and sucked it down as the door ahead of him opened, and a servant poked her head out.

Arthur plastered on his most lascivious expression and moved to push past her. "Please excuse me for my haste, kind lady. If I hadn't been summoned with all speed by the King, I sense you may have a place where I may sheath my longsword."

The servant blushed and dipped her head, opening the door to let him past. He deliberately brushed against her as he went through, even though the slightest touch made his skin burst into agony.

"Arthur, leave the girl alone."

His father, Uther, stood by the flickering hearth, his face thunderous. The Prince was unsure he had seen any other expression from that quarter for years.

If he had hoped that his near-death experience would bring them closer, he had been crushingly disappointed. If anything, Uther's demands on his son had increased in the days and weeks following the siege of Tintagel. Never had the fragility of the kingdom of Dumnonia been made more apparent, and therefore, the strength of those who ruled it needed to be underlined - in fire and blood - to anyone who watched.

Messengers had been sent the length and breadth of the British border to ensure that those allies that owed their fealty to the Pendragon were kept in line.

Uther had just returned from visiting one of the petty kingdoms whose reply to that message had been less than full-throated support.

Some nice new ornaments were on spikes above Tintagel's battlements.

Sensing this would be another one of their more testing encounters, Arthur took a settling breath and raised his chin defiantly.

"If you will keep all these buxom lovelies hanging around, Father, what's a red-blooded Knight to do?"

Uther's scowl deepened. It was approaching being at the soul level at this stage. "How fares the Princess Guinevere?"

"Oh, you know. Still a colossal bitch. Sorry, I forgot. You actually do know, don't you? Didn't you choose certain death on the battlefield rather than attempting to bed her yourself?"

Uther flushed, biting back an angry retort.

The truth was, Arthur knew exactly why his father needed to see him.

It had been decades since there had been any suggestion that the King of Dumnonia might not be the *de facto* ruler of the Britons. An awful lot of blood had flowed under the bridge to make that so, and the suggestion—post Isca and the arrival of a Saxon army at the gates of his own castle—that this may need to be re-examined had taken him by surprise.

Almost as much as how tired he had felt leading an army in the field. Nothing brought home to you how many years had passed when you nearly caught a peasant's pitchfork in your throat.

An uneasy silence settled between them. Arthur was damned if he was going to be the one to break it. His father was the one who'd requested this bloody audience, after all.

"The Saxon retreat was a respite, not a victory," Uther's voice was like far-off thunder, quiet but threatening more storms. "Your timely arrival with the wizard turned the tide, but their strength remains poised to strike again."

"You're welcome, by the way."

"I'm welcome?"

"For the save."

Uther crashed his hands into the stoneware above the fire. "This is not a game! The Saxons were here! We were fighting them on the bridge. Do you understand how close we came to being wiped out?"

"I was at Isca, father. I have some conception."

"But you weren't, were you? You were fucking a farmer's daughter while our people burned."

Uther regretted the words as soon as he said them. But that was no matter. It was as if he saw fresh wounds open on his son's soul, and yet the Prince did nothing to fight back. That was the thing that worried Uther most about his son. The spark seemed to have left his eyes.

"Was there anything else, father?"

Arthur moved to leave, but Uther grasped his arm. "Without an heir, Arthur, this respite means nothing. They will come again, and we need Leodegrance's spears."

The weight of his father's oft-repeated words hung around Arthur's neck like a millstone, and he nearly staggered. Did Uther not think he knew all this? The importance of lineage, of securing a future for the kingdom, was all he'd thought about since he'd been healed.

"The Princess has her own mind on the matter," Arthur said quietly, the raw edge of near-death softening his voice. "And, as you know as well as I, her will is not toward motherhood."

Uther's stare hardened, and he struggled to keep his anger under control. "We do not have time for her to find her feminine instincts, boy. Even now, I hear reports of boats filled with Saxons arriving from over the sea. Just weeks after driving them from our walls, their numbers replenish. There is talk - not just low murmuring but open discussion - that a new Pendragon may need to be chosen in order to secure the British line. Money flows across the borders of Cardigan, of Powys, of Deheubarth, and I can see no other reason, but they are preparing to challenge for my throne. We are approaching disaster because your wife's womb lies barren. Do not leave us in such a situation again."

"Was there anything else? It's just I feel we've explored every version of the 'go and fuck your wife' conversation a father and his son can realistically hold. It's becoming a touch weird."

The King's jaw worked as if he sought to grind the impudence of his son's response out of existence. They both knew they were pushing the boundaries of their relationship too far. That was all either of them seemed able to do lately, yet the gravity of the situation would not let either of them back down.

Arthur wondered how it would be if he shared the reality of his minute-by-minute agony with Uther. Would that make a difference to the bitter war they now fought? The saddest thing was he knew it would.

He just couldn't bring himself to say it.

Fathers and their sons.

After what felt like forever, Uther broke the silence, his voice a low growl. "Get out of here and do your duty, Prince Arthur."

Well, he guessed that was that.

With the finality of closing time, Arthur turned on his heel and strode from the room, the heavy wooden door slamming shut behind him. He moved with such alacrity that he almost forgot to wink at the girl who waited for him in the corridor. Almost, but not quite.

He had an image to maintain, after all.

Outside, the air was crisp, the cold biting at his cheeks, a stark contrast to the stifling atmosphere of the throne room. Each step took him further away from the King's presence, yet the weight of his father's expectation clung to him like a drowning man.

As he walked, he clenched and unclenched his fists, the phantom pain of his burns flaring with each movement. Phantom pain. Ha, the banality of those words almost made him smile.

Britain needed an heir. That fact was as accurate as it ever was, yet the thought of Guinevere, with her cool indifference and sharp tongue, made the prospect of his bed chamber as appealing as a draught of poison.

A glass of which he'd found himself contemplating in the dark hours of late.

He suddenly stopped and threw back his head, roaring to the sky. "Fuck!"

The healing that had sealed his wounds had not dulled the memory of the fire that had ravaged his body.

The desolation that had threatened to consume his spirit had as powerful a hold on him now as it ever had. Arthur remembered the look of sheer terror in his men's eyes as they had witnessed his agony. He was the Once and Future King. This sort of thing happened to other people. Morgan's timely intervention had saved his life, and for that, Arthur was begrudgingly thankful. But the healing had left him changed, not just in his resolutely bald head, but in his soul.

He stopped at the edge of the training grounds, where the rhythmic clang of iron rang out. With the death of so many of his Marghekyon, the call had gone out for anyone who sought revenge for the predations of the Saxons. So far, they had yet to unearth anyone of the calibre of those lost, but he knew Bors lived in hope.

At least one of them did.

Arthur had once found solace in the simple clarity of swordplay, in the honest exertion of physical combat. Now, he felt no enthusiasm for such things.

If I'd known you were going to be this much of a fucking sad sack, I'd have gone hunting with the girl.

The Prince did not know why he'd taken to strapping Drynwyn to his back. He'd relinquished Wynebgwrthucher to the armoury, much to the shield's chagrin, so he couldn't quite explain why he'd decided to retain the sword that was the cause of his pain.

Or maybe that was why.

Trust me as one who has spent significant time around a fucking masochist. You ain't that. If you want my opinion—

"I really don't."

Well, that's a fucking shame, ain't it? Because you're getting it. As far as I can see, you're good at two things. Fucking and fighting. And I haven't seen you do either since the Saxons ran for it. Why's Morgan out there with Bors tearing them a new one? Seems like the sort of thing the Prince of the Britons should be fucking taking the lead on.

Arthur ignored the sword. Sometimes, that was the only way to deal with the truth.

He could blame his pain. He could say his father had forbidden him from leaving Tintagel. He could even say that the prospect of facing Guinevere, of enduring her sharp words, cut more profoundly than any physical agony could.

And maybe it was all of those.

But the truth was he just did not want to do any of it anymore.

Arthur's eyes drifted to the battlements, the flags above snapping in the wind. Each banner stood for a house, a family, a lineage - all bound together under his father's rule. He knew he was letting them all down.

With a sigh that seemed to carry the weight of his burdens, Arthur turned from the training grounds and made his way to the relative solitude of the stables. The calm, quiet sanctuary offered a reprieve from the clamour of the world outside.

Here, in the dim light filtering through the windows, with just Llamrei's solid presence for the company, Arthur could hear the whisper of his own thoughts. He sank onto the floor, the straw familiar beneath his fingers.

In the silence, Arthur allowed himself a moment of weakness; his head bowed not in prayer but in a search for clarity. How could he lead a kingdom when his life felt like a battlefield? How could he give an heir to the kingdom when that notion felt like an act of war?

He had to find a way through this, not just for Britain, but for himself.

Rhydrech always said, never meet your fucking heroes.

"I never wanted to be a hero. I never had any choice."

Well, boo, fucking, hoo. It must have been a fucking nightmare growing up with every door and shapely pair of legs falling opening for you. My metal heart bleeds.

"I wouldn't expect you to understand. No one does."

Fucking sad sack, the sword murmured.

And in that, Arthur felt the sword had it pretty much spot on.

CHAPTER 3 – IN WHICH MY UNBROKEN STREAK OF HETEROSEXUALITY IS CHALLENGED

"The King demands your presence,"

I'm going to be honest here, there are any number of five-word phrases you hope never to hear. "Have you gained weight recently?" is one. "I'm not angry, just disappointed," is one with which I'm intimately acquainted. "It's not me, it's you," is another that's come up over the years more than I might have been hoped.

However, I'm going to say that being summoned to meet the father of the mythical Prince you kind of burned to a crisp pretty much up there too.

"Dude, you don't have to look so happy about it."

Bors grinned back at me. "I've been telling you to get this over and done with for the best part of a month. It's not like he's going to have you executed or anything. You healed his son."

"After my sword barbecued him."

"Sure. And if you want some advice, don't lead with that. Might not set the right tone. Maybe run with the hundreds of Saxons you've been helping to mop up. Or do a magic trick. He always liked it when Merlin did that. Or, I don't know, show him your tits. Although, as I think Queen Igraine will be there too, maybe not."

I was following the big man down a corridor lined with elaborate tapestries. Most seemed to depict Uther slaying various foes in ingenious ways, but they did little to calm my growing nerves.

"It's alright for you, she's your mate. I've never got a good vibe from her ..."

Bors shrugged. "Don't let the icy, heinous bitch exterior fool you."

"You're saying she's really warm and cuddly underneath?"

"Goodness me, no. Inside, a rabid wolverine's scrabbling to get out. But as Mrs Bors will tell you, I'm a sucker for a strong woman."

"I can confirm, my dear, that Queen Igraine is not an especially easy person. It may serve you well not to mention me too much. We never really saw eye to eye. I think she - entirely unfairly - blames me for ruining her life." Merlin said.

I thought back to what I knew about the Queen from Arthurian mythology. "Didn't you help Uther catfish her?"

"If by 'catfish' you mean did I shapeshift Uther into the likeness of her actual husband so that Uther could impregnate her and then steal her away from their castle, then yes. Yes, I did that."

"I can see why she might hold some negative energy towards you. What happened to her husband?"

"I think we can take it as read that I don't come out of any part of that story too well and leave it there."

"You know, at times like this, I do wonder whether I'm on the side of the good guys."

"And then you think back to some of the atrocities you've just seen committed by the Saxons on innocent people and stop being such a fucking wet blanket?"

I'd kind of forgotten Bors could hear me.

"What he said."

We'd reached the outside of the throne room. "So, the advice I'm hearing about this audience is to not bring up Drynwyn's role in Arthur's injuries, to try not to anger Queen Karen and to avoid giving Uther an excuse to bend me over the banqueting table because, basically, as he's the king no one will bat an eyelid."

"Yeah. And if all else fails, whip your baps out. You know what? Don't know what we're mithering about. Sounds like you're all set."

***

Uther did not know what to make of his new Court Wizard.

Apparently, she was in constant communion with Merlin - not that he could mention that in Igraine's hearing. She was already not exactly on 'Team Morgan', and the final nail in the coffin would be letting that little snippet of information slip out.

Bors spoke highly of her capabilities in the field, and the gods knew - in the absence of his son stepping up - they needed every advantage they could gather to them there. He still was unclear on the details, but he knew she had been primarily responsible for the destruction of the giant bridge the Saxons had been preparing to use to storm Tintagel. But although she had healed his son of catastrophic injuries, most of the stories he'd been able to pin together suggested she'd been to blame for them in the first place ...

So, this Celt was a puzzle.

"I am unsure what to do with you, Morgan Le Fay."

"Story of my life."

"Your Highness," Igraine's voice could have frozen a jacuzzi.

"Ah, bless your heart, but there's no need for that. Morgan's fine."

Bors snorted out the mouthful of wine he had just sipped. This did little to improve the atmosphere.

Uther sighed and gestured for a servant to come forward and clean up the mess. He had hoped to get through this with some of his dignity intact. He appeared, once again, to be destined to be disappointed. "Queen Igraine means that the correct way to address the King and Queen of the Britons is 'Your Highness.'"

"Right. Sorry, Iggy. I'll remember in the future."

"My dear, are you actively trying to make this go as badly as possible? Or are you just, you know, being you?"

I pulled a ball of Qi to my hand and flicked it towards the goblet Bors had knocked over, trying to suppress his latest bout of sniggering. It caught it on the rim with a ding and righted it instantly.

The King and the Queen both started at my casual use of power.

"Look, let's cut to the chase. You want to know how the land lies, so here's the skinny. Following his murder, Merlin pulled me back from the future to try to keep the timeline intact and kill some Saxons. I've done my best so far - sorry about Isca, by the way - and I'll keep pitching in however I can. I have skin in the game, in the form of my sister, to try to keep the idea of Camelot alive. So, you know, I'm not lacking in motivation. From how Merlin tells it, though, I will soon be hitting the cultivation wall quite hard, so I need to spend some time working on that. But apart from that, I'm pretty much at your disposal. Oh, and sorry about frying your son."

Uther blinked at the torrent of information and then turned to the big knight. "Sir Bors, if you cannot control yourself, I would ask you to leave."

Bors wiped his streaming eyes. "Sorry, Your Highness. It won't happen again. But I did tell you she was a handful."

"So, you did. What I am trying to decide is if she is a useful handful. Or whether to throw her in a dungeon."

Bors leaned forward and stage-whispered. "Might well be tits time."

I glared at him and let my Qi leak through my skin. I felt people took me more seriously when they remembered I was a cultivator. "Look, I don't expect to be lavished with thanks, but I'm fairly sure if I hadn't arrived when I did, there'd be a blue-painted twat on your throne right now. So, how about we all put our dicks away, take a breath and start over?"

***

"I didn't think that went too bad, all things considered."

I think you would need to not consider quite a few things that have just occurred to believe that meeting went well, said Merlin.

"By the end, I think Uther quite liked me."

I think if we are using as our baseline whether he threw you into the deepest dungeon in Tintangel, then yes, he liked you.

"They're both worried."

I glanced up at Bors, who had followed us from the throne room.

"Worried?"

"About Arthur. He's not been the same since he returned."

"I told you, get him a hat he can wear at a jaunty angle, and he'll be as good as new."

Bors stopped and looked around. Seeing no eavesdroppers, he leant closer. The effect was of a mountain looming over me, and I instinctively stepped back. "It's one thing to push the Saxons out of our territory, it's quite another to secure the land from internal threats. There was already significant opposition to Arthur succeeding Uther, and that was before the invasion; it's only getting worse in the last few weeks." Having seen the nice new heads on stakes that Uther had brought home, I felt I could agree with that assessment.

Bors was on a roll. "The rumours about the delay in reaching Isca aren't pretty, and there are not that many of his friends left around to make them go away. I love the guy, but at the moment, he's his own worst enemy. People are saying he's lost his nerve, and to be honest, I'm not sure I disagree. But the more pressing issue is that the longer the realm goes without an heir, the louder those voices will become."

"I could be wrong, but are you trying to involve me in someone else's sex life? Because, as I've had to tell more partners than you'd hope, I'm a strictly one-in-one-out kind of girl."

Bless his heart, I think the big guy blushed. "No. Nothing like that. But the brutality of the invasion has left Uther's position weak. He's King because he's shown himself to be the biggest swinging cock in the land. People will fight for him against the Saxons because he's earned that right. But that was a long time ago, and most of the other British kingdoms now have someone new on their thrones since he came to power. In the normal run of things, this wouldn't be a problem. But right now,

19

enough voices are asking whether they are really up to bending the knee to an Arthur who doesn't seem to be ticking many liege lord boxes. He's the Party Prince that was getting his cock wet when Isca burned. With most of the Marghekyon slain, he's vulnerable in a way he hasn't been his whole life. Guinevere's father has promised the realm enough spears to make all those problems go away. But he won't send them until his daughter is pregnant."

"Again, I'm not sure where I come into this. Do you need me to invent the turkey baster?"

"You come into this because someone needs to help my husband."

I spun around at the new voice. "Princess Guinevere, I hope you are well?"

"As well as someone can be whose urine is tested every morning for traces of a new Pendragon."

I wasn't sure what the correct response to that would be.

"That sounds ... intrusive."

Guinevere turned her green eyes my way, and I was, once again, left wondering what Arthur was playing at.

I had a reasonably long, unbroken streak of heterosexuality behind me - Ibiza in the summers of 96, 97 and 98 didn't count - but if my mission in life were to get this woman pregnant, I'd be feeling pretty cheery about the hand dealt to me by fate.

She was tall. Not Bors tall, because that would be ridiculous, but my eyes were about level with her extremely present bosom. She had long, dark hair plaited to her waist in a thoroughly complex braid that clearly needed the attention of a dedicated team each morning. And she was athletic. Like, full-on Katee Sackoff athletic. And I'm talking her at her peak-Battlestar Galactica best, not sadly wearing a headband in some poor, sub-Star Wars schtick.

Basically, what I'm saying is that in a world where women appeared to be primarily cast in the role of soft, fleeing victims, this was a motherfucking bad Amazonian bitch.

I liked her. And I wanted her to like me.

"It is what it is. However, I am not here to speak to you about me."

"What is it I can do for you, Princess?"

Guinevere looked at me steadily for a few moments as if weighing up whether to continue. I don't know what she saw in my eyes that made up her mind, but she nodded to herself and took my hand.

Be still my beating heart.

"My husband is in pain. Not physical pain. I understand I have you to thank for healing that. But I can see something is dying behind his eyes. Regardless of everything else that has gone wrong between us, I cannot sit by and watch him waste away. From everything I understand, Britain needs Arthur. And I want to play my part in making that happen."

"I hear you. But without being rude, unless you need a fluff girl, I still don't know where I fit into this?"

"You fit in, wizard because I have a quest for you."

CHAPTER 4 - IN WHICH I GIVE A SPEECH OF SUCH CLASS AND SOPHISTICATION IT WOULD MAKE JANE AUSTEN WEEP

Far be it from me to criticise, my dear ...

"Mate, ninety-nine per cent of our time together has, basically, been me doing some stupid shit, and then you are going, *'Actually, my dear, that was spectacularly ill-advised.'* It's kind of like the bedrock of our entire relationship."

Did you just do an impression of me?

Reader, I did.

"Obviously, I'm only getting half of this extremely weird conversation," despite that, Bors still decided he had an opinion worthy of being shared. Oh, for the confidence of being a straight, white man, "but I have to agree with the part I can't hear. I am presuming that Merlin is telling you not to touch this steaming giant turd of a plan, even with someone else's shit shovel."

Well, that was a metaphor worth waiting for.

Having outlined the quest, she wished me to go on, the Princess Guinevere had left us about half an hour ago. We'd been discussing the pros and cons of her rather ambitious scheme ever since.

I say 'discussing', Bors and Merlin had spent most of that time ragging on her. To tell the truth, it was getting on my nerves. I was wondering if I could get away with calling her Xenia moving forward.

I am fucking loving her plan.

There're times when you want your squad to back you up on a scheme. And then there are times when it's not that helpful to have the most psychotic, least rational team member in your corner. I instinctively felt this might be an example of the latter.

Oh, pray tell, Drynwyn. What part of Guinevere's plan that has us smuggle her out of Tintagel, pretend she's been kidnapped by some fictional bad guy, and then encourage Arthur to join us on a lengthy quest to recover her from a foe who doesn't exist most pleases you? Apologies, I missed the vital context that the realm is at war, and there's a chance this sort of security breach might be remarked upon negatively.

I liked the bit when you fucking shut your mouth.

Stellar comeback. I can see why we should absolutely take your opinion on this situation seriously. Do you have any more words of wisdom? Merlin bit back.

I don't know. Is 'fuck you' wisdominy enough for you?

"Guys, let's all calm down. When you think about it, it's not actually that bad an idea. Arthur needs a win. Bors, you were just saying that his reputation has taken a knock. What better way of fixing that than an honest-to-goodness quest? You never know; it might even be the reset their relationship needs, and if Guinevere is happy to play damsel in distress to reboot things, I really don't see the problem. There's no real bad guy involved, so no harm, no foul. I can use the time to focus on my cultivation. Big wins all around."

"With all due respect, Morgan ..."

"Bors, mate. Nothing is more guaranteed to get my back up than some jacked-up gym bro giving me my 'due respect.' I cannot tell you how often I've heard it over the years. It's patronising, dude, and means, 'you're a fucking stupid little girl and here's why.' You get me?"

Bors was giving me the look of every door-to-door salesman who had ever risked ringing my bell. He knew he'd seriously fucked up. He just didn't know how badly yet.

You are missing the point here, my dear. The job of Princess Guinevere is not to run around the countryside playing hide-and-seek with her husband.

"And what is her 'job', Big M? What should this smart, capable, and eminently fuckable woman be doing with her time?"

No way is he walking into *that* beartrap ...

She should do everything she can to supply the realm with an heir.

Okay. So he is that fucking stupid. Been nice knowing you, Merlin.

"Oh, I'm sorry, Merlin. I hadn't realised that the only role women should play in your vision of the world is to be barefoot and pregnant. You should have mentioned it! Is there a particular dick I should be having in me right now? I didn't know I was breaking some sort of massive cultural taboo walking around with a completely empty vagina."

"What about you, big boy," I sashayed towards a clearly terrified Bors, "did you want a go? Apparently, it is some sort of massive red flag that I'm wandering around here with my legs closed. Apologies. Who knew?"

"No. You're alright." He could not have pressed himself firmer against the wall without merging with it.

My dear ...

"Will you stop with the paternalistic 'my dear' crap? My name is Morgan!"

Strictly speaking, it really is not. You chose that name when ...

Dear gods, for a smart guy, he really does not know when to shut the fuck up.

"It doesn't matter what I want to call myself, you colossal fuckwit! You don't get to override my chosen name with some cutesy, chauvinistic derivative crap. Why don't the two of you just admit it? If either of you had come up with this idea to break Arthur out of his bad mood, we'd already be halfway to Devon by now. It's only because the little woman came up with it herself that you're standing here taking the piss. And do you know what? As the only one of us who both a) has magical powers and b) is alive, I'm saying we're going to do exactly what she asks, and the rest of you can fuck off all the way back to Misogyny Town. Population, you."

"Apologies for interrupting, but you are being rather loud. Could anyone explain exactly what Princess Guinevere has asked you to do?"

I turned to look into the ice-blue eyes of Queen Igraine, who looked like she absolutely wanted to talk to the manager.

***

Igraine had led me to her private quarters - Bors was pathetically relieved to have been summarily dismissed - where she had me outline Guinevere's scheme. When I had finished, I looked at her expectantly. I really had no idea which way she was going to jump here.

"It's a terrible plan."

Hah!

"But that does not mean we should so easily discard it."

I may have taken this opportunity to indulge in an unnecessarily vigorous victory dance.

"Please do not do that in my presence again."

"Sorry, Your Highness."

"Although, can I just check? Did my siding with you displease a certain ex-cultivator?"

"Absolutely."

"Excellent. May I offer you some wine?"

***

Day drinking with the Queen of the Britons was a pretty intense experience. Every time I kind of thought I knew where I stood, I seemed to step on one taboo topic or another, and she ripped my head off.

I was loving it.

I felt like Sandy in Grease with Rizzo tearing me a new one every few scenes. If Igraine wasn't careful, I was going to Qi her up a pink jacket any moment.

Please don't use the phrase 'Qi her up' ever again.

I ignored him. I figured I was about eight bottles in, and while booze didn't seem to affect me in the same way as before, I was undoubtedly in the making-poor-life-choices-at-midnight-in-a-dark-nightclub territory.

"If this plan is to work, you must tell no one else. Not Uther. Not any other member of Arthur's Marghekyon. No-one. Bors is scared enough of me to stay quiet if I tell him to, so we do not have to worry there."

I figured I needed a slightly clearer head, so I pulsed some Qi into my liver. The effect was, disappointingly, almost instantaneous. "Do you really think we should do this? I know Bors and I have been clearing up most of the warbands still hanging around Tintagel, but from what I hear, there's no lack of Saxons out there. It was quite the effort to get back behind these walls relatively unscathed. Feels like we might be asking for trouble."

Igraine fixed me with an imperious expression. "I know the pressure upon Guinevere better than anyone else alive. I was, I suppose, lucky. I was with child the first time Uther rutted with me. But, for whatever reason, I have been unable to supply the realm with 'spares.' So, believe me, I understand her pain. And I understand the weight on Arthur's shoulders in the absence of anyone else to share or understand his burden. I have had to watch him destroy his marriage, with all the disastrous repercussions that it has for the realm. When we thought we had lost Arthur ... Let me just say that this was a bleak time for us all. Thus, I am heartened to hear that she understands that my son is hurting, and despite everything else, she seeks to find a way to remedy that. What would I not like about that?"

"Do you think we can pull it off?"

"Do I think that giving Arthur an urgent, important martial adventure to save his Princess will ... get his juices flowing? I would be very much surprised if it did not. For all his flaws, no one doubts his prowess in the field. This could well be the perfect task for him to regain his confidence."

23

I hesitate to put my head in the lion's jaws again, my dear, but can we please remember that the whole point of you being in this realm is to ensure nothing untoward happens to the timeline. Call me cynical, but it will probably be easier to achieve that if Arthur and Guinevere are not traipsing through Saxon-infested woods, rekindling their relationship."

The Queen obviously saw something on my face change when Merlin was speaking, as she took my hands and leant forward. "Is that old goat really in your head?"

I shrugged. "He is."

"How do you stand it?"

I smiled. "Oh, you know!"

Her expression darkened. "No. I don't know. That was why I asked."

Oh. Yes. Need to remember this is not a nice, old lady. "Apologies, Your Highness. Merlin knows things I need to understand better in order to save someone I love. He's kind of a dick most of the time, but he's also saved my life over and over again. I was only able to rescue Arthur because of him. I know he did you dirty, but I need his help. And he's good."

I think that is quite possibly the nicest thing you have ever said about me, my dear.

"Don't let it go to your head."

Igraine was nodding, as if in thought. "Okay. I can appreciate naked self-interest. But understand, nothing good has ever happened to me, or those I love, at the hands of Merlin. He has great power, and power can be infinitely seductive. But when push comes to shove . . .

"He will kill your friends and family to remind you of his love?"

"What?"

"Sorry. Don't know where that came from."

"Okay." Igraine stood and beckoned a servant who was either deaf or in possession of the single greatest poker face of all time. "I think we should ask the Princess to join us to discuss the matter further. We have quite a lot of planning to achieve before the morning."

"Merlin, I didn't hear you just describe us as the three witches under your breath, did I?"

Goodness, Morgan, as if I would ...

CHAPTER 5 - IN WHICH A TERRIBLE, TERRIBLE PLAN IS UNVEILED

"For clarity, just because I want to make sure I have this all straight in my own mind, let's run through this one last time. Do you mind? Oh, good, I'm so glad." As Uther was clearly ticking like the angriest alarm clock in all the world, I thought it wise to keep schtum.

"You are suggesting that sometime in the early morning, an unknown assailant somehow infiltrated the walls of Tintagel. This brave soul succeeded in avoiding the notice of any number of methods - both physical and magical - that I have paid a not-insignificant sum of gold to put in place to prevent just this type of nefarious activity."

I didn't say anything.

"It's probably worth flagging at this stage that Merlin was responsible for developing most of those protections so, goodness me, that is going to make it hard for us all to sleep soundly in our beds ever again, isn't it?"

I still didn't say anything.

"Whoever this spunky burglar was, they ignored my treasury. The armoury. They did not even, the gods forefend, attempt to assassinate me. Instead, having demonstrated themselves as being able to achieve a feat of startling stealth and ingenuity, they chose to break into the bed chamber of Princess Guinevere and seem to have stolen her away from the boundaries of the castle. In doing so, they took with them a not-inconsiderable portion of her wardrobe and any number of personal items that - and I do not possess to be an expert in such matters - might be considered non-essential in the cut-and-thrust of frenzied escape. But, as I say, I am not a kidnapper. What do I know of such things?"

On the plus side, my dear, while he is being sarcastic, it means he is not pulling off anyone's fingers. I saw him do that once. It can get pretty messy. And loud. But mostly messy.

"Not. The. Time." I hissed through gritted teeth. Fortunately, I think Uther was too busy enjoying his rant to notice.

"Oh, and let us not forget that, as if that was not enough, whilst executing this improbable task, they also took the time to write a very detailed ransom note, which helpfully included clear instructions as to how a motivated Prince with access to a number of skilful followers might be able to follow and recover his missing lady. If he was minded to and wanted to make an issue of said kidnapping." Uther's eyes slipped from me, to Igraine, to Bors and back again. "Have I summed everything up appropriately?"

After an awkward silence, I cleared my throat and offered: "Indeed, my Lord." To be honest, I was feeling pretty damn salty about ending up the spokesman for our little band of miscreants.

But here we are.

It's the fingers, my dear. Unfortunately, you're the only one who is likely to be able to regrow them if Uther gets all ... pully. This is the very definition of taking one for the team.

"Dude, I know you think you are being funny, but if you keep this up, even if it's my last act on this earth, I will exorcise you so hard Father Merrin himself will provide me with a fucking St Joseph medallion and ask for tips. Do you understand me!"

Indeed. Although...

"What?"

I think you're mixing up your Exorcist clergy. Merrin has the heart attack, Karras goes out the window when possessed, and Dyer ends up with the medallion.

"I know I say this a lot, Big M, but I want you to understand that I truly mean this from the very bottom of my heart. Fuck off. And keep fucking off. And when you think you can fuck off no further, I want you to reach down inside, find some hitherto unexplored mental resources, and then seek to fuck off a bit more."

Uther was glaring at me. "I'm so sorry to be interrupting you, mage. Would you like me to hang on for a minute whilst you finish chatting with your invisible friend? Or does Merlin have any words of wisdom for us that would be useful at this juncture?"

Nope. Not going anywhere near this one. You're on your own.

I put on my most winning smile. "He says he thinks you have this all completely in hand and just wanted to tell me that."

"Okay. Then I have just one remaining question, if I may?"

"Of course, my lord."

"Are you FUCKING kidding me!"

Even Bors took a step back at Uther's roar. "We're at war! We've barely scraped the last pieces of Saxon off Tintagel's lawn, and there are still hundreds of the buggers running amok the length and breadth of the country. Merlin's dead, Arthur's turned into some sort of soppy wet blanket, and he's still not managed to impregnate his bitch of a wife. I have only just returned from having to kick the arse of one of my so-called bannermen who was communicating with Bennoc of fucking Powys about changing his allegiance. And I doubt he is the only fucking one, just the one stupid enough to put it down on paper.

I went to bed thinking what a fucking shambles things were, but at least - I reasoned in my naivete - we were now probably at rock bottom. But no. Here you three clowns are, and - what do you know - you've turned up with fucking pickaxes and shovels."

"Do clowns traditionally use shovels?" I asked with what I now recognise was foolish, nay suicidal, abandonment.

"Do not try my patience, mage. The only reason you still have a head on your shoulders is that not even you - a woman who, in the space of a few days, burned my son three-quarters of the way to death, healed him, oversaw the massacre of the cream of the British force and then destroyed an entire Saxon army - would think this was a good idea.

No, for this type of genuinely fucked-up thinking, there's only one place I'm going to look."

"Can I just check? You don't mean me, do you?" Bors' voice was rather strained.

Uther ignored him. "Igraine. What the fuck have you done?"

I might have mentioned it, but I have, at times found Queen Igraine to be somewhat of a cold fish. However, in the face of Uther's white-hot fury, she was *magnificent.*

"Tantrum quite over, my dear?"

"Tantrum! How dare you -"

"Uther, I accept that it was probably unwise to have enacted this plan without running it by you first. This was an oversight, and we are willing to address that now. However, you are behaving exactly as you did when I told you I was no longer willing to wear that particular costume you were so keen on. And I should not have to remind you how that unfortunate episode was resolved."

There was an awkward silence that quite simply dwarfed all other awkward silences of which I have partaken. And I was once caught blowing my therapist. By his kid. In a Toys R Us.

Then, as if all the air was sucked out of Uther - again, like ... nope, too crude - he sat down heavily on his throne and ran his hands through his hair.

Igraine crossed over and patted him lightly on his head. "Now that you've got that off your chest, and we've all calmed down, why don't we talk about this like grown-ups?"

***

Just to catch you all up.

Late that previous evening, I'd fast-travelled Guinevere to the village of Beocca and Sæþrȳð. Remember them from the whole Knockers sub-quest?

Well, we'd - Igraine. This is all on Igraine. I'm absolutely not taking any more flak for this bollocks - figured this was far enough away that Arthur would seriously need to get his quest-groove on in order to save her properly, but not so far out of the that too much could go wrong.

Full disclosure, we were all perfectly aware of how much we'd just tempted fate as soon as I'd said it.

While packing her things, I'd tried to engage the Princess in some mild bantery of small talk, but after a couple of false starts, I realised, with a crushing sense of disappointment, that we probably wouldn't ever be gal-pals.

Of course, it might have been the whole 'cultivator' thing that meant she wanted to keep her distance. Or the 'being the wizard whose sword set my husband on fire' could have contributed to the slight chilliness in her behaviour towards me. Or, and let's be honest, this probably played a significant part, she just might not have been too keen on swapping sewing patterns while preparing to flee a castle in the middle of the night.

I'm trying not to take it personally, as I'm sure you can tell.

Her and Sæþrȳð, on the other hand? It was like they were long-lost friends who'd been unexpectedly reunited. Within minutes, they were walking, arm in arm, around the village, Sæþrȳð pointing out the - admittedly few - sights to be seen and Guinevere cooing appreciatively. Beocca trailed a little way behind them with the look of every man dragged along on a shopping trip. He was in hell, and he knew he wasn't getting out of it any time soon.

Watching the two of them casually bond, I'm big enough to note that I felt a touch jealous. I'd never had that 'knack' some people had of easily getting on with others. It was like I'd been off that day at nursery where the teacher had put everyone in their friendship groups. And when I got there, I had no space to slip into—that kind of felt like a metaphor for my life.

God, I've gone all maudlin.

All caught up, now?

Excellent. Back to Igraine quietly humiliating her husband.

"It might not be the perfect plan, but we hope this will allow Arthur to rediscover the spark he lost due to his wounding. You must admit, it has more chance of success than just constantly berating him."

Uther shook his head, but - fortunately - he was much less angry than before. "Do you really think he will fall for this?"

Bors nodded emphatically. "Without wishing to cast aspersions on the intellect of my best friend, he really has no sort of deductive mind. Give him a bad guy, a quest and a firm pair of tits, and he won't ask many questions." This big man suddenly seemed to remember his audience and went a very amusing shade of blush.

"Not unlike his father in that respect," the Queen added, deadpan.

Did I mention Igraine is fucking awesome?

Uther took a deep breath and slowly blew it out. I don't think this confrontation had worked out quite how any of us had expected. "Okay. Fine. The die is cast, and we're going to need to make the best of it. Even if we wished to, there's no way to undo what's happened. Too many people know the Princess is missing, so we probably only have a few moments before Arthur comes crashing in here. What do you see as the next steps?"

I stepped forward. "As soon as Arthur finds the ransom note, we figure he will want to suit up and get straight on the road after... sorry, what did we call the kidnapper?"

"Maleagant."

There was another awkward pause following Uther nearly choking on his own rage. "Seriously, Igraine?"

I sensed I was missing something. The Queen smiled and shook her head. "Not to worry, it's just the name of an old flame. Uther has never quite managed to get over it."

I sensed the King and Queen had some significant issues that needed working through, but I wasn't going anywhere near that particular nest of vipers. "Anyway, we know some Saxon stragglers are hanging around out towards that village - nothing too problematic - so we figure we'll 'track' Guinevere through them, work off some excess tension and then 'find' where this Maleagant has stashed her, rescue her and then Bors and I will make ourselves scarce whilst Arthur and Guinevere make passionate post-kidnap make-up sex. I hear that's a thing. And it's supposed to be glorious."

Uther chose to ignore my colourful commentary. "So, just you, Arthur and Bors?"

"Yep. Judging by the quality of Saxons we've been wiping out as of late, we probably won't even need the three of us. Honestly, Your Highness, this is no more interesting than one of those filler episodes you see in US dramas where the budget has run down, and a couple of the main characters wander around in the woods talking about their feelings to fill an hour or so. Genuinely, and I mean this with all sincerity, what's the worst that can possibly happen?"

And, yes, other than the complete bafflement at what I'd just said, everyone in the room was instantly aware again of how much I'd just tempted fate.

CHAPTER 6 - IN WHICH I RECEIVE THE SPANKING I SO RICHLY DESERVED

I wasn't delighted with the way Arthur reacted to the news his wife had been kidnapped.

I'd heard he'd been struggling since his little mishap with Drynwyn, but I'd not had much of a chance to catch up with him. I'd either been out and about with Bors culling Saxons or working on my cultivation with Merlin. In our few conversations, though, I didn't think I'd noticed anything to cause me concern. But, then again, I wasn't sure I should be anyone's bellwether of good mental health.

Nevertheless, I don't think I was the only one who'd expected him to snap into action immediately. Like, full-on Bruce ripping his shirt off Angry Dude Mode. So confident was I that we were going to making our way sharpish, I'd even arranged for a borrowed horse to be saddled in expectation of a rapid deployment to the road.

Thus, the quiet nod, pained expression, and the dropping of his eyes to the floor wasn't exactly on point.

"Did you hear me, dude? Guinevere's been kidnapped." I didn't quite give it the whole dum-dum-derrrrr, but the implication was there. My eyebrows alone gave it some serious welly.

"I heard you, wizard. And just how do you propose to proceed?"

I glanced at Bors, thinking this might be more of a boy-thing. Perhaps he was embarrassed to be speaking about losing his wife in front of a girl? Who knows how these things work. It wasn't exactly like I was a penis whisperer.

At least, not lately.

Bors took the hint and tried to run with the conversation. "Well, we were thinking we're going to want to get out and about sharpish. You know? Kick ass. Take names. Maybe indulge in some light torture until we get some answers we like." No one could quite do a 'hail-fellow-well-met' voice like a seven-foot tall, strategically shaved gorilla in plate armour. If the man's voice were any deeper, it'd be excavating the earth's core.

Arthur looked up in surprise. "Sorry, I must have misunderstood. It's not just going to be you two going after her? You need me to come with you too?"

"Mate, it's *your* wife. If anyone should be tooling up for this, it's you. Aren't you anxious to get her back?"

"As I am sure you are aware, wizard, Princess Guinevere is more than capable of looking after herself. I would be amazed if this ... this Malageant is not already regretting his actions in kidnapping her. In fact, I would anticipate we will hear from him again shortly, begging to return her."

Sighing, I dropped into my Artist's Studio and called on Merlin. "I don't know what's the matter with him, Big M. We were sure he'd leap at the chance to ride to Guinevere's aid."

There's an awful lot of pain emanating from him.

"Really? I didn't know. Should I give him back the healing mana stone?"

I do not believe it is a physical pain, my dear. Arthur has taken a number of significant blows of late. He blames himself for the loss of Isca. He and his men should have been within its walls when the Saxons arrived. They were late due to a dalliance.

"But there wasn't a battle at Isca. The Saxons went full Hiroshima on its arse. What does he think he could have done? As later events have proved, he isn't especially fireproof."

Indeed. But you need to remember that there is nothing logical about despair. Of everyone that is a force in his life, I think you will probably appreciate that better than anyone. Arthur feels - and feels deeply - he let those people down. Then, as if that was not traumatic enough, shortly after Isca, he led his Marghekyon in a terror, guerrilla campaign against the invading Saxon army. I hear even Sir Bors finds the weight of the deeds committed there a touch heavy for his conscience. Unless I am mistaken, a poet from close to your own time period will note that 'war is hell'. Arthur would be the first to voice his agreement.

Merlin's words made more sense than I would have liked. More than anything, they reminded me that the version of Arthur I was stuck with here was not the one I'd read so much about growing up. Camelot was not a shining beacon on the hill - at least not yet - and this Prince didn't have all the answers to the world's ills. Actions had consequences here, and wounds - no matter how well they were magically healed - echoed onwards.

And then, let us not forget, we have the slaughter of most of his childhood friends whilst he lay incapacitated. He's lost men before, for sure, but I don't think you quite understand the scale of the disaster that befell Britain when he was too injured to lead. If he could not forgive himself for Isca, imagine how he feels about the eradication of his Marghekyon. The British lost their greatest fortress in that fire, but it was robbed of its future might in the battle with the West Saxons. Even when fully healed and back to the peak of his powers, Tintagel itself would have been lost without your intervention. For a man who has always revelled in his status as the realm's foremost warrior, I am sure that cannot have been an easy series of blows to accept. Following my . . . passing, this was Arthur's opportunity to truly 'be the man'. That he had to be saved by another cultivator? Well, I can understand how this will have shaken him. Thus, if you ask me what is wrong with Arthur, I must say that I am unsure where to start.

I let Merlin's words percolate around my head for a moment. "Okay. So, when you put it like that, I'll admit that he's had a pretty shitty time of it."

He most certainly has. Do not get me wrong; some aspects of Arthur's personality are not especially admirable. I think how he has treated Guinevere during their marriage has been, at best, casually cruel. I had told him as much, and repeatedly, when I was alive. We both know the role the Princess will play in the rise and fall of King Arthur, and I think we can each see how the seeds for that betrayal are being sown. However, regardless of that behaviour, Arthur has ever had a strong sense of honour and duty when it comes to Britain. No matter what else he is feeling, that drive to protect the realm will always lie at his core.

"I hear you: honour and duty. Well, we need to wake that part of him up, don't we? Do you reckon it might be time for some tough love?"

A word of caution, my dear. If you bear in mind who his mother and father are, I think we can assume the Prince is well versed in 'tough love.' Perhaps it would be sensible to try something a bit more subtle?

I mentally winked at the wizard. "Subtle is my middle name."

Opening my eyes, I returned to reality. Only a few seconds had passed and Arthur was still standing in front of me looking like a wet weekend in Brighton. "Listen to me, you sack of shit. Your wife, the woman you have spent a decade screwing around on, has been kidnapped. This is a big deal and it's one that needs you to step up and act like the leader everyone tells me you are. It's time for you to break the habit of a lifetime, remove your head from your arse, and look after her for once."

The silence that fell around us absolutely convinced me that I was doing the right thing. Nothing like watching all the servants run for cover to make you confident in your choice of action. Pleased with the success of my approach, I blundered onwards. "Mate, this isn't a job you delegate to a lacky while you vanish off to fuck a milkmaid. Your wife, the Princess of Britain, is missing. The people need to see that when the chips are down, the Once and Future King wipes away his whiney tears, pulls on his big boy pants and takes care of business. So, no. Bors and I will not be taking care of business for you here. We will be there for you – dragging you along if necessary – but I swear by whatever god you guys believe in, that you will be out in the trenches with us. You hear me, you fucking wet wipe?"

By any chance, is your first name 'Not Remotely.'

***

Say what you like - and Merlin certainly said plenty - my words appeared to have the desired effect. After staring at me for a few moments, eye twitching, Arthur summoned back one of the servants who had run for cover when I went off on one.

"Could you please inform the King I will shortly be leaving the castle to pursue Guinevere's kidnappers. I will, of course, keep him informed of my progress. If you could make sure he remembers that someone must inform King Leodegrance that his daughter is missing. As time is pressing, I would appreciate it if my father would do that in my stead. Please apologise to them both that I was not able to deliver this message myself. I have just been informed that time is very much of the essence."

With that, the Prince turned on his heels and walked away. Bors and I glanced at each other, and then hurried to follow him. Bors took the lead in the questions. "My Lord, where do you plan to start the search?"

Arthur held out a piece of paper to the big man but did not stop walking. "It would appear that the kidnapper has left me a note. I found this pinned to the door of my bedchamber." Bors took it and read the note aloud.

"To Arthur, the so-called 'Prince of the Britons',

Revel in your turmoil, for I, Malageant, have spirited away your beloved Guinevere into a realm shrouded in darkness. She now resides within the Dark Tower, a place known only to me that exists between the realms. To reclaim her, you must undertake a quest and here are the dire stages you must traverse:

First, you must venture into the mystic Forest of Enchantment, where reality blurs and illusions abound. Here, you shall encounter a mysterious guide and three perplexing challenges. Seek the wisdom of a mystical hermit whose cryptic advice will set you on your path.

Secondly, I invite you to cross the Bridge of Slaughter, a structure that distorts reality and tests your self-image. Confront the reflection of your truest self and conquer the inner demons that assail you. Only then may you proceed.

Finally, you will arrive at the Dark Tower, where Guinevere's captivity is shrouded in mystery. Battle sinister adversaries and confront the dark secrets that bind her to this place. Only through courage, sacrifice, and unwavering determination can you hope to rescue her from this accursed fortress.

31

Time slips through your grasp, Arthur, and Guinevere's fate hangs by the thinnest of threads. Succeed in these trials, and you may yet hold her in your arms once more. Falter and darkness shall claim you both.

With ominous intent,

Malageant"

As Bors read out the note, I couldn't help but wince. I'd offered to write the ransom note, but Guinevere had insisted she knew what she was doing. It seemed to me that her prose was a touch heavy on the schlocky melodrama.

From the look on his face, Bors agreed. "So, my Lord, our destination is the Forest of Enchantment?"

Arthur did not answer, and in a few moments, we found ourselves in the stables. I frowned to see that Llameri was already saddled, Wynebgwrthucher strapped to the saddle bag, and Drynwyn in a scabbard on the other side. It looked like Arthur had already prepped to ride.

That thought had barely registered when the Prince's hand was on my throat, and I was lifted two feet off the ground and pinned to the wall.

"I know you have not been in this realm long, wizard. So, you are getting your one and only pass from me. I am not your friend. I am not your whimsical sidekick. And I am not a minor character in the rich tapestry of your exciting saga. I am Arthur Pendragon, the Once and Future King of Britain. My destiny is written in the stars, and my name will echo through the ages. At my birth, Merlin himself prophesied that the very heavens would bend to my will and I have dedicated my whole life to that goal. Do not presume that you have some special place at my side because you once saved my life. You are not Merlin. That man bounced me on his knee and counselled me through some of my darkest moments. Bors has stood at my shoulder more times than I can count and has earned my trust a million times over. What is more, he is now one of the last remaining links to my childhood. I have a closer kinship with my fucking horse than I feel for a random Celt that turned up at the precise moment my life fell apart. If you ever speak to me in such a way again, it will be the last time you ever say anything at all. Do we have an understanding?"

Funny thing is, it's pretty difficult to access your Qi when someone has you by your throat. For the first time since I'd arrived in the Dark Ages, I felt absolutely helpless. My vision began to darken.

"I asked you a question, Celt."

I was dimly aware that Bors was there, trying to break Arthur's grip. The fact that the giant was making no impression added to the rapidly increasing list of things I was reassessing about the Prince.

On the edge of passing out, and with great difficulty, I gave a little nod, and, with a final squeeze, Arthur released his hold and dropped me to the floor. Immediately, I was sucking in as much oxygen as I could, cycling Qi to repair the significant damage the Prince had caused.

I recognise that it would be cheap and unnecessary to say 'I told you so' in this situation, so I won't. Imagine instead that I'm smiling smugly and ruefully shaking my head.

Damn. That was fucking brutal. So, I guess you're his bitch now?

I chose to ignore them both.

CHAPTER 7 - IN WHICH AN ARGUABLY UNNECESSARILY AMOUNT OF PROSE CONCERNS HORSE DICK

As journeys go, this one was proving to be pretty awkward.

Arthur and Bors were riding way out in front, and – quite regardless to the state of my and Arthur's relationship - the atmosphere between the two was decidedly frosty.

Bors had made his opinion on his Prince's hands-on behaviour with me very clear - Arthur was sporting a black eye that I was damned if I would be healing - and it seemed sensible to let them work through their issues in their own distinctly male way.

By this, I mean squashing down all the emotional turmoil and never speaking about it ever again. You know, all healthy like.

It had not gone unnoticed that the only one of my companions who thought Arthur had crossed a line was the guy I knew least well. As a consequence, Bors had gone right to the top of a very exclusive list of people who I thought of as 'not too bad, really'.

Merlin and Drynwyn, on the other hand . . . Let's just say I have another list - a fairly extensive one - of those I wouldn't piss on if they were on fire and note everyone else in our little quest group was on it.

My mood thoroughly soured, I shifted uncomfortably in my horse's saddle. It might shock you to learn that this was my first time riding one. I know! I absolutely give off the vibe of someone whose daddy paid for his Little Princess to have lessons every Saturday, don't I?

Well, shockingly, not. I have some dim and distant memories of various farm visits when I was pretty young, but that's about it. For me, animals serve a very limited purpose in the world, most of which is to taste delicious. I was happy to have grown up at a time and place where only chinless wonders used them as modes of transport, and the less said about people who kept pets, the better.

The horse I was sitting on was called Forca. He was big and dark brown and appeared to find the very idea of someone on his back to be a massive imposition. We'd only been going for a few hours, and he had already landed me in the mud six times.

But on the plus side, that vantage point gave me an excellent view of his comically enormous penis. So, swings and roundabouts, I guess.

What with all the brooding silence - punctuated by my swearing at Phallic Forca when he shook me off again - we weren't making especially fast progress towards our first Quest destination, the Forest of Enchantment.

On the one hand, the vast majority of the party knew this whole thing was a ruse, and Guinevere wasn't in any danger, so why would we hurry? On the other, though,

Prince Wanker was still seeming pretty chill about the whole 'saving my wife from a dastardly kidnapper' thing. I've been on pub crawls that moved with more focus and intensity.

I know you are angry, my dear, but I must insist you refer to Arthur appropriately.

I ignored the wizard - I had been doing a lot of that lately - and dropped into my Artist's Studio.

To pass the time between unseatings, I'd spent most of the journey observing the manner in which my Qi cycled around my body. By hook or by crook, I knew I'd ended up with some pretty insanely overpowered channels, and I sensed I wasn't really making the most of what this state of affairs allowed. From what I understood, the time and effort it would have taken to get to this level of smoothness should have unlocked all sorts of cultivator goodies and knowledge. By progressing so quickly to **Ron**, I'd missed out on many vital experiences and was clearly the worst off for it.

It would obviously help to have a legendary wizard offer their thoughts on this, but I was not asking Merlin for any more advice right now.

In lieu of anything better to do right now, I directed a handful of Qi to a fresh, white page, watching as the purple blob landed and then held its spherical structure on the sheet. It was a perfect globe and was, and I don't know a better way to say this, vibrating with potential.

Given enough time, it felt like I could do pretty much anything I wanted with this power. I'd been getting a much better feel for all this stuff during the 'hunting of the Saxons' phase of my development, and I sensed I was on the edge of . . . some sort of breakthrough.

I could still remember a vision Merlin had given me of him utterly devastating several armies outside of Carlion. I would be lying if there wasn't a significant part of me that didn't want any piece of that action. Having the Prince of the Britons slap me around and there being little I could do to stop it didn't hurt my motivation much either.

For now, though, I wanted to work on my control, not change the universe. Or vapourise a bald twat with too high an opinion of himself.

Settling myself down – I found the more worked up I was, the less effective I was working my Qi - I rolled the blob around the page. As I had hoped, it left a pleasingly solid line behind, which meant I could move on to the second part of my plan.

Qi doodling.

In no time, I'd directed the blob around with enough skill to leave a drawing of a rudimentary horse in its wake. After a moment's consideration, I went back and added a huge dick. Forca's magnificence needed to be documented, after all. When I was finished, I let the excess Qi return to my channels and properly looked at the picture.

I mean, it wasn't my finest work - Gainsborough wouldn't be hanging up his brush in despair at the bar to which I had raised equine artistry - but I was happy enough with it. No one would fail to recognise that this was a priapic purple horse.

So far, so good. However, the point of this exercise wasn't to refresh my drawing skills. I wanted to see if I could do anything else with a Qi drawing.

From all the reading Merlin had been forcing on me since the battle in front of the walls of Tintagel, it seemed that anything I produced with my Qi was basically mine to command. I had a distinct memory of Melehan – the Saxon wizard who had sacrificed himself to save Arthur and me – throwing Qi around like lightning bolts.

It wasn't a skill I had managed to make use of yet, and I was keen to find ways in which I could externalise Qi outside my body.

So, having sketched out Randy Ronny, I was hoping I would be able to animate him in some way and have him follow my commands.

Annoyingly, though, I didn't quite know how.

Trying to pick the Qi drawing up didn't cut it - although I could feel that there was something more tangible to the drawing than it simply being painted on paper, that didn't mean I could simply lift it clear.

Likewise, no amount of Magic-Eyes achieved anything especially noticeable. Again, it was clear there was more to it than just being a drawing, but I couldn't work out what I was missing. It was quite a quandary.

I can help you if you want.

For a moment, I almost gave in. I know I wasn't going to be able to ignore Merlin forever, but he'd definitely earned a good while longer of the cold shoulder.

For whatever reason, we'd not really been on the best of terms since the Saxons were sent packing. However, it was going to take me quite some time to get over his whole 'you asked for it' attitude regarding Arthur's hissy-fit in the stables.

Say what you like about my Dad - and believe me, I'd said plenty over the years – but he'd been very clear about what would happen to any man who put his hands on his little girl.

Merlin, though? Look, I wasn't looking at him as a substitute father figure, but it was causing me more pain than I'd like to admit that my two closest friends in this realm were taking the opposite view than a man who social services saw as 'a danger to himself and others'.

My dear, I'm sorry if you are upset about something I've done.

I hated that style of apology. I'd heard it far too many times over the years. It's not 'I'm sorry I did something wrong'. It's 'I'm sorry **you** are upset about what I did.' It's not contrition. It's sorrowful you are proving to be emotionally incontinent about whatever minor snafu has your little girl panties in a bunch.

I could feel I was going to lose my temper.

Rather than give the Big M the satisfaction, I focused back on my drawing. And this time – and it might have been the building rage - I sensed that there was another dimension to the horse. There's probably a better way to put it than that, but that's what we're going to run with.

My Qi drawing wasn't quite 'solid', but neither was it just lines on a page. It was like it had . . . inflated somewhat.

Apparently, angry Morgan had more cards to play than a contemplative one.

Drawing on my fury with both my sword – Drynwyn hadn't stopped with the unnecessary commentary about a woman's place, either - and the wizard, I poured that emotion into the horse, gasping as it blew up like a balloon filling with helium.

In no time at all, the Qi drawing lifted clear from the page and stood, rigid and upright, on the page.

It was still manifestly a picture, though. But now it was more like a cardboard statue. I pushed a bit more of my anger into it - honestly, this was some of the best drawing therapy I'd had in some time - and it came alive.

So, this was the weirdest sensation I had ever experienced. One moment, I was playing around with the doodle of a purple horse with a big dick, and the next, the fucking thing was alive and cantering around inside my head.

Just to say, my dear, you are doing something quite impressive at the moment, and I am very proud of you.

"Fuck off, Merlin."

No, honestly. Well, done you.

My little purple Qi horse reached the end of the page and reacted like it had hit a wall, quickly turning, and setting off to the other side. When it got to the edge over there, it turned again and set off at a tangent. It could have been my imagination, but it seemed to move faster each time.

Whilst acknowledging just how fantastic this manifestation of your power has been, my dear, are you open to just the tiniest bit of advice?

After a few more collisions, the horse was now careening about the page at an astonishing speed. Each crash against the edge made my artist's studio shake. I was beginning to wonder about the advisability of rage as an energy source . . . Speaking of which, I could not help but notice that keeping the horse 'alive' was draining my Qi stores.

I tried to cut off the source from my Artist's Studio, but very quickly got nowhere. As I watched, the levels of available Qi paint continued to drop down towards zero. Remembering how terrible I felt when this had happened before, I overcame my need to ignore my only source of advice.

"How do I make it stop?"

Well, that is an excellent question. I'm very pleased you have thought to ask it.

"Merlin ..."

At your stage of development - not that you haven't made astonishing progress. Because you have. I am very proud of you - any object you create with your Qi has a reasonably finite lifespan— five, ten minutes at most. So, you have two choices. You can wait it out –

My Artist's Studio shook with another colossal impact of a supersonic horse against a page. And, as I was down to the final inch of available Qi, I could already feel the exhaustion headache coming. "Or?"

You let it out.

"Just like that?"

You need to be aware that the potential for devastating damage to be caused by an out-of-control Qi construct is likely to be significant. But . . . well, we are near the edge of the Enchanted Forest. They will have seen worse.

As loathe as I was to put others at risk, I did not think I had much choice. I didn't get any sense of malevolence from Randy Roger; he just wanted to run. He was only getting antsy because he was trapped in a small space. I figured of anyone, I should be able to dig that. "So, how do I let him out?"

It really is quite simple. All you have to do is release the construct from its bonds.

"I love it when you say things like that. 'Release the construct from its bonds'. Absolutely. No worries at all. Why didn't I think of that? Honestly, Merlin, you are one of the lousiest teachers in the known universe." I felt like my entire head would be shaken off at any second.

Many apologies, my dear. It is easy to forget when you perform such wondrous feats that you are still quite new at all this. It would be best if you visualised your construct, not held within you, but in the world outside. This will pierce the veil between the two, allowing it to surge to freedom.

Annoyingly, it was pretty much exactly like that.

I imagined Randy galloping free on the track next to me, and - poof - there he was.

My own horse reared up at his unexpected companion, depositing me again on the ground. Bors and Arthur turned at the noise and narrowly avoided being unhorsed themselves as a purple streak flashed between them and off into the forest beyond.

Fare thee well, Roger. I really hope you enjoy your brief time in the world.

Bors was looking at me with barely concealed horror.

"Did you do that?"

I shrugged.

"Fuck me," he puffed his cheeks appreciatively, "did you see the size of the cock on that thing?"

CHAPTER 8 - IN WHICH THERE IS NOTHING CLOSE TO AN APOLOGY OFFERED

The light was just starting to fade when we set up camp for the night. This was another one of those times that I was blown away by how desolate the Dark Age world was. When I say, 'set up camp', I don't mean that we pulled off a well-trodden path and into a nice clearing in the woods that existed for just that purpose. I mean, we simply just stopped travelling and set up a fire.

There was nothing that marked a dividing line between 'path' and 'camp' other than us just deciding this was where we were holding up. A thousand pounds on the table and the keys to a new Ferrari on offer, and I couldn't tell you the difference between this part of the forest and anywhere else we'd travelled through.

Basically, if Bors and Arthur wanted to run off and Hansel and Gretel my ass, I'd be stuck out here making a gingerbread house for the rest of my days.

It was amazing to think that in less than two thousand years, all of this greenery would just be badly maintained roads, poorly constructed housing and the odd rundown shopping arcade. 'Amazing', yeah. I think that was the right word.

On the plus side, there'd been no further sight nor sound of my Qi construct, so I had to assume Merlin had been right and poor Randy Roger had faded from existence. I idly hoped he'd gone out like the Cheshire Cat, with his dick being the final thing to fade from existence.

The experience seemed to have had quite an impact on Forca, though. He hadn't made to unseat me since. I guess if this wizarding thing didn't work out, I had a future career in taming wild horses.

Although, once Bors had talked me through all the daily chores I now seemed to have around keeping this bloody thing fed, clean and happy, I wasn't sure I ever wanted to see one again.

I'd been working away for some time, when a voice interrupted me. "If you want that horse to hate you, Wizard, you're going the right way about it."

I paused in my vigorous brushing of said animal and glared over at Arthur. We'd still not spoken since the incident in the stables, and if he thought we were about to have some light horse-related banter and then everything was going to be okay, he was very wrong indeed.

He started to walk towards me, and I felt my body stiffen at his approach. If he noticed, he didn't show it. As he drew near, I hurriedly stepped back from Forca, giving him space to rest his hands on the beast. "Horses are much more sensitive to pressure than people realise. When you groom them, thinking about how you'd want to be massaged in their place is helpful. The idea is for it to be soothing and comfortable, not -" and he paused - "not whatever violent act of brutality you're committing here. May I?"

He held out his hand for the brush I was using. I had an impulsive moment where I wanted to throw it into the trees rather than hand it over. I managed to restrain myself.

Excellent, my dear. You really are showing impressive maturity lately. Clear personal growth. Well, done.

I'd thought there was nothing worse than Merlin's incessant criticism and picking at me. Turned out I was wrong. Cheerleader Merlin was several magnitudes worse.

Arthur accepted the brush and took over the grooming. "Every horse is different, and some might even enjoy a firmer touch, but it's always good to start gently and watch how they react. If you notice your horse seems tense or tries to move away, it's a sign to ease up a bit."

Forca, the disloyal bastard, was clearly enjoying the Prince's attention. He whinnied softly and pressed against him, giving me the epic stink-eye. I was reminded that Drynwyn seemed to prefer Arthur's company to mine. Perhaps there was something in that? Maybe it wouldn't be the worst thing in the world if I tried to get to know him a little better. Or perhaps that particular thought could fuck right off.

"You should brush in the direction of the hair growth. It feels more natural and comfortable for the horse. Oh, and always be extra gentle around the face and legs. Those areas are particularly sensitive."

He was so absorbed in what he was doing that I didn't know if he was even talking to me anymore. "I've found that grooming is a great time to bond with a horse. It's not just about cleaning them but also about building trust and understanding. Grooming gently, we show them respect and care, strengthening our connection. If you would like, I can show you some techniques I use with Llameri. It's amazing how small changes in how we groom can make a big difference in how they feel and respond to us."

Are you fucking kidding me?! Since when did Arthur Pendragon, the Once and Future King, turn into some sort of soppy nature lover?

I could feel my feminine instinct to go all weak-kneed at this hitherto hidden personality trait at epic war with my white-hot anger towards him. If I wasn't careful, I was going to end up forgiving him . . .

"I'm not sorry about what happened."

Well, that certainly helped with my dilemma.

Arthur's whole focus appeared to be on the horse, but every softly spoken word carried to me. "You have only known me since . . . my injury. But I hear others talk about how much I seem to have changed. Sometimes, I think I am on the mend, but others? Well, there are times I cannot see how to make it through the day."

His movement of the brush, coupled with the lilting tone of his voice, was almost hypnotic. "I have never been a good man. I know that well enough. Give me a sword in my hand and a group of warriors to command, and I doubt you'll find anyone better on the field of battle. Likewise, I am told I can be fine company. Give me a drink and fire burning in a hearth, and I can tell a fine tale. But am I a good man? No."

He paused Forca's grooming and turned to face me.

"I'm sure you have heard of some of my sins. And it will only have been some of them. You know I've cheated on my wife since the moment of our betrothal. I've bedded the wives of more than half the nobles at court, and none dare - at least openly - to call me to account. There are probably enough of my bastards running around Britain to raise my own army should I be so inclined."

The fire cast shadows across his face, giving his expression somewhat of a Satanic quality. More of a Fuesli depiction than Bosch, if I was honest, but, you know, the night was yet young.

"I've spent my life bending the rules and flashing a winning smile to get away without any consequences. And I'm always forgiven because I'm Arthur. But, no, that does not make me a good man. But you know what? It does not seem to matter to anyone because I am the Once and Future King. I am the one who will bring peace to the land, not just now but forever. Isn't that a wonderful thing? And because of that, there seems to be no limit to the depths I can sink without censure as long as I have that fucking prophecy around my neck."

I was aware Bors had stopped what he was doing to hover at the edge of our conversation. Which of us he would protect if things went south, I wasn't sure.

"So, no. I don't apologise to you. I lost my temper and did something I would like to think was out of character. I hope others would tell you the same. I am not given to bouts of expressive violence. At least not off the battlefield. I also do not make a habit of striking women. But I'm not sorry it happened. Because you need to know that is who I am. I have heard the servants chatter of the tales you spin for my father of the deeds of King Arthur and the legend of Camelot from your own realm. They make for good stories. I enjoy hearing them and thinking about what might have been. In a different world. But I am not a fairy-tale prince. I am not the man you hope I will be. I am not a good man."

Our eyes were locked when he finished. It seemed it was my time to talk.

"You do anything like that again, and I'll kill you."

Arthur nodded. "I would expect nothing else."

That caused a flutter of unease. As somewhat of a connoisseur of invasive, destructive thoughts, I caught more than a touch of familiarity in his tone.

By attacking me, Arthur hadn't attempted suicide by wizard, had he . . .

No. I squashed down that thought. I wasn't in a mental space to begin to forgive him yet. Let alone start to feel sorry for him. This wasn't even any sort of apology. It was basically, "I'm a dick. You got dicked on. Stop your moping. What did you expect? Prepare for more dick. From me. The dick."

I'd heard more than my fair share of this type of conversation over the years. And to be honest, it usually worked on me. But that was the old Morgan. The me who had retreated to a world of shadows and pharmaceuticals. Not the me who could literally rip someone to pieces using only the power of her mind.

This me was awesome. And she didn't need to forgive anyone.

"Do we have a truce?" He still sought to hold my gaze.

I didn't know what to say. Since arriving in the Dark Age, I felt like I'd been in a non-stop struggle for survival. Saxons. Dragons. Knockers. Angry Scotsmen. It'd been a lot.

But the only time I'd ever really been afraid was when the Prince of the Britons had me by the throat.

I could sense Bors and Merlin, and maybe even Drynwyn and Wynebgwrthucher, wanted me to draw a line under it all. To be a good little girl. To not make a fuss. Boys will be boys, after all, and you couldn't blame them for occasionally pulling pigtails. I'd been asking for it. Shake hands and move on. Be the bigger person.

But do you know what? I was so fed up with having to be the person who accepted shitty behaviour and excused it. Just because he was good in a fight, was a laugh to have a drink with, and knew which way to stroke a . . . a horse didn't mean he got a permanent free pass.

I was about to tell him all that when - looking into his eyes - I felt another tug of . . . something.

Fucking fragile men . . .

"My lord, I spoke harshly to you, and you reacted poorly. I'm not sorry for what I said, and you're not sorry for what you did. I doubt that's the stuff of a truce, but if you want to call it such, I won't argue."

I held out my hand. Arthur took me by my forearm. I held his eyes as I squeezed, pushing a little bit of Qi in that direction just to make my point.

"For me, I prefer to think we're both on notice. I'll watch my tongue, and you watch out for doing anything that'll get you incinerated. Again."

I saw little beads of sweat pop on his forehead. Maybe I was squeezing a little too tightly. I just didn't feel like stopping right now.

"All friends again?" Bors was at our side. He banged us both on our backs in a 'hail-fellow-well-met' kind of way. He was trying too hard to dispel the tension.

"No." I released Arthur's arm, and he did his best not to rub it immediately. "But I know how to groom my horse better now." I plucked the brush from the Prince's hand and turned away to focus on Forca.

Bors shrugged and led Arthur back towards their side of the fire.

Well, done, my dear. I think you handled that very well, indeed. Honour to both sides, without anyone losing face. Excellent work.

"Merlin, mate. We need to talk ..."

CHAPTER 9 - IN WHICH WE DO A LITTLE GARDENING

I *have a bad feeling about this.*
On the one hand, I was pleased that Merlin and I had reached an understanding as to the immediate cessation of the stream of praise he'd been sluicing down upon me during this journey.

I say "understanding" . . .

What I mean is that he understood if he kept it up, he would be banished back to the place between the realms. I still wasn't entirely clear how I'd managed it the first time, but I'd made it clear I was feeling pretty fucking motivated to give it another whirl.

So, the cheerleading had abruptly stopped.

In its place, though, he seemed to have developed a cloying need to ingratiate himself through the incessant delivery of pop-culture references.

I was finding it bloody annoying.

Especially as I realised that this method of making friends was basically my entire personality. I was starting to understand a bit more about my lack of a healthy social life.

We were stood at the very edge of what I was told was the Enchanted Forest. It was not especially clear to me what was different about this particular collection of trees and bushes as opposed to those we'd been travelling through for the last few days.

But, you know, I was currently in the company of King Arthur, Merlin, Sir Bors, and a sword and a shield viciously disagreeing about the rules of the card game, 'Beggar my Neighbour.'

Some things you just have to take on trust.

For fuck's sake, how many times! If an Ace is played, the next player must turn over four cards, one at a time. You've been hit on the head too many fucking times.

And you've been spending too many hours stuck in places you shouldn't. Who cares about an Ace? The King is the most important card. An Ace just means you turn one over. Four turnovers for a King, three for a Queen, two for a Jack and ONE for the ace. You pointy-headed, taboo-spouting tease of a prick.

It was undoubtedly a vibe.

"Will everyone shut up!?" Say what you like about Arthur, and I've been saying plenty, he could undoubtedly command a silence. He looked over at Sir Bors. "Can you feel it?"

Bors nodded. "The Forest doesn't want us here."

I kind of understood the Forest's point of view.

"No," Arthur jumped down from Llameri and dragged his spear, Rhongomynyad, free from her saddle.

Of course, he takes the spear. Two magical, speaking weapons at his disposal, and the thing he takes is just a sharp pointy stick. He's basically a caveman. Don't know why we bother.

I wish I could find it in me to like Wynebgwrthucher. She gave Arthur so much shit that I felt like we would be natural allies. But, man, she was a mood hoover.

My least favourite character in The Hitchhiker's Guide to the Galaxy was Marvin. I couldn't help but feel Wynebgwrthucher's vibe kill would be the final nail in his little metal coffin of despair.

"You're sure the track of the kidnappers leads through here?" Arthur said.

Both Bors and I did our best not to exchange glances. Since kicking off in pursuit of Guinevere and those who stole her, we had not had a moment to discuss how we wanted this to play out properly. The big man had been doing an excellent job of selling his hitherto unheralded tracking abilities, but I worried the act was all starting to feel a touch thin.

Thus far, Arthur had seemed happy to accept his directions - with my occasional sotto-voiced "Merlin agrees" as an added backup - but there was surely a limit to how many times Bors could stare at a bush, nod sagely and go 'they went thataway.'

Nevertheless, despite my misgivings, we had reached the Enchanted Forest, our first destination on this little quest after Malageant. I wasn't totally sure why Guinevere had felt the need to have a properly dangerous place as the first of our little quest destinations, but the time to ask those questions was probably before actually enacting the plan.

The ransom note had directed us to enter it and find a mystical hermit within who would have a clue to our next stop of the Bridge of Slaughter. Queen Igraine had told us to leave the "little details to me", but I couldn't help but feel that now we were actually about to go into the Forest, a bit more clarity about things like 'who', 'where', 'when' and 'how' would be of help . . .

Fuck me, this plan SUCKED.

Bors sniffed ostentatiously - trust me, it's a thing - and then spat on the floor. "A small band of warriors came this way, and they're holding a hostage. If it's not Malageant and Guinevere, it's a pretty big coincidence."

Arthur took a few steps forward and prodded at the ground experimentally with the length of his spear. Immediately, a shimmery green barrier sprang into life, and a coil of vines shot out of the undergrowth. These vines, covered in tiny thorns and leaves, snaked their way towards Arthur.

He swore and stepped backwards, but they pursued him, twining and twisting around each other, forming a writhing mass. In moments, they reached the tip of his spear and wrapped around its shaft.

No, this was not as sexual as it sounds.

The vines spiralled upwards, binding the spear in a tight embrace, their thorns never quite piercing the wood but gripping it with a strength that clearly surprised the Prince. He attempted to pull Rhongomynyad free, but the more he struggled, the tighter the vines seemed to hold on, as if each tug only encouraged their determined grasp.

This would seem a good moment for the group's wizard to offer some assistance...

To be honest, I wasn't against watching Arthur struggle a little. On the other hand, letting him become a snack for Audrey II would seem a touch counterproductive to the whole journey.

And, you know, the whole reason for your existence in this realm.

I suppose when Merlin put it like that . . .

I condensed a ball of Qi into my hand and refashioned it using my connection to the Fire element. This was one of the techniques I'd been trialling on my various wandering Saxon hunts of late. Apparently, this sort of usage was fairly rudimentary in the grand scheme of things, but I enjoyed the feeling of turning the blobs of purple paint into something different.

I couldn't quite externalise my Qi in the way I wanted yet, but — fortunately — I had a very helpful flaming sword that was the perfect conduit for my power. Merlin had said that the reason most cultivators had a wand, or a staff, was in order to help them cross this conceptual threshold when they weren't quite strong enough to do so themselves. As with so many things that had occurred to me in this realm so far, I appeared to have had lucked out by picking up a legendary weapon I could use in this way.

Hey, it's not like I didn't need the advantage.

With a mental flick of my Qi, I directed a fiery glowing ball through Drynwyn to the mound of vines, slowly dragging Arthur towards the trees - despite Bors' best efforts at pulling him back.

The moment my Qi struck the greenery, there was a soft *whumph,* a screech that sounded uncannily like a giant anthropomorphic Venus Flytrap getting its fingers burned and not liking it one bit, and the vines let go and vanished.

"What the fuck was that about?" I asked.

The legends of the Enchanted Forest speak of the need for those seeking entry to demonstrate their worthiness. I doubt we will likely be allowed access unless we can show the purity of our intent.

I relayed Merlin's words to the rest of the party. I managed not to include my commentary as to how that sort of information would have been pretty damn useful a touch earlier.

My dear, you have barely talked to me for the last few days. You can hardly complain about not having the information you need when being as talkative as Bartleby, the Scrivener.

"Who?"

Bartleby the Scrivener. Famously taciturn character from a Melville short story.

"Melville?"

Without wishing to be condescending, you moan about my using pop culture references to bond with you, and then you display ignorance of more literary references. I have only so much time and effort available to parse my conversational style to your requirements.

"I'm glad you weren't seeking to be condescending there. Otherwise, you would have been quite an arse."

I realised Arthur had asked me something whilst I was busy internally duelling with a colossal dickhead of a wizard.

"Sorry, I missed that. What was it again?"

Arthur paused as if swallowing down a sharp retort. "I asked, wizard, if you had any words of advice?"

I don't know why, but Arthur's continued failure to use my name was starting to get to me. It didn't help, I kind of thought he was doing it on purpose. "We're pursuing the kidnappers of your wife. I'm not sure there's much purer intent than that? Maybe try again?"

I mean, the whole quest was bollocks, but Arthur didn't know that. Maybe the Forest would let him in if he truly believed it was true? If there was some sort of psychic barrier of 'pure intent' that triggered the vines, he should be able to overcome it by thinking about his quest.

Hopefully, Bors and I would be able to slip in after him. Maybe.

Fucking hell. This was yet another terrible element to a terrible plan in a long line of terrible plans. Sometimes I had visions of Monty Python and the Holy Grail and feared we were not living up to that level of efficiency and professionalism.

Arthur nodded, then pointed at Drynwyn. "I have a better idea. Will your sword let me bear it for a few moments?" He replaced the spear in Llameri's saddlebag.

Abso-fucking-lutely!

I unbuckled my scabbard and threw it over to Arthur. He caught it and unsheathed the blade in one smooth movement. Despite everything, I had to admire the man's balls. It wasn't so long ago that holding on to this sword had pretty much killed the guy. Now, here he was, risking it happening again to save a wife he really did not care that much about.

The man was a steaming pile of contradictions.

And it took one to know one.

Arthur spun the sword one-handed in an entirely unnecessary way, which made Drynwyn giggle in pleasure. Not a sentence I ever want to think about again.

He then held the sword upright in the guard position, the blade resting a few centimetres from his lips. I saw his lips move as he whispered some instructions.

I realised what he had planned a little too late as Drynwyn ignited, and Arthur tossed it across the shimmering barrier to the Enchanted Forest.

We watched the fire blossom and listened to the screaming for a good half-an-hour before silence again returned to the woods.

It was only broken by Drynwyn's voice calling back to us.

All done. There was some sort of fucking big-arsed tree thing back here. Pretty flammable, though.

The Guardian of the Enchanted Forest has stood for millennia. I do not believe I have seen any versions of reality where it was slain in such a manner.

I wasn't sure whether there was more awe or horror in Merlin's voice.

I fear what has just occurred will have significant repercussions.

Bors and I fell in behind Arthur as he crossed over the place where the ethereal green barrier had stood.

"I have a bad feeling about this."

Hypocrite.

CHAPTER 10 – IN WHICH I HAD TO GOOGLE THE MEANING OF 'HENTAI' TO CHECK THIS GAG WORKED

I've come across some sad sights in my time.

You don't regularly find your drunk self on the mean streets of Birmingham in the early hours of Sunday morning without developing a high tolerance for the terrifying, the broken and the outright bizarre.

In my early twenties, for example, I once rescued a hedgehog from a hotdog bun a homeless guy was toasting over a campfire.

I seen me some shit.

Even so, and even with all those dissolute years of battle-hardened, gin-soaked grimness behind me, I'm going to struggle to forget the image of the blackened corpse of the Forest Guardian.

I wasn't sure why I was so affected by the sight. It could have been my developing sensitivity to Wood Qi. Maybe it was the unholy smell of napalm that lingered around the body. It might even have been the troubling way the little body looked to have suffered greatly in its last - fiery - moments.

Basically, what I'm saying is, as far as I was concerned, we'd murdered Groot, and I was going to be losing sleep over it. And I didn't think there would be any cutesy regrowing of a clone from these charred remains.

Using my foot to free my sword from viney ash, I stooped and picked up a rather too pleased for itself Drynwyn. Without a word, I dropped it back in its scabbard, and followed behind Arthur and Bors.

Even before we set out on this quest, Merlin had been ragging on me for my overreliance on Drynwyn for all my death-dealing needs. I was beginning to see what he meant. It wasn't that I was ungrateful to the sword. It had gotten me out of more than my fair share of scrapes since I'd acquired it. And I'm fairly sure the Saxons would have been able to take Tintagel if it hadn't burned down that giant bridge and the cultivators conjuring it.

It was just . . . I couldn't help but feel I was supposed to be advancing past the stage where 'throw a magical sword at it' should be the solution to every problem.

At the risk of being accused of cheerleading again, my dear, what you feel is very encouraging. It shows that you are, even if it is just subconscious musings at the moment, recognising your potential. You instinctively recognise that you should have been able to defeat the Forest Guardian in another way. I should note that had you done so, you would doubtless have enhanced your cultivation.

"I'm not convinced thinking arson shouldn't be the go-to method for saying 'hello' is evidence of mystical growth, Big M."

In that, we can agree to disagree. Some people go through their entire lives thinking that just because they have a giant hammer, every problem must be a nail. I hope it goes without saying that this approach does not lead to successful cultivators. Without wishing to overstate the point, I would further note that the Morgan I met back in a field of corpses would not have spent too long agonising over the manner in which she dealt with hostile wildlife. Whether you like it or not, you are growing.

A vivid memory of ripping a wolf in half sailed across my vision.

Perhaps Merlin has a point, after all.

I idly wondered if the reason I had been keeping the Big M at arm's length of late was not that I found him to be a gigantic dickhead - *ouch* - but rather that I did not really want to have this 'progress on your journey' conversation. Because if I was going to admit that I was changing into a 'better' person, it kind of behooved me to do a little more to unpick what was different now compared to the old me.

And that was a scab I wasn't that keen to dig into.

I was not so filled with self-loathing that I didn't see that I had been making—largely—better choices since my reincarnation in the Dark Ages. Zizzie was always saying that if I could just break myself free of my doom spiral of chaos, I could actually have a chance to be happy.

Well, there were few more comprehensive breaks with twenty-first-century cultural malaise than being hit by a lorry and being reincarnated into the body of a Saxon spearman.

When you are ready to explore it further, my dear, I'll be here for you, like I've been there before. Just know that you are a very different person today than you were just a few weeks ago.

Hand's up, who had Merlin going all The Rembrandts on me...

A surprised shout from up ahead saved me from a clapping montage. I ran forward to see what was up.

It was bedlam.

Bors had pushed Arthur behind him, brandishing his axe in a defensive position. For his part, the Prince held Rhongomyniad braced before him as if in preparation to meet a charging boar.

I had another flashback of Morgan vs Wildlife. The great outdoors *really* did not seem to like me.

I quickly filled my hands with fiery Qi death and reached Bors' side, looking out for whatever enemy had so spooked them. I was unsure what I expected to be so threatening to these two exceptionally capable knights that they were white with fear.

But - and I cannot stress this enough - it was certainly not a tiny, deformed man in a dress sitting on a green, miniature, pot-bellied pig.

I let my Qi flow backwards and reached out to dip Arthur's spear towards the ground. "I know we're all on edge here, but shall we chill the jets a little?"

However, Arthur's eyes were wide with genuine terror, and he shrugged me off - refocusing his spear and cowering behind it. Baffled, I glanced at Bors and saw the same horror etched on his face.

These two were absolutely shitting themselves.

I've not always been known to read the room—I vividly recall singing 'I will survive' karaoke at my Auntie Dot's funeral —but even I could sense something was not quite right here.

Assuming that the newcomer was the cause of whatever was going down, I went down on my knees to be eye-to-eye with the little man in the dress.

Okay, so first things first, this wasn't quite a man.

On closer inspection, I could see his skin was rough and bark-like, almost camouflaging him against the gnarled trunks of the trees surrounding us. Yet, on the other hand, his eyes were bright and impish beneath a tangle of wild, twiggy hair. And that's not a colourful adjective. His hair was actually made out of twigs.

Moreover, the little dude was wearing a dress made entirely of leaves and moss, which - and I need to be clear here - I could tell was absolutely my style. When we were done here, we were going shopping together.

"Giles is a boggart."

I'm not going to lie. I've become pretty comfortable with all manner of oddness since finding myself in Dark Age Cornwall and even I wasn't expecting the pig to speak. In response to these softly spoken words, Arthur and Bors both drew closer together and took a step back as if the porker had just shrieked a terrible battle cry.

I looked down further and met the eyes of the little green pig. It looked right back at me and then winked.

It seemed rude not to talk back. "Giles is a boggart?"

"Yes. That's why they're acting like that. Boggarts are annoying little shits for the most part, but they do have the useful ability to create potent auras of fear around them."

I looked back at the terrified figures of Arthur and Bors, and that made quite a lot of sense. The two of them were acting as if they were facing off against a dragon - I speak from personal experience that this is a uniquely terrifying thing - rather than . . . whatever this was.

"Do you mean when they're looking at him, he becomes whatever each of them most fears?"

"What? No. Don't be fucking stupid. Giles has a gland in his arse that stimulates insane amounts of adrenaline and cortisol. One whiff of his farts and, basically, it's Fear Town, population you. It's just your standard defence mechanism to an external threat. 'Becoming whatever you most fear' Fuck me. How would that work? With the best will in the world, Giles is basically a bunch of primal impulses in a nice dress. It's all he can do to stay sat on my back most of the time. Instantly decoding an individual's innermost fears and then projecting them outwards in a psychically linked terror spell is a task slightly above his mental capacity. You get me?"

"Right. I understand. And you are?"

"I'm a pig."

I could sense Merlin trying very hard to get my attention. However, I couldn't quite focus on what he was saying for some reason. "Right. You are a pig. And, let me just check this, you can apparently talk?"

"That's me. A talking pig. I'm also fucking green and of a species not known for being native to these isles."

"Okay . . . "

It seemed to me that Merlin was shouting quite loud now, but for the life of me, I couldn't decode the words.

"I mean, I could tell you my name was 'Hal the Distracting Hallucination' if that would help the penny drop?"

I'd like to say that it was at this stage that I snapped out of the spell I was under and immediately set about freeing Arthur and Bors from the vines that had sneaked out from the woods to wrap around them.

Unfortunately, despite every instinct crying out for me to wake up, I could not quite seem to manage it.

I watched as more dark green tendrils emerged from behind the Boggart/Pig combination and began reaching towards me. They slid across the forest floor in an unsettling way, reminding me of nothing so much as snakes on the hunt. There'd been an absolutely traumatic David Attenborough show - I think it was *Planet Earth*

II - I'd seen a year or so back where a baby marine iguana was captured by some racer snakes. Google it. Now. And prepare to cry.

Now wipe your eyes and buckle up. Because that's basically me at this precise moment. These slithering things looked a little different from the vines of the Forest Guardian, but I couldn't help but feel they were likely to have a similar intent.

"Not quite," said the pig, "The Guardian would have pulled you into its maw and digested you over the next thousand years. We like to call that Sarlacc Style around here." There was a loud thump behind me as Bors, who had been making a pretty decent effort to fight back against what was happening, was eventually dragged down and toppled to the floor.

Without the added defence of the big man, Arthur quickly followed, and they were dragged past me to vanish into the trees.

"So whatever has us isn't planning on eating me?"

"Oh, it's absolutely planning on eating you. Eventually," said the pig. "But first . . . well, I suppose you will find out soon enough. How familiar are you with hentai?"

Bet you wished you had a flaming sword round about now, right?

"Oh, do fuck off, Drynwyn."

CHAPTER 11 - IN WHICH WHATEVER YOU THINK HAPPENED BETWEEN CHAPTERS SAYS MORE ABOUT YOU THAN ME

"So, we're all agreed that we never need to speak of this again?"

Bors spat out a mouthful of green slime. Slime. That substance is absolutely slime. Slime. And grunted his agreement.

Arthur mutely nodded along with his friend's words. He hadn't opened his eyes for quite some time.

I can't say I blamed him.

I know this has been a pretty traumatic event all around, but there is something quite exciting about the form of mind manipulation that took place here. The implications for—

"Merlin?"

Shut the fuck up?

"Spot on."

***

We made our way back to the path from... where we had been.

In doing so, we left behind the cleaved-in-two body of Giles the Boggart and something that might once have been a pig before a very angry knight with giant fists pounded it into sausage meat.

Oh, and fluids.

So. Many. Fluids.

Fun fact. If your magical, sentient sword gets up off its arse and eviscerates the little monster secreting psychotropic drugs from its arse, the people being affected wake up pretty damn quickly.

Particularly if they're being . . . interfered with.

To be honest, I was feeling pretty sorry for the next inhabitant of the Enchanted Forest we came up against. I sensed both of my companions had some things they would need to work out of their systems.

It was fair to say - what with one thing and another - we'd not been the chattiest of questing groups before the attack of the invasive vine, but we were now moving through the forest in complete, awkward, horrified silence.

Rhyddrech Hael would have fucking loved this forest.

"When I say 'silence'—"

Since the . . . incident, I had been taking the point position. Arthur was taking some processing time and seemed perfectly happy to go along with my half-arsed efforts at 'tracking' Guinevere's kidnapper. In doing so, I'd decided to pull a little ahead of the others. Drynwyn and subtle sensitivity were not close relations, and he did tend to muse aloud.

"Mate, how many times? Let's leave what we saw alone. Don't swords have some sort of bro code? You know. What goes on in the glade of the cactus with the big stalk, stays in the glade of the cactus with the big stalk."

I'm not talking about that. But, for the record, abso-fucking-lutely would he have been up for some of that. All day, every day. No. What I meant was how quiet it all is. Usually, when you are in a forest, you can't move for birds singing, wolves howling and all that. But here? You can hear a pin drop. Rhyddrech was always saying he would have been alright if he could just get some fucking peace. He'd have loved it here.

I pulled Forca up in his tracks. I wouldn't say I liked it when Drynwyn had a point. But he was right; there was absolutely no noise at all.

Bors had caught me up. "What's up?"

I glanced down the trail to where Arthur was leading Llameri slowly over some brambles. We were all on foot, and I imagine – for the boys – that would be the case for the foreseeable.

"It's too quiet."

Bors grimaced. "I know what you mean. It's like the whole forest is holding its breath. From what I know about the Enchanted Forest, we should be encountering all manner of creatures. I doubt the complete absence of wildlife means anything good."

Checking Arthur was still out of earshot, I leaned close to the big man and whispered. "Do you have any idea where we are heading?"

"No. The Queen said to leave the destination to her. But," and Bors looked sheepish for a moment. Which was quite the expression on a face more setup for belligerent rage, "it's been ages since I saw any sign of a track to follow. I think, to begin with, someone had been moving ahead of us, leaving a pretty obvious trail. But I've not seen anything like that since we encountered the Forest Guardian. If there's someone following us who's planning to jump out and point us to the Bridge of Slaughter - or whatever the fuck foolish thing you all came up with - I don't know where they are."

"What are you telling me?"

Bors grimaced. "Look, I think we need to get ourselves into the mental place where we understand we are actually completely lost. In the Enchanted Forest."

I rubbed my brow. Goddam it, Guinevere. This was truly the shittiest plan since - no. I don't actually think there is a comparable shitty plan I can invoke here.

This is the gold standard for all shitty plans.

There has never been, nor will there ever be, a plan that is shittier.

We were leading Prince fucking Arthur on a wild goose chase through the Enchanted Forest, somehow hoping to stumble across someone that Queen Igraine - who didn't like any of us - had primed with directions for the next made-up stopping point on this completely made-up quest to rescue his wife.

Who hadn't actually been kidnapped.

Arthur joined us. "Everything okay?"

Bors and I exchanged a look. To be honest, I was pretty much on board with confessing the whole thing right now. Any lingering resentment that I felt towards the Prince had somewhat receded during the time it took to free him from . . .

Nope. Not going there.

I opened my mouth to speak when the forest went from utterly silent to very loud indeed.

"Greetings, mortals!"

The deepness of the booming voice made the very ground tremble. The reverberations ran right up to my feet and turned my legs to jelly. And not in a good way. Obviously, all three of our horses reared in panic and bolted into the woods. Because, of course, they did.

Strike Seven Hundred and Fifty-Three for ways in which this quest was well and truly borked.

"Leave them!" Bors yelled, yanking Arthur backwards, who had instinctively moved to follow Llameri. Not knowing where the voice had come from, we formed a defensive triad, our backs to each other and weapons out.

There was a tense moment of silence, and then the voice 'spoke' again.

"Few dare to enter my grove. What is it you foolish ones seek?"

And this is where our shitty plan really did its best to shit the bed. Because how were we supposed to know whether this was what the Queen had set up for us? If it was – and I recognise this would suggest a signifcant increase in the investment into her FX budget – we should try to play along. "Oh, we're looking for Princess Guinevere who has been stolen away by some terrible cad. Please give us advice."

On the other hand, every single thing we had come across in this bloody forest had either wanted to kill us or fuck us or both, and we shouldn't bother conversing and instead run away as fast as possible.

Arthur decided for us, "Who are you?"

An amused note entered the voice. "I am someone so far beyond your understanding that even to begin to try and answer your question would cause your brains to leak from your ears." Having been forced to sit through every episode of Lost, I could kind of see what the voice was getting at.

My dear, I would try not to anger whatever this is. There are things within this forest that would have given me pause in my prime.

I was very much on board with Operation Don't-Piss-Off-the-Unseen-Monster. Arthur, unfortunately, seemed not to have gotten the memo. "If you are so powerful, will you help us find that which we seek?"

Whoever was speaking laughed. And not a 'oh, how funny you are. Let's be friends' kind of laugh. It was more of a 'Oh, it's going to be such fun to wear your head as a hat' giggle. "Little Prince, it is clear you believe yourself to be on a quest of no small importance. Interestingly, though, I wonder if that is true of all in your party?"

Bors and I quickly put on our best 'no idea what he's chatting about, boss' expressions. I'll have you know that's a very tricky piece of mummery to get right when preparing to fight an invisible forest creature. It seemed we nailed it, though.

"My friends and I are on a quest to recover my wife, who has been stolen from me. Do you know where we can find her?"

There was a pause.

The eerie silence of the forest was not doing much to settle my nerves. Nor was the fact that Merlin had gone very quiet - as if he was doing his best not to draw any attention. Then, the voice boomed out again. "You seek that which is not lost. You will not find Princess Guinevere within this wood. There is only death for you here."

If he was daunted - or remotely suspicious - Arthur managed not to sound it. "If she is not here, do you know where she has gone?"

"Such knowledge comes at a price."

"Name it. We will gladly pay it."

Oh, goodness. My dear, you need to ensure Arthur is very careful indeed here. We should not so quickly make deals with those of the fae.

The voice chuckled. This was not an especially calming sound. If you imagine the laugh of the Wicked Witch of the West, voiced by James Earl Jones, you'd be in the right ballpark.

"Three there are of you. The Warrior. The Mage. The Lord. Thus, I propose three trials. Pass them all, and I will give you the answers you seek. Fail, and . . . well, let us say that I shall eat my fill."

For some reason, I decided to add my voice to proceedings at this stage. "Just to say, Mr. Forest, that does not seem especially balanced. You answer a question if we win, and you eat us if you win. Perhaps you should sweeten the pot a little on our end. You know, maybe we each get a weapon of mythical properties or something like that?"

"You seem to think you are in a position to make demands. It is a custom of the Enchanted Forest that I offer this opportunity to you. However, this is merely good manners, not a hard or fast rule. Should you prefer, I could just liquify you now?"

"No, that's fine. We're all about honouring quaint folk customs and practices here. Please ignore me."

A note of amusement had dripped into the voice. I didn't need Merlin's hiss of concern to see things were not going well. "Three trials there shall be. A trial of strength. A trial of thought. A trial of honour. Complete them, and you may ask your questions. Fail just one, and the consequences shall be dire."

Okay, so far, so RPG. This was your common-or-garden quest structure, and despite Merlin's doom-filled warnings, I was pretty sure we could handle it.

Bors was obviously 'the Warrior,' and considering I'd recently seen him rip out a Saxon's spine with one hand while simultaneously disemboweling another with a spoon, I felt pretty good about him coming through any fight with a win.

Arthur was clearly 'the Lord', and it seemed likely he could handle whatever the trial of 'honour' would be. I mean, he was Prince Arthur. Honour was literally his one job.

That left me as the Mage with the Trial of Thought.

And - let's be honest here - I would be cheating like a bandit.

CHAPTER 12 - IN WHICH GUINEVERE GETS TO WORK OUT SOME OF HER FRUSTRATIONS

Guinevere stood her ground as the Saxon horseman urged his mount up the hill towards her. Her hair, braided tightly, fluttered like a golden banner in the wind, and she held the pose for a second longer than strictly necessary just to ensure anyone watching understood she was not afraid in the slightest.

To be fair, her attacker - a lad barely out of childhood, in all honesty, all awkward limbs and spotty face - was not an especially impressive sight, and she was already upgrading him in her mind for when she would retell the story later. He was a hulking figure, clad in chainmail that glinted with each powerful stride of his steed. The horse, a massive black stallion, thundered across the grassy plain, its hooves tearing up clods of earth. The Saxon's face was a mask of rage, his beard wild, and his blue eyes burning with the fervour of battle. A broad-bladed axe was clutched in his right hand, ready to strike . . .

Okay, she might need to dial that back a bit. The wizard had said her prose was a little overdone on the ransom note. Maybe she had a point.

It was enough that she, a lone Princess, was being chased across a desolate moor and had turned to face her pursuer.

No need to overwrite the whole thing.

With a fluidity that spoke of many hours of practice, she turned sidewise to minimise her profile and settled into her stance, feet shoulder-width apart. Memories of an old soldier kicking her legs into their 'proper position' whispered through her mind, and she found herself grinning as she shuffled her feet a touch wider into the stance he had called 'whore fucking a dwarf'.

Funnily enough, she hadn't shared that with her father.

The drumbeat of the approaching hooves gave her a rhythm to further still her mind, allowing her to smoothly go through her work.

Guinevere raised her longbow, which, at six feet tall, stood taller than she did. This size allowed for a full draw, maximising the potential energy stored in its yew limbs. She drew the string, her fingers finding their familiar places. The size of the bow meant the draw required significant strength, not just in her arms but also in her back and shoulders. Arthur had never liked how well-developed her muscles were. But, as she'd explained, years of rigorous training will do that to you.

What exactly did he expect? But no. Why would he value that aspect of her? He much preferred his women soft, helpless, and damply grateful.

The bowstring came back smoothly, stopping at her anchor point — the corner of her mouth — ensuring the angle and direction of the shot would remain consistent.

The hoofbeats drew closer, and she matched her breathing to their rise and fall, slowing her heartbeat and settling into the perfect state of mind for what was coming next. She recognised the irony that she was probably calmer right now as death - or worse - rapidly approached than she ever was in the presence of her husband.

No more of that. Once this was over, there would be time to ruminate on the state of her marriage. She had another, more pressing issue before her right now.

Guinevere paused and waited for the precise moment to release – as with so many things, timing was crucial. Too early, and the arrow would miss its mark; too late, and the horseman would close the distance.

Whilst not as skilled as she was with the bow, she had no little ability with the spear she carried on her back. But close-quarter fighting was to be avoided wherever possible.

"Yer strong for a lass, but most men will be stronger. Prick them from distance unless you want them pricking you up close."

Now she thought again of his words, what on earth had her father been doing, allowing a man of Bryntag's demeanour to train his eight-year-old daughter? It was a wonder she'd turned out as well as she had.

Said the Princess, who'd set up a wholly fictional kidnap narrative to make her husband love her again.

Probably best not to pick at that scab right now.

As the Saxon neared, Guinevere calculated the lead necessary to account for the speed of the horse. It was a complex, split-second calculation involving the arrow's trajectory, the horse's pace, and the distance closing between them. Her eyes, long trained to make such judgements quickly, made subtle adjustments to her aim.

With a decisive, almost imperceptible movement, Guinevere released the arrow. It screamed outwards, aimed not just to strike the Saxon but to take him in the head.

It was a ridiculously complicated choice, but she needed to unseat her foe from his horse before he reached her. This seemed the most likely way to achieve that.

With a sound as noiseless as a soft sigh, the shot went through the horseman's left eye, and he toppled from his saddle. The horse, suddenly free of the weight, shied off to the left, fouling the progress of the second horseman that Guinevere had chosen, by necessity, to ignore.

At the speed they were travelling, the accidental collision led to the other Saxon being unhorsed and - judging by the cracking sound of bones he made as he hit the ground - out of the pursuit.

Guinevere nodded. Pleased with herself. "Two for the price of one arrow. Not bad."

Of course, she was now down to her final arrow.

And there were still three Saxons out there somewhere. But she quite liked those odds.

With a smile on her face, she went back to climbing up the hill, scampering on her hands and knees over the uneven terrain.

If anyone had been able to ask her, she would have told them she was having the time of her life.

✳✳✳

The plan, such as it was, had started to unravel almost the moment Guinevere was beyond Tintagel's walls. She had refused all offers of support or accompaniment that Igraine had suggested. And, as soon as that clingy wizard had left her alone in the little village, she'd made her excuses to her hosts, retired to bed and, when everyone else was asleep, made a run for it.

55

Quite simply, she did not trust any of these Britons to keep their word.

If her plan was going to work, she wanted to ensure all the parts that depended on her went precisely as intended. She would make sure she was where she was supposed to be when the time came, and Igraine and the rest of them could focus their attention on keeping Arthur on the right track.

Leaving Guinevere on her own.

Exactly how she liked it.

Ironically, though, she'd miscalculated the extent of the turmoil in the land around the castle following the Saxon invasion. She'd barely been travelling a few bells before being forced to abandon most of her baggage when bandits showed far too much interest in a richly dressed lady travelling the road on her own.

And then, two days later, she'd attracted the attention of a band of roving Saxons and needed to take evasive action.

Unfortunately, they had proved oddly committed in their pursuit of her, and this had become an unwelcome distraction that had pretty much destroyed any hope of Operation Rescue Guinevere actually coming off as intended.

Thus, as Guinevere fled uphill away from the last three of a group that had once numbered ten, she had no idea where she was, how she would get back on track, or even if anyone knew things had gone awry.

But she was sure it would all work out okay. One way or another.

***

As night began to fall, Guinevere congratulated herself on somehow staying ahead of the remaining Saxons and reaching a copse of wood to hide within. A small voice in the back of her head kept trying to point out this was because they were letting her run herself to exhaustion, but she had no truck with that sort of defeatest thinking.

Guinevere had found a small area where trees grew close together, and the ground was particularly uneven. Exactly the sort of place she had been trained to turn to her advantage. They'd need to lead their horses through this bit. If it was in a single file, so much the better. To that end, Guinevere chose a narrow path, bordered by two large trees, knowing she could easily lead them through this natural choke point.

Dropping to her knees, she selected a sturdy, flexible sapling that could bend significantly without breaking. She carefully bent it over, using its natural tension as the driving force for her trap.

The technical challenge here was to bend the tree just enough to store ample energy but not so much as to snap it or make it obvious. There was an obvious innuendo to make, and, not for the first time, she regretted not having anyone around to share it with. She guessed that was why her husband constantly travelled with a large band of friends. She bet Arthur was never short of an appreciative audience for a good 'bending the sapling over' gag.

As a consequence of her musings, she may have whittled the sharpened piece of wood to attach to the sapling with a little more vigour than was strictly necessary.

Guinevere then anchored the sapling in its bent position - another wasted opportunity for jolly japery - using a tripwire made from vines she had hastily weaved together. With that all done, she placed the tripwire across the path and camouflaged it with leaves and debris to ensure it remained hidden from sight.

Finally, Guinevere attached a trigger to the tripwire and set it up in such a way that, when disturbed, it would release the sapling. The engineering behind this was precise; the trigger had to be sensitive enough to activate at the slightest touch, yet stable enough not to go off prematurely.

"That's what she said," she said loudly.

Nope.

It just wasn't the same without an audience.

Her words, though, had the effect of drawing the three Saxons to her, leaving their horses behind to run after her. They were, as she was pleased to note, in single file as intended. Men could be so predictable. She ran through the choke point between the two trees, turned and prepared her bow to shoot.

As expected, the leading Saxon stepped on the concealed tripwire. The sapling was released in an instant; its stored energy propelled the spear forward with lethal force and speed. The warrior, caught completely off guard, could not react in time.

Arterial spray filled the air.

The one following behind paused just long enough in horror at the demise of his friend to provide a nicely static and well-lit target for her to place her final arrow in the centre of his chest.

Two down, one to go.

She discarded the bow and reached for her spear.

The remaining Saxon looked at the bodies of his friends and then up at her. He did not look exactly afraid - she doubted he had the imagination - but he could recognise something was not working out exactly as it should.

He was bigger, stronger, better armed and - well - he was a man. His worldview did not really have space for this working out any other way. And he held on to those convictions right until the moment Guinevere kicked him in the groin and pinged the head of her spear through his throat.

Blowing away a tendril of hair that fell across her face, the Princess efficiently looted the corpses, recovered her own kit and, with a satisfied step of knowing a job well done, carried on her merry way.

As she went, she wondered how Arthur's quest was going.

She presumed he was having as much fun as she was.

CHAPTER 13 - IN WHICH WE HEAR A RIDDLE YOU WILL ALL BE ASKING AROUND THE DINNER TABLE TONIGHT

"Oh, come on! You cannot be serious!"

Call me cynical, but I was beginning to think the all-powerful, disembodied voice of a monster from the Enchanted Forest might not be seeking to wholly embody the British sense of fair play.

***

In preparation for the first challenge, a giant warrior in plate mail had manifested out of nowhere and clanked forward to stand in the middle of a softly glowing circle.

The three of us exchanged confident nods, and I fist-bumped Bors. "Trial of Strength. You're up, big guy." As I immediately needed to cycle some Qi to heal three broken fingers, I felt we'd probably picked the right horse for this particular challenge.

Bors yawned and stepped forward into what was clearly a fighting ring, swinging his arms forward and back and cracking his neck from side to side.

Stood opposite the giant mailed knight, Bors was perhaps a head smaller and a touch less wide. However, what he may be giving away in size, Arthur and I were confident he would make up for in unbridled, batshit crazy aggression. When in his battle fury, Bors made a dog-less John Wick seem positively chill.

"Who have you selected for the first trial?" The booming voice felt like it was coming from all around. I was beginning to suspect we might be talking **to** the Enchanted Forest rather than to someone within it . . .

"Me. Sir Bors the Younger."

"So be it."

At those words, the ring of light around Bors glowed brighter, rose upwards, and then went over the top of the two opponents to form a sealed dome.

"Although your champion can no longer hear you, you can listen to how he fairs in the Trial of Thought."

"Hang on," Arthur stepped forward, then realised he didn't know where the voice was. "The Trial of Thought? We want Bors to do the Trial of Strength."

"I imagine you did." And the voice did its creepy laugh again.

I did warn you, my dear. Do not make deals with the fae.

As helpful as yet another 'I told you so' from Merlin was in this situation, there was nothing more for us to do than settle down and watch Bors compete in a mental challenge. Having repeatedly seen him put his jerkin on the wrong way around, it would be fair to say my hopes weren't high.

***

Bors knew people thought he was stupid.

And he didn't mind. To be honest, he'd encouraged the perception.

His size and reputation for brutal insanity made most people he met feel highly uncomfortable around him. So, if it helped smooth things over for him to play at being a bit thick sometimes, that was a price worth paying.

In his heart, Bors liked people and liked people liking him. If they needed to feel superior to him for that to happen, he was okay with it.

So, he felt less immediate concern than Arthur and Morgan when the words "Welcome to the Trial of Thought" boomed out across the glowing cage that had appeared around him and the big streak of piss opposite.

"This trial is a test of your mental acuity. Your opponent will ask you a riddle. If you can solve it, you will be allowed an undefended strike upon him. Should you be unable to answer it, he will be allowed the same. Should the competitor who is struck survive, they will have an opportunity to ask their own riddle, and the pattern will continue. This trial will only complete when one of you is dead."

Bors raised his hand. "I have a few questions."

He was sure he heard the voice sigh. "Ask your questions, little mortal."

"You say 'strike'. Are we talking a bitch-slap, or can I use my axe?"

"You can interpret the instruction in any way you wish. You will, however, note that your opponent, whilst mailed, carries no weapon."

"Fair enough. And, just to check, what are we talking about going on under the armour? Is it mortal? Not that I'm calling you out or anything here, but my boy Gawyne will tell you that just because you cut someone's head off, there's no guarantee it will stay off. If you know what I mean?"

In response, his opponent flicked up the visor of his helm. His voice was deep and raspy. "While I have lived for many centuries, Sir Bors, I am as susceptible to violence as any mortal. Be warned, though. I have undertaken the Trial of Thought countless times over the years. That I stand before you should be all the warning you require. It is not too late to concede and go on your way."

Bors smiled and shook his head. "Nah. Let's play this out."

The knight sighed ruefully and dropped his visor. "As you wish."

The dome's glow changed to a vivid green, and it looked as if a spotlight focused upon the mailed knight.

"Hear my first riddle:

On grēne mǣdum ond wudu swāðe,

Ic licge stille, sumes gest.

Ic blǣse nāt, hwæðre ic geseo līf,

On fugol ond blōstma, on lēaf ond trēow.

Menn tredað ofer mē, hwæðre hīe mē ne fielað,

Þurh winteres cyle ond sumeres hātu.

Ic bewege nāt, hwæðre fare ic feorr,

Under sunnan, beneoþan steorra."

*

"What the fuck?"

Hang on. It's a weird, old-fashioned form of Saxon. I felt Merlin move some of my Qi to my ears and shivered. The more control I gained over my own powers, the more his doing this sort of thing creeped me out.

Okay. You should be able to understand that going forward.

"What did it mean?"

I jumped as Arthur spoke from behind me.

"In meadows green and forests vast,

I lay in wait, a silent guest.

No breath I take, yet life I see,

In bird and bloom, in leaf and tree.

Men tread on me, yet feel me not,

Through winter's chill and summer's hot.

I do not move, yet travel far,

Under the sun, beneath the star."

By the look on Bor's face, he had as little idea what it meant as I did.

"Any ideas?"

"The answer is a shadow," Arthur said, his eyes glued on his friend in the glowing dome. Bors was shaking his head.

***

"No idea. Go on then, clanky. Give it your best shot."

The mailed knight stepped out of the spotlight and quickly closed the distance between them. His fist blurred, and Bors flew backwards to crash into the magical walls around them. He lay still for a moment, then slowly clambered to his feet, spitting a bloody mouthful of teeth out as he did so.

"Okay. Nice one. Is it my turn now?"

The mailed knight had returned to his spot and raised his visor again. "Sir Bors, you have shown great courage in this endeavour and exemplary resilience in seeking to carry on after my initial strike. Few survive, and fewer still seek to invite a second blow. Please, let us end this now.

"But I want to ask my riddle."

Shaking his head, the knight replaced his visor. "So be it. Should I solve it, I will strike again. I fear you will no longer be alive following that."

"I better make it a good one then.

In the hall, I sit in silence,

Guarding treasures without violence."

"A key," the knight answered immediately and closed the gap. The blow he struck Bors lifted him a foot off his feet.

***

The mailed knight asked four more riddles without answer and immediately solved the three Bors had asked back.

Arthur's fists clenched and reclenched. Neither of us had any idea how the big man was still alive. His face was a ruin. Most of his teeth had been knocked out, and both his cheekbones were shattered. By his stumbling about, it was apparent he could not easily see out of either of his swollen eyes. Having once endured an evening's company of a big fan of all things boxing, I felt I had the mansplained knowledge to state Bors was 'fucked'.

After each blow, the mailed knight had tried to persuade Bors to quit, but the big man simply shook his head and pressed onwards.

It was now Bor's turn to ask the riddle.

"I've been saving this one until I needed it." His head lolled forward, and I think he briefly lost consciousness. But then he stood upright again and swayed back and forth. There was no doubt this was pretty much over.

Bors licked his bruised lips, and a smile formed on his face. As blood leaked down his chin, he forced out the words.

"I am a wonderful help to women,
The hope of something to come.
I harm no one except my slayer.
I stand rooted on a high bed.
I am shaggy below.
I remember a peasant's daughter grabbing my body,
Brushing my red skin, holding me hard,
And claiming my head.
Last night, Mrs Bors caught me fast.
She felt our meeting. Her eye was wet."

For the first time, the mailed knight paused. Just as I hoped there might be some respite to the one-way battering, he nodded and said, "An onion. I am sorry, Sir Bors. You have been a worthy opponent."

He moved forward to deliver what would clearly be a lethal strike when Bors' voice croaked out. "No. That's wrong."

The knight stopped and tilted his head in question. "The answer is clearly 'an onion.' Helpful to women in cookery, gives hope of a coming meal. Harms its slayer by causing tears when cut. Has a rooted top and shaggy roots below. Peasants' daughters dig it up, remove the skin and chop them up. Your wife used one in your meal last night, and her eyes streamed."

"Not the answer I wanted."

"What other possible answer is there?"

Bors cleared his throat and hawked another bloody globful to the ground. "My dick."

The knight did not say anything for a moment. Then, he quickly returned to his place. "In recognition of your sacrifice this day, I will allow your answer fits your riddle more completely than my response. You will be allowed to strike me. You should know, Sir Bors, that I have not been struck in nearly three hundred years. You have truly shown yourself to be amongst the greatest of men in this Trial of Thought. I am sorry that you will die on my next question."

All things being equal, we might have hoped that a single punch from Bors would have a decent chance of ringing this dude's bell. However, looking at the swaying, stumbling figure of what was left of our friend, it was obvious he had nothing left. He wasn't so much punchdrunk as punchparalytic. I doubted the mailed knight would even feel the contact through his armour.

"Cheers, mate."

Bors stumbled towards the knight and lifted both arms above his head as if preparing to try a double-fist downward blow onto his opponent's helm.

I don't think any of us expected him to pull his Great Axe from behind his back to chop downwards with all the momentum of a meteorite with a grudge against the dinosaurs.

The mailed knight was split entirely in two, both sides vanishing in a puff of light as they hit the ground.

There was a moment of silence, and then the unseen voice boomed out in outrage. "Sir Bors! Your opponent merely struck you with their hand. You should have replied in kind."

Clearly, the only thing keeping Bors upright now was that he was pressing all his weight down upon the axe. He looked up to the sky in his reply. "Weren't the fucking Trial of Honour, was it?"

CHAPTER 14 - IN WHICH THOSE QUIBBLING WITH THE PHYSICS NEED TO REMEMBER ALL THE FUCKING MAGIC ABOUT

As soon as I'd reached the mountain of minced beef that was Bors, I'd passed him 'Melehan's Rock of Continous Curing' and did what I could to push my Qi in and around his injuries.

Even with all that going on, it took a good couple of hours for the worst of the obvious damage to start to fade away. Watching facial bones shift and reconnect together is quite a trip - kind of like watching a week-old helium balloon suddenly reinflating and looking for a fight.

"Should I be worried about internal damage?" I asked Merlin. "That artefact seems pretty nifty in repairing bones and skin, but I don't know if it addresses brain trauma."

I looked over to where Bors was, for the hundredth time, re-enacting the whole fight for Arthur with two dead squirrels.

"I mean, the riddle was about my dick. How did he not expect to get fucked?"

I feel great affection for Sir Bors, so it pains me to note I am unsure how we would be able to tell if he was cognitively impaired.

"Meow, Big M."

There was a flash, and then the glowing trial circle on the ground reappeared. However, this time, there was not an opponent within it, but three stones of granite about the size of a big cow and what looked like another one in a deep pool of water.

Interesting.

"There's a lot of different interpretations of that word, mate. Is that 'interesting' like you're going to really enjoy this Trial. It's a fascinating way to spend a few hours. Or 'interesting' as in fuck me, I didn't see this particular nightmare coming. We're screwed."

Little from Column A. Little from B, to be honest.

Before I could process that bit of deep and meaningful advice, Arthur stood and strode into the circle.

"Dude! Aren't we even going to talk about which of us does this one?"

He looked my way, and I was struck by how sad his eyes had become. We'd still not properly sorted out what had gone wrong with our relationship of late, but I was beginning to suspect it might have a little less to do with me, and a bit more about him in general.

As a card-carrying narcissist, this caused me physical pain.

Seemingly unaware that he was failing to treat me as the centre of his universe in the very creepy way I clearly needed, Arthur shrugged and gave me an odd smile. "Do you think it matters? The force that challenges us has proven itself to be capricious in the extreme. Should we decide I should do the Trial of Honour, and you should do the one of Strength, I am sure a way will be found to frustrate that choice. Sir Bors has set us on the path to victory, and I will look to continue that tradition."

At that, he turned his back on me and faced the centre of the ring.

In case you missed it, the unsubtle undertone there was that if he let you go next, he thinks you'd fuck it up.

"Cheers, Drynwyn."

No worries. Happy to help translate. I've spent quite a lot of time with that fucking grumble-cunt of late. Picked up his 'tells', you know what I mean?

I was saved from further 'help' and advice by the disembodied voice of the Enchanted Forest swanning back into town. "I see the Lord has chosen to undertake The Trial of Strength. This is a brave, nay foolish, decision. In my long experience, whilst a Lord is used to achieving their desires, they rarely do so through the power of their own arm. Should you wish to back out and let the Mage take your place, I shall, in recognition of the success of the Warrior, allow this substitution. Just this once.

I'd barely had a chance to open my mouth to speak before Arthur had replied in the negative. "No. I will do this Trial. Let's fucking get on with it."

"Fine words, little mortal. Let us see if you are any different from those who came before you. To complete this Trial, you simply must move each of the stones outside of the challenge circle."

Arthur did not respond to the goading. He simply stood and looked at each of the objects before him.

The first stone was embedded in the ground. On it was carved a triple spiral pattern that I was pretty sure I had on a bunch of jewellery.

It's a triskelion, my dear. It can be thought to symbolise many things, but in the context of this challenge, I imagine it means Earth.

A second stone floated about ten feet above the others, and in its centre, it had a stick with a snake wrapped around it - *a Cadeceus. The symbol of Hermes. This probably is intended to suggest Air.*

The rock hovering in the sky has a symbol meaning 'Air' carved on it? Fuck me, it's a good job you're here, Merlin. Not sure any of the rest of us could manage that level of advanced cryptology.

I'd always liked Drynwyn.

The third rock was lying on the ground but was surrounded by a ring of white-hot magical flames. On it was a triangular symbol, which, and I know I'm going out on a limb here, but I'm going to hazard that might mean 'Fire'.

Are you really siding with the sword against me, my dear?

There was no sign of the final rock, presumably because it was at the bottom of the pool of water. "Can I just check, Big M. Do all your years of cultivation experience give you any clue what the symbol on the final rock may be?"

You jest, my dear. But it is clear that this Trial would have been wholly facile for you, with your growing connection to the elements. Who - or what - is running these challenges deliberately seeks to ensure you fail.

"Awesome. And Arthur's chances?"

There was a pause. *It is unlikely that anyone who is not a cultivator will be able to move even one, let alone all four of those stones.*

"So, we're fucked?"

Perhaps. However, Prince Arthur is not just 'anyone'.

***

"Do you understand the challenge?" The disembodied voice boomed out.

"Pick up a rock and move it outside the circle. Is there a particular order I need to do them in?"

"No."

"Is there a time limit?"

"Not really. However, should I become bored, I may review that. You must give it your best endeavours. Be entertaining, and I will allow it to play out."

"Generous of you. Any other rules?"

The voice did not answer for a moment. "I can sense that one of your companions has significant power at their disposal. Should I sense any external magical interference in your Trial, I will treat that as a failure with all the attendant consequences for you and your party. You can, however, use any non-magical equipment you may possess."

Arthur nodded. "Fair enough. Your arrival scared away my horse earlier. Can you bring her back? There are some things in her saddlebags I think I will need."

Arthur had barely finished speaking when Llameri appeared beside him in the circle.

"You have everything you requested. The Trial begins . . . now."

***

I watched as Arthur rested a hand on his horse's neck and whispered softly to her. She quickly calmed down - what with one thing and another, she was not exactly having the best day of her horsey life thus far - and allowed Arthur to retrieve a thick coil of rope from a pack on her back.

Still speaking quietly to the horse, he crossed to the Earth stone and tied one end of the rope around it. He gave it a few experimental tugs, but there was no discernible movement.

The voice laughed its creepy laugh. "If you think it will be that easy, little mortal, you are sadly mistaken."

In my best stage whisper, I said, "Big M, I can't help but think whatever is running this Trial is a bit of a twat."

Indeed.

Arthur turned to me and smiled. Then he moved over to the Air stone and stood looking up at it. After a few moments of consideration, he asked, "Can I leave the circle for a moment?"

The Enchanted Forest replied instantly. "You can. If you look to escape, though, I will immediately kill you and the rest of your party."

"Understood."

Still carrying the rope, Arthur stepped outside the circle and made directly for a giant tree at the edge of the clearing that was halfway between the two stones. He scaled it with some hitherto unremarked ninja skills and looped the rope around an especially thick branch. Then, sitting on that branch, he looped the end of the rope into a lasso and tossed it over the Air stone.

I say he 'tossed it over the Air stone.'

To be clear, he missed the first forty-nine times. After each failure, Arthur needed to climb down from the tree, retrieve the rope, climb back up, loop it over the branch and throw it again.

Ultimately, I'm not convinced the disembodied voice didn't cheat a little just to move the whole thing along. Eventually, he managed to get the coil of rope where he intended it.

"My patience is growing thin, little mortal."

"Okay. I think I'm set."

Having achieved his aim, Arthur had returned to the circle, braced himself next to the Earth stone, and began to try to pull the Air stone out of the sky.

He obviously got nowhere.

Even using the rudimentary pulley system he had set up, with the Earth stone as an anchor, he simply didn't have the raw strength.

"A good try, little mortal. However, . . ."

Then Llameri grabbed the rope between her teeth, and things got a bit more interesting.

***

Fundamentally, no matter how pretty the symbol is carved upon them, giant rocks do not especially enjoy being suspended in the air.

While the full might of the Prince of the Britons leveraging every rule of mechanical physics available in the sixth century was not enough to get things moving, two and half thousand pounds of prime, motivated warhorse was a different matter.

The Air stone fell from the sky.

As it swooped downwards, its newly freed weight pulled on its end of the rope, ripping the Earth stone from the ground, finishing its swing by crashing into the Fire stone, knocking it out of its flaming circle.

All three rocks were thus in motion.

In a moment of barely believable coincidence, each crashed into the pool containing the Water stone, and then the world's biggest game of marbles began. The combined weight of all three stones and the momentum of the swing were enough to cause a significant splash, emptying the pool, and dousing the flames that had been around the Fire stone. Each of the stones ended up rolling towards the edge of its pool.

There was a chilly silence, broken only by Arthur whistling a jaunty little number as he lassoed the rope around each stone (again, I'm skirting over the hours this took. Arthur did not have a future as a cowboy ahead of him). He eventually had Llameri drag them outside the circle.

The light on the challenge circle faded.

"You know, Big M, it'd be cool if Arthur made some sort of Roger Mooresque 007 quip right about now."

Something like, "Well, that's not the first time I have done four at once and ended up utterly soaked. Though never before with a horse."

"Fucking hell, mate. Where did that come from? No. Nothing like that at all."

CHAPTER 15 - IN WHICH I, UNFORGIVABLY, MISS THE OPPORTUNITY TO INCLUDE MUPPETS

"Welcome, little mortal, to the Trial of Honour, a challenge as ancient as the cosmos and as revered as the virtues it seeks to unearth within you.

I, who have watched the rise and fall of civilisations and witnessed the turning of the ages and the dance of destiny, stand before you not just as your judge but as the custodian of a tradition that has tested the mettle of heroes since time immemorial."

"Dude, no one else had to put up with a massive cut-scene intro. Can't we move things along?"

Can I just point out it might be best not to antagonise the all-powerful disembodied voice?

"You, who stand on the precipice of this hallowed rite, bear more than just your hopes and dreams. You carry the legacy of those who walked this path before you, the aspirations of those who will follow, and the expectations of the very essence of Honour itself."

"I really don't. I'm just a girl standing in front of - well, nothing. There's literally nothing here, and I'm talking to thin air. But, basically, I'm just a girl, standing in front of an immortal Enchanted Forest asking for directions to a fucking bridge. A bridge, I need to point out, that has no real fucking peril associated with it, because the whole quest we've come up with is made up. Literally, the only threat here comes from you being a twat. You're the one who conjured up all this Trial bullshit for us. I can't help but feel you're making more of this than it needs to be. Can we just spool on through to the bit where I improbably blag my way through whatever over-elaborate game you have set up, and then we get what we need?"

"This Trial is not merely an assessment of strength..."

"Nope, because Arthur physics'd the shit out of that one."

"Or a measure of thought..."

"Bors' dick sorted that."

"Little mortal!" Ah, there it is. That particular tone of frustrated impatience I can bring out in the best of them. Even Enchanted Forests, apparently. "Can you please let me finish without the commentary? I do not get to deliver this speech very often, and I'd appreciate not being interrupted."

Seriously, my dear. There's a bigger picture here we need to remember and as fun as it may be to annoy this being, it does have the power to vapourise you. I'd rather we avoided this if at all possible.

Yeah, I could see where he was coming from on that one. I think I was letting my inner 'me' out a touch more than was ideal. "Sorry. That's my bad. That's on me. Please continue."

"Thank you. Now, where was I? Ah, yes. This Trial delves deeper into the very core of your being. It seeks the truth of your character, your spirit's resilience, and your heart's integrity. Only those who embody the most authentic ideals of Honour, who can rise above the baser temptations of their mortal coil, shall find glory here.

"So, let your heart be steadfast, your mind clear, and your spirit unyielding. For the Trial of Honour begins now, and with it, the chance to etch your name into the annals of eternity. May your actions reflect the nobility of your purpose and may your journey through this Trial reveal the brilliance of the Honour that lies within each of you."

There was a long silence.

"Do you not have anything to say in response, little mortal?"

"Sorry. I zoned out there for a moment. I was thinking about the end of The Shawshank Redemption. Have you seen it? No? You absolutely should. Banging movie. Right at the end, Tim Robbins secretly tunnels out of prison, and he's hid his escape hole with a poster of some long-limbed bimbo. But, when you think about it, how did he manage to reattach the poster to the *outside* of the escape tunnel after leaving through it? I mean, how did he do it? How?"

Sigh.

There was more than just a slight peeved tone when the disembodied voice boomed back. "The Trial of Honour starts now."

It would appear I had once again misread the mood of a social situation.

***

When I woke up, it was so dark that, looking out of bed, I could scarcely distinguish the transparent window from the opaque walls of my chamber until suddenly, the church clock tolled a deep, dull, hollow, melancholy ONE.

Hang on a minute . . .

Light flashed up in the room upon the instant, and the curtains of my bed were drawn aside by a strange figure - like a child: yet not so like a child as like an old man, viewed through some supernatural medium, which gave him the appearance of having receded from the view, and being diminished to a child's proportions. Its hair, which hung about its neck and down its back, was white as if with age, and yet the face had not a wrinkle in it, and the tenderest bloom was on the skin.

"Oh, for fuck's sake."

The little old man stared at me, as if he were paused waiting for me to say something else.

Well, he could bloody well wait.

"A Christmas Carol? Seriously? This is the best you can do? The Trial of Honour is 'A Christmas Carol?' Look, spoiler alert, but I'm perfectly happy to fork out for the Cratchitts to have a big fucking turkey without needing any further ado. Boom. Job done. Honour satisfied all round."

There was no reply.

The creepy little old child-man stayed frozen at the end of my - well, Scrooge's - bed. I was starting to regret not treating the disembodied voice with the respect he clearly felt he deserved.

If only someone could have warned you, my dear...

Fuck off, Merlin.

I stayed where I was for a while, but nothing else happened. Apparently, I was going to have to play this one out. Fortunately, I'd been in a God-awful am-dram version of Dickens' book a few years back. It wasn't really my scene, but, you know, I rock a corset and bustle, so it seemed rude not to. From the dark of the wings, I ended up doing a lot of prompting - and a bunch of the cast, buddumtish - so I had most of the words down pat.

The next line was: "Are you the Spirit, sir, who's coming was foretold to me?"

The Ghost suddenly sprang back into life. "I am!"

"Who and what are you?"

"I am the Ghost of Christmas Past."

Awesome. Such happy times.

***

From what I could tell, the Trial of Honour was about showing me things that had happened in my life and highlighting occasions where my choices were aligned with or deviated from the path of 'Honour.' Apparently, I was expected to acknowledge my past mistakes and vow to learn from them, demonstrating humility and the willingness to grow. Oh, and buy everyone a fucking big Christmas turkey at the end of it all.

The problem was, after a while, my past mistakes seemed to have seriously bummed out the Ghost of Christmas Past.

In fact, he'd got so upset we needed to have a break from popping in on a succession of moments that I freely admit were not my finest hour. We seemed to be running through things chronologically - by my reckoning, we'd only got up to the mid-nineties so far - and my next 'memory' should be me about to make a series of poor decisions in a graveyard with several people who did not have my personal wellbeing at the heart of their thinking. From what I could remember that night was somewhere in between stealing Nan's just 'in-case' money tin and planting a bag of . . . herbs on Zizzie rather than owning up to the cops about them being mine.

That had been a busy weekend.

The Ghost, however, was currently sitting on the edge of Scrooge's bed, rocking himself backwards and forwards. "These are shadows of the things that have been," he said. "That they are what they are, do not blame me!"

"I don't blame you, mate. Sometimes, bad things happen to bad people. That's just the way it is. Some things'll never change. That's just the way it is." I may have started humming at this stage.

"Enough!"

At that booming shout, the Victorian bedroom vanished, and I was back stood in the Trial Circle.

"You are making a mockery of the Trial of Honour."

"Mate, it's not my fault your Ghost has a queasy stomach. I wish my past was all dances at the Fezziwigs and choosing focusing on work rather than pursuing love, but it wasn't. Did I do my share of fucked up things? Damn straight. Probably did the share of most of my street, too. Some of it I wished I hadn't, and I'd like to think I've learned from them. But I'm not saying if you put me back there right now, I'd be Little Miss Perfect and choose the road less travelled. Life doesn't work like that.

69

I'm me because of those fucked up things, not despite them. There. What more do you need from me?

There was a noise like the whole forest breathing in, and then a chalice appeared on the ground in front of me.

Shit. Don't go near that.

I, of course, walked forward and picked up the cup. It was filled with a deep purple liquid - looking not unlike my Qi.

"You speak of Honour as if it is a thing, you can choose or deny. Well, then, let us test your commitment to that. The chalice you hold contains the purest essence of sacrifice. Drinking it will induce a vision of a significant personal sacrifice that you will need to make in the future for the good of others. It could be a foregone personal desire, a relinquishment of a cherished dream, or accepting a deep personal loss that will ultimately benefit those around you. The nature of the sacrifice required is such that it does not demand immediate action but requires a commitment to a future choice, a constant reminder of your duty and the price of Honour."

"I'm going to be honest, as slogans go, that's no 'Red Bull gives you Wings'. You could do on working on your marketing patter."

My dear, you do not need to drink this potion. By any measure, in confronting and accepting your past choices, you have passed the Trial of Honour. The quest setter cannot simply add another stage because he does not like how you achieved that.

I looked down at the purple liquid and swirled it around the cup. I guess Merlin was right. But who wouldn't want a vision of the future? It wasn't like it locked me into anything.

I knocked that drink back like Tommy just burst in the door whippin' Pam's ass worse than before.

"Fuck. I really am a shitty person, aren't I?"

And the vision began.

CHAPTER 16 - IN WHICH THERE IS A VISION OF CAMLANN

I wasn't a big fan of this vision.

I'm not unfamiliar with the concept of imbibing an unknown substance and then being taken somewhat out of myself. However, this would be the first time I'd partaken and then been transported to the aftermath of a massive battle.

Given a choice, it goes without saying a beach in Bali with Jared Leto fulfilling my every need would have been much preferable.

However, we are where we are.

And where we are is obviously Camlann.

For those of you who are here for the knob gags and are thus not Arthurian scholars, it's probably worth catching you up here. Basically, in our timeline Arthur has a bastard child who grows up to hate him - I know, who would have thought it? He seems so chaste and reliable! But, after a lot of chivalric shenanigans, various things happen, leading to a massive battle at Camlann, loads of knights you will have heard of die, and Arthur and Mordred go mano a mano. Oh, and depending which source you are following, Lancelot isn't there to help because he's been banished due to the whole fucking Guinevere subplot.

Anyhow, father and son fight, Mordred dies, Arthur gets mortally wounded, and the Lady of the Lake arrives to spirit him away to Avalon to heal him up. He's then supposed to be waiting until Britain needs him to come back and save the day.

All good? Then, let's get back to it.

In my vision, the sun was dipping below the horizon, casting long shadows across the battlefield. The Enchanted Forest had clearly decided to go all out on the pathetic fallacy. So much so that I feel confident making an early call that someone will drop to their knees, shouting 'noooo!' in the near future, at which point there will be a massive crash of thunder.

There are bodies everywhere.

I see people I recognise from in and around Tintagel to my left - in keeping with the primary school level of visual metaphor in this vision, they all seem to be in white armour. I'm sure some of them are still alive, but the vibe is very much 'last moments of The Cabin in the Woods'. To my right are a bunch of guys and dolls I've never come across before, but they're wearing black armour and have made huge investments in goth eyeliner. Might just be me, but I don't think they're on the side of the angels.

Standing opposite me is Arthur - and he's seen better days. And I say this as the woman who oversaw him being deep-fried. His armour has been completely battered out of shape and he looks like Carrie seconds after her closest friends had performed a jolly jape. He's carrying a glowing sword that isn't

Drynwyn, so I'm going to take a punt, it's Excalibur. It hangs limply in his grasp, its blade dulled and chipped.

Then it starts to rain.

Because of course it does. Because this is England, where the pathetic fallacy comes pre-packaged with the weather and a complimentary cup of lukewarm tea.

Under the sudden deluge, blood starts to run in rivers through the trampled grasses, and the field turns into mud. And in about one hundred and fifty years, I can hear John Bunyan going, "ah, that's exactly what I'm going for in my Slough of Despond."

Arthur's gaze finds its way to me, and it occurs to me that, in this vision, I seem to play the role of Mordred. Well . . . that's unsettling. Is the suggestion that I'm actually going to be the one here fighting him at the end - I look down, and it's definitely Drynwyn I have in my hand - or is this more of a subconscious final battle?

We engage in a few moments of tense eye-fucking and then I hear a voice intone, "In that moment, the world narrowed to the expanse of ground that separated Lord and Mage, king and usurper, the end and the beginning."

Unless I was mistaken, our friendly narrator was the voice of the Enchanted Forests.

With a speed that defied the number of mortal wounds I could see he had received, Arthur advanced towards me, Excalibur raised. Mordred - no, it's me - ran to meet him in the middle, their clash of swords echoing like a thunderclap of fate.

I'm not saying I've watched Kylo versus Luke too many times, but if you're not quite feeling this fight, maybe flick the movie on in the background.

The only key difference is that rather than it turning out that Luke isn't really there, Arthur makes the point he is entirely present rather forcefully. He bats a slash from Drynwyn away with his hand, runs Mordred (me?) through and then decapitates us on the return swing.

Disconcertingly, my p.o.v remains from the eyes of the now unattached head as it sails through the air to land in the mud.

From this stage, my perspective on things becomes somewhat unclear as the rainwater, blood, and general shite slowly rise to cover my eyes.

I can just about make out that Arthur falls to his knees, and Excalibur slips from his fingers. He looks up into the twilight sky, where the first stars begin to twinkle, like silent witnesses to the end of an era.

With his last breath, Arthur cries out in frustration, and lightning crashes around him.

So, Fucking. Predictable.

As the final light of day gave way to night's embrace, King Arthur Pendragon, the Once and Future King, breathes his last.

***

"Well, that was cheery."

Indeed. I am unclear, though, as to the point of it. To my understanding, this was supposed to be a vision of a sacrifice you need to commit to make in the future. I do not see any such honourable choice here.

"Maybe I'm supposed to let Arthur slay me? Feels all a bit Obi-Wan, though. It looks like he dies straight afterwards, so it's not like there's a huge win there. But, for me, surely the bigger question is, why am I standing in for Mordred?"

Merlin began to answer me, but then my head swam, and I was back in the vision, but this time from a different perspective.

***

I was rowing a boat towards the shore of Camlann.

In the distance, I could see two warriors kicking ten bells out of each other. The one was in battered white armour, and the other - the smaller of the two - had gone all in on a nifty black number.

As I drew closer, the guy in white pivoted and swept his opponent's head off its shoulders with all the badassery of Samuel L Jackson with a glowing purple stick. However, rather than celebrating, he fell to his knees and gave it the full 'Platoon' scream to the heavens.

I knew that was my cue to swoop in, collect him up before he died and head for Avalon.

However, just as my oars dipped into the sea, a different destination opened up for me. It seemed that rather than pulling onto the beach, gathering up the dying body of King Arthur and then transporting him to a mystical resting place where he would heal, I could instead choose to go home.

Home.

But not to my fucking awful bedsit. Not to a life where my only consistent relationship was with a bottle. And not to a world where I'd burnt every possible bridge with everyone I cared about.

No, the 'me' I could see in this world was . . . happy. In the eons that stretched between a sweep of the oars, I saw a woman with secure roots. With a job she enjoyed - working in a gallery that, on occasion, allowed her to display her own art. With a small group of friends that had more in common than who could reach oblivion first. With a . . . yes, there was a family there. And a radiant, much-loved Aunt Zizzie sweeping up laughing children in an embrace.

"Fuck me, Merlin. Is this an option?"

He didn't answer me straight away. In a way, I found myself respecting him a little more for that. Because - obviously - what I was being shown here was that the only way I could achieve this version of my life was to royally screw over his plan. The Enchanted Forest offered me a life I could have if I didn't care too much about anything else.

In all honesty, my dear, I do not know. That Arthur will fall at Camlann is no surprise to either of us. Indeed, in a strange way it is pretty much what we are working so hard to achieve. On the positive side, that would suggest that despite everything, we may have an excellent chance to keep the settled timeline intact.

"But then I will get a choice? To take him to Avalon or . . . what? Pick the life I always wanted?"

Again, the Big M was silent for a few moments. When he spoke, it was with careful precision. *It would appear, at some point in the future, there will come a moment when you need to make a significant decision. I doubt it will come to pass as demonstrated in this vision, but I am sure the sentiment will be the same. You will have to choose whether to do the right thing or have your dreams fulfilled.*

"Dude, I'm not being funny, but you have to believe I'm picking Option B."

And I doubt there would be many that would blame you. You have suffered considerable trauma throughout your life. Should, when the moment comes, you choose to reset your existence along the lines shown today, I would wish you well."

"But?"

But in stepping into that version of reality, you will doom this realm. Whilst I object to the melodrama in this vision, it is clear on one thing. If you are not present at Camlann to transport Arthur to Avalon, he will die. And with his death, Britain will be transformed. These will be small, minor changes to begin with, but as centuries roll by, without the legend of the promise of the return of the Once and Future King, the resilience, exceptionalism and . . . basic pluck of the people of these islands will be much reduced.

"You're saying that unless I row Arthur to Avalon, Churchill wouldn't have the oomph to want to fight them on the beaches?"

No, my dear. I'm saying without the prospect of Arthur's return as a foundational myth for your culture, it would never occur to the British to fight the Nazis at all. There are, of course, many such foundational myths upon which a view of Britishness is formed. But none are more important than the Once and Future King. When the time comes, you can choose to let Arthur fall and seek out a better life for yourself, but I cannot promise you the world you find yourself in will be anything like the one you expect.

And then I was back in the forest, standing in the Trial circle.

CHAPTER 17 - IN WHICH, YAY, GUESS WHICH TORTURED AND MUTILATED WIZARD MAKES A COMEBACK!

Guinevere would be the first to admit that things may have gone a touch awry with her escape plan.

Gritting her teeth, she shuffled so that her back was pressed against the low wall against which she had fallen. Rubbing mud into her face with one hand and piling a bunch of leaves over her legs with the other, she tried to avoid looking too intently at the gaping wound in her thigh.

She'd bound it tightly with strips torn from her dress, and the gushing blood that had made her feel *quite* light-headed had slowed to a trickle. She hoped that was a testament to discovering unexpected medical prowess rather than the fact she was bleeding out.

It kind of felt odds and evens at this point.

She'd got sloppy.

Her success against those initial Saxons had gone a touch to her head. But it was one thing to waylay some overeager kids on horseback but quite another when running into the rear guard of a whole fucking army.

By rights - and she was clutching at straws here, she knew - she was not sure she could have reasonably anticipated how slowly the Saxon retreat from Tintagel was going. To listen to Bors and the wizard tell it, they'd been picking stragglers off the beaten remains of that fleeing army for weeks.

So, she'd imagined that she'd - give or take the odd game of lethal hide and seek with a few waifs and strays - largely have this part of Cornwall to herself until Arthur figured out the clues and came riding to her 'rescue.'

Turned out not so much.

Guinevere had thought there would be little risk in stopping overnight at a little village sat picturesquely on a riverbank. She'd positively skipped over the rough stone bridge, imagining actually sleeping in a bed for the first time in far too long.

That was her excuse for missing the first of the bodies.

In Guinevere's defence, she actually saw the Saxons who had slaughtered the entire population of the hamlet just before they saw her.

Unfortunately, the word 'just' didn't get her out of the very deep brown smelly stuff.

Bedded down in her hiding place, Guinevere held her breath as a burly, heavily armed man thundered past her, not giving her so much of a second glance.

Holding back her panic, she kept telling herself that as long as she kept confounding their expectations, she'd be okay. Probably. After all, as her sister was fond of saying, "no one ever became poor betting on the stupidity of men."

That felt like a decent way to live your life when the worst thing that could happen was your husband somehow figuring out he was eating a slightly healthier cut of venison. It hit a little different when your margin for error was an axe to the forehead.

But, fingers crossed, it had worked for her thus far since her colossal fuck-up. When she'd blundered right into the middle of their sentry line, they'd expected her to surrender. So, she'd attacked. When she'd taken a mortal wound, they'd thought she'd fall crying to the floor. So, she slew her attacker and ran for it. And now they were seeking her; the last thing they would anticipate would be for her to double back the way she came.

But there was something about these Saxons wearing wolf cloaks that unnerved her. Although she'd not spent much time with Arthur since the battle at Tintagel's walls, Bors was a regular visitor. She liked the big, bluff man who seemed able to take her as he found her rather than judging all the ways in which she failed at being a princess.

It was Bors who had spoken of the confrontation in the woods against Cedric the West Saxon and his very motivated warriors. It didn't feel ideal that she was coming across these guys deep in Dumnonia's territory.

Another Saxon ran past her hiding spot, howling to the moon as he went. She'd seen more subtle hunting parties.

That said, they wouldn't need much subtlety if they spotted her. She'd left her short sword behind in the belly of the first sentry that reached for her and her dagger in the eye of the second. Then she'd had to use her spear as a crutch as she'd limped away, and it had got caught in some fucking badger hole and twisted away from her.

If push came to shove - excuse the pun - she'd back herself hand-to-hand against most opponents her size. However, as most of the Saxons she'd seen this day looked like they could eat her in one sitting, she felt fisticuffs would be best kept as a last resort.

Timing would be everything.

She knew she needed to work her way back through the sentry line and away from whatever the fuck was going on here. Were they planning to have another assault on the castle? That would need to be someone else's problem.

She needed to get away, and with luck, they would be all too busy looking for her in the other direction.

She was just preparing to stand - and my word standing on this leg, let alone running, was going to suck - when she heard approaching voices and froze.

"You have until I finish my own piss, wizard. Do whatever it is you need to."

And a horribly mutilated body was thrown at her feet.

Guinevere clamped her teeth down tight on her hand to avoid gasping at the terrible damage that had been inflicted upon the poor man.

But that wasn't the worst thing.

No, that was the fact he was still alive.

***

All alone in her tower high above the rest of Tintagel, Queen Igraine sat in stately silence.

This room, bathed in the soft glow of the afternoon sun, was her refuge from the hustle and bustle of court life. It was here that she could forget about her role. And about the interminable struggles at court. And about her husband.

She smiled to imagine how Uther Pendragon would react if he knew that, when she retired to her room, she was not plotting sedition or brewing deadly potions but rather surrendering to the quaint simplicity of sewing.

For Igraine found quiet joy in the rhythm of her needlework.

The iron needle, slender and sharp, was her loyal subject in the realm of fabric and thread. She threaded it with a precision that spoke of years spent mastering this delicate art. The thread itself was a rich hue, contrasting beautifully against the pale linen stretched across her lap.

She was stitching a gift for Guinevere.

The needle plunged again and again through the fabric, reemerging with a consistency that bespoke of her focus and discipline. Igraine worked in a pattern, each stitch following the last in perfect succession. The thread twisted and turned, forming intricate shapes and patterns.

Around her, the room was adorned with embroideries showing this had been her escape for years. However, she knew the symbolic importance of her latest creation eclipsed anything that had come before.

Since becoming Queen, the act of sewing had become more than just a pastime; it was a silent language through which she expressed herself. The rhythmic motion of her hands, the steady pull of the thread, and the soft rustle of the fabric were the only sounds that filled the air, creating a symphony.

As she sewed, Igraine's severe expression softened, revealing a side seldom seen by her subjects. Or her husband. Or, if she was honest, her son.

Her eyes, usually sharp and piercing, now reflected a gentle concentration. The furrow of her brow eased as she navigated the needle, each stitch a tiny victory, a moment of peace.

The fabric gradually transformed. It was as if, with each thread, she was weaving a part of herself into the fabric, a quiet legacy of the woman behind the crown.

This creation was to be a wrap for Guinevere's baby.

Not that there was one yet, of course. But steps were being taken, and she had no doubt they would come to fruition.

They had to.

Although they had not given voice to it, this was to be the Princess's last chance to bear Arthur's child. The realm had become perilously close to disaster in the previous few months, and the need for an heir had become manifest.

Should this elaborate scheme fail, Arthur was to be persuaded to dispose of her quietly. Not that she thought he would take much persuading. There were convents aplenty in which she could be stowed away if she went willingly and holes in the ground to host her if she did not.

Of course, they would miss Leodegrance's dowry of spears, but that was what it was. She had already curated a list of available women to fill the void. Or, she smiled humourlessly, with a void for Arthur to fill.

But no more of that. Such plotting was for the future.

She liked Guinevere. Truthfully, she saw more than a little of herself in that young woman and wished this latest adventure well. But she would be failing the realm if she did not have an alternative plan. And Queen Igraine had never let the realm down in her life.

She was musing on that when she heard hurried feet thundering up the stone steps of her tower, and she quietly put aside her stitching.

She was facing the door when one of her favourite household guards - Beckwith - burst in.

"My Lady," he stopped to suck in lungfuls of air. She liked Beckwith because he had just enough intelligence to be utterly loyal but not enough to - for example - realise walking up steps and having enough breath to tell the tale was more efficient than running and then needing significant recovery time.

"Take your time. I'm sure the message that has caused you to burst into my private chamber so unexpectedly cannot be that important. Why, I might have been up to anything . . ."

If anything, that worsened the situation as the poor man now had blushing and spluttering to contend with.

Eventually, though, he was in a sufficient state to share the unwelcome news that not only had the men tasked with supporting Arthur, Bors and the Celt lost track of them somewhere near the Enchanted Forest - something about a giant purple horse with a massive cock appearing from nowhere and rogering their own mounts - but the company of prime spearman shadowing the Princess had been found slaughtered a short distance from Tintagel. The name 'Cedric the West Saxon' was being mentioned in dark tones.

"So, to summarise. Rather than the heir to the throne conducting a rigorous but ultimately danger-free quest for his wife, which would bring them closer together, we find ourselves in the situation of having no Arthur, no Guinevere and no fucking idea where either of them is."

Ignoring any potential response from Beckwith, she swept past him and started descending the stairs.

"Where are you going, my Lady?"

"I rather think it is beyond time someone looped my husband into what is occurring. Can I suggest you hang around in case I need someone to heroically save my life?"

Going rather green around the gills, the exhausted young man began retaking the steps.

CHAPTER 18 - IN WHICH THERE IS A U2 JOKE OF WHICH I AM SO PROUD, I PHONED A FRIEND TO SHARE IT.

"I don't want to talk about it."
I did not say anything, my dear.

"I know. And your ability not to say anything is louder and more expressive than most rock concerts. I'm just saying you can be as passive-aggressive as you like, but I'm still not going to talk about the end of the Trial."

And that is entirely your choice. Which I absolutely respect.

"Good. I'll hold you to that. We do not need to talk about Camlann. Ever."

Good.

"Good."

If it helps, I've got no fucking idea what either of you are talking about."

Despite the disembodied voice clearly being pissed off I'd passed the 'A Christmas Carol' test, it had been true(ish) to its word.

"That which you seek cannot be found within this Forest. Nor, I will tell you, was your wife ever to be found beneath our canopy. Retrace your steps and leave us dwellers in the woods in peace."

"Is there no more you can tell us?" If Arthur had questions about how we'd managed to track Guinevere into these woods if she'd never actually been there, he decided not to air them. I wondered how long that was likely to be the case. "We were expecting directions to the Bridge of Slaughter."

"There is no such place."

Probably not that much longer, if I was being honest.

Arthur turned to stare at me and then cast a significant look at Bors. "No such place?"

"Forgive me; your language is hard for me to parse. I mean, that is not the name of your intended destination as you know it. In order to recover your wife, you should head to Slaughterbridge. In the spirit of the vow, I made and in recognition that each of you passed your respective Trials - albeit each in a somewhat unusual manner - I will note that the Princess Guinevere is in grave danger."

***

Our horses were waiting for us at the edge of the Forest.

Forca seemed absolutely delighted to see me still alive and affectionately took a chunk out of my forearm when I went to stroke him. There is nothing like the bond between a warrior and her noble steed.

Apparently, everyone else knew exactly where we were heading. And at quite some speed. On the other hand, while hanging on to the neck of my fucking demon animal, I was having local geography wizardsplained to me.

It turns out that Slaughterbridge isn't as much fun as it sounds. It's as simple as 'slohtre' meaning 'marsh' and there also being a few piled-together stones over it. So, the upshot was we were heading for a bridge in a marsh that - according to Merlin - crossed the River Camel.

"Camel?"

Camel.

"Don't you think that's an unusual name for a river in this part of the world?"

How so?

"Maybe I'm being unfair. Because I, for one, cannot move for all the large, spitting hairy beasts I keep falling over in this famously hot and desert-like area of Southwest of England?"

I have no idea what you are talking about. Kammel means 'crooked'.

Ah, well that was much less fun.

I was still reeling from having those dreams dashed when Bors drew up next to me and tossed me back the Curing Rock. "This is all so fucked. Arthur's not an idiot. He has to know we've been playing him."

"I know. But I don't think it makes much difference right now. The plan was to help him get his groove back by swooping in and saving Guinevere. Obviously, something's gone wrong if she actually needs our help, but Stella still gets to dance," I said.

I don't understand what you've just said, my dear.

Join the fucking club. Although I don't think she does most of the fucking time.

"Look," I said, " what I'm getting at is that it doesn't matter how we get there if we end up at the place we need to be."

Not to be all judgey, but I distinctly remember we had a significant falling out about the ends justifying the means. It resulted in me being banished to the netherworld.

"Totally different situation, Big M. We told Arthur a few little white lies. No harm, no foul. You fed me to a dragon."

Ask Arthur how 'little' some of those tendrils were...

"Not helping, Drynwyn."

"I just want to say," Bors broke in, "in case you're wondering, it really doesn't do much for your reputation for being fucking insane that you keep having conversations the rest of us can't hear. With that noted, the point I'm making is at some stage, we're going to need to explain the circumstances surrounding Guinevere leaving Tintagel, and that's going to be a shit show."

"Don't worry, I'll be right there behind you when you have that chat, mate."

"Fuck you, Celt."

"Not my type, dude. Besides, what would Mrs Bors say?"

***

"Remind me again about how the Saxons are in full retreat?"

I could be wrong, but I sensed Arthur was ticking a little bit.

He obviously knew there was more to the 'quest for Guinevere' story than we'd let on. But I wasn't too worried about that right now. I wasn't even too bothered that the atmosphere between us was about as chilly as anything I had experienced with someone I hadn't screwed - either literally or metaphorically. Haters can hate. I have enough friends.

You really don't, my dear.

No, what I was worried about was that we were looking down at a village wholly emptied of Britons and replaced by an awful lot of Saxon spears - somewhere within which was apparently the Princess Guinevere.

And her husband, my liege Lord and a legendary future king I was currently seeking to keep alive was seeming a bit . . . fighty.

Bors crawled to our position, moving with all the stealth and grace of sandpaper over an eyeball. "I thought I recognised their standard. It's those wolfy fuckers again. Maybe two hundred of them."

This was not exactly great news. We'd tangled with this particular warband before, and the result had not been great. And by that, I mean that scrap wiped out most of the Knights of the Round Table you will never now get to hear of.

On the other hand, we knew that their war leader - Cedric - really hated wizards. So, there was a chance I was the only spellflinger around.

"Any ideas why they're still on this side of the border? Weren't the two of you supposed to be mopping up anyone who hadn't crossed back over the Tamar?"

Bors and I looked at each other and silently agreed there was no way I was answering. "Sure, we've been on clean-up duty. But that was just wiping out the ones who had panicked and broken away from the main body of the retreat. That's not what this is. This feels like a main event."

"Are you saying you missed two hundred fucking Saxons a couple of day's ride from Tintagel?"

An edge crept into Bors' voice. "It's entirely possible, my Lord. You see, for some reason, our most capable commander couldn't be persuaded to suit up for the job, so it was left to me and the ginger to take care of business. Now, we both have our various skills - I'm good at the killing and she's . . . I'm not really sure what she's good at, but the Saxons are fucking terrified of her. But, anyway, tactical planning and strategy isn't really in either of our wheelhouses. No offence." He nodded towards me.

"None taken. Although maybe we find a different nickname than 'the ginger'."

"Understood. I guess what I'm saying, *sir*' - there was now more than an edge to his voice. There was an entire Irish rock band tuning up for 'Where The Streets Have No Name' - 'is that some of us have been knee-deep in Saxon viscera for the last few weeks, and some of us have been wandering the corridors of Tintagel and sighing a lot. Within that context, I'm not sure the latter should be casting aspersions as to the competence of the former."

I suddenly understood what kept Mrs Bors barefoot and pregnant.

Arthur and Bors locked gazes for quite some time.

"Not that I'm not loving all the homoerotic posturing going on here, but can I suggest we focus more on the problem at hand? Lots of Saxons. Not so many of us. And somewhere down there is Guinevere."

Look at you and your growing diplomacy skills.

"Cheers, Big M. Whilst I've got you, I know I can track other cultivators, but I don't suppose there's anything I can do to, I don't know, Cerebo onto the Princess?"

No.

"Really? Not even a little bit? It kind of feels like the plot needs me to be able to find her right about now."

There is no power of which I know that would allow you to zero in on the location of a non-cultivator. Think of the implications! With sufficient power, a cultivator would be able to eliminate almost anyone without ever needing to leave their tower. Now, I'm not saying that doesn't sound lovely, but it simply isn't the case...

I zoned out a little from this monologue. Firstly, because it was boring me. But also, because my spidey senses had picked up a cultivator amongst those Saxons.

Now, knowing Cedric, that was odd but not exceptionally so. However, it was strange that it was a cultivator with a power signature I recognised.

It was Melehan.

CHAPTER 19 - IN WHICH GUINEVERE DOES NOT HAVE TIME FOR ANYONE'S BULLSHIT

"I imagine you're the 'fucking bitch' they're all so riled up about."

Guinevere didn't say anything - although she thought she could get on board with that being her epitaph.

"If you're remotely interested, Tidhelm is still hanging on. But gut wounds are nasty. I'd give him a day at best. Hildred, well, not so much."

She was not sure she really needed the names of the men she'd fought in her head right now. Especially as the only thought she could summon was 'still hanging on? Fucking hell. Do it properly, or not at all. How many times? Twist the blade when it goes in. Rupture those intestines.'

The horribly mutilated man rolled over to face her, and she could see - as well as everything else that had been done to him - someone had put out his eyes. And done . . . other things to his face. This did little to dissuade her from her point of view that being captured by these guys would probably not be a relaxing experience.

He spoke again. "There's something not quite right with your aura. Are you injured?"

Guinevere tried to stretch out her leg and winced. She either had the most epic pins and needles known to man or . . . yeah, she wasn't going near the alternative when looking at what happened to those these Saxons captured.

Then what the man - she guessed it was a man. There wasn't any awful lot left that wasn't scar tissue to make that distinction matter - had said about her 'aura' hit home.

Dropping her voice as low as she could, she whispered, "Are you a wizard?"

"Ah, I was starting to worry I was talking to myself. That's happening more than I'd like of late. Glad you are really there. It's been a while since I had a proper conversation. Yes. I am a wizard. Or, at least, I used to be."

For the first time since receiving her wound, Guinevere felt the stirring of a little bit of hope.

Growing up over the sea in Cornouaille, she was much more used to being around wizards than anyone on this forsaken little island. The way her father had explained it, when outlining the various woes of the British race, Merlin took up so much of the available Qi that it was almost impossible for any others to flourish in his vicinity. Even on their side of the sea, the impact of Merlin's thirst for power was felt, with their cultivators being weak things in comparison. However, there had been five or six wizards of various quality at court at any one time.

Leodegrance had sent one of their most powerful with her when she had married Arthur. The plan was that Nimue would be able to determine when she became pregnant, open the portal for the ten thousand spears Leodegrance had promised as her dowry and then return to her father's side.

And hadn't that plan worked out just wonderfully ...

No. Now was not the time.

Dragging herself back to the present, Guinevere took a careful look at the wizard. Surely, if he had any power at all, he wouldn't have let the Saxons abuse him so much? Even the weakest of cultivators should have been able to escape.

As if he was reading her mind, the wizard spoke again. "To escape, you need two things. The means to achieve it and the will to want to do so. I find myself somewhat lacking in the latter right now. How about you?"

He gave what might have been a smile. They'd broken each and every one of his teeth . . .

"I think my issue is probably the other way around. The will is there, but I fear the means may well be beyond me." Blood was leaking through the leaves she had bundled over her legs. She didn't think she could possibly have much more of it to spare.

"And where does that will come from?"

Guinevere snorted. "Living is better than dying. Fighting is better than giving up. What more is there to it than that? Not being tortured is better than . . ." She stopped herself there. She probably didn't need to tell him that.

"I admire your clarity of thought. However, believe me when I say that it is not always so simple. What if you had done something that was unforgivable? Is it better to live then?"

It might have been the blood loss, it might have been the stress of being hunted, it might even have been the weight of several years of crushing disappointment in a marriage for which she had had such hopes.

It might even have been a bit of all three.

But whatever it was, Guinevere found that she really did not have any time for this torn-up man's bullshit. "Look, not that I'm not loving the opportunity to debate the meaning of life, but there's a time and a place for everything. And I'm fairly confident right here, and right now, is neither of those. You're a wizard. And I'm hurt. Is there anything you can do anything to help me get out of here?"

There was a beat. Then, the ruined face gave a little nod.

"Time's up. Cedric will be wanting his favourite plaything back, especially if we still don't have a fucking bitch to substitute in for some variety."

From out of nowhere, a scrawny-looking Saxon had appeared, bending down to pick the wizard up. With the ease he managed it, throwing him over his shoulder with a casual effort, it was clear that being overfed was probably not one of the tortures the Saxons were trying.

Guinevere froze as, in the act of turning around, the Saxon's eyes rested upon her. She could feel her heart pounding in her chest and was sure he'd be able to hear it, too. But, no, his glance slid off her, and he started to walk away, carrying the wizard over his back.

She was just starting to relax when the Saxon suddenly threw the wizard to the ground, looked back her way and reached for a hand axe hanging from his belt.

"I see you, my lovely. Heardweald is going to get some love from Cedric for this."

Guinevere realised three things as he swaggered towards her, no doubt pleased to note the volume of blood the Princess was lying in.

First, she did not want to die right now.

Second, knowing the names of random Saxons she was going to kill felt entirely unnecessary.

And third, her leg was feeling an awful lot better. Almost magically so.

She stood up, which, it would be fair to say, somewhat surprised her attacker. However, he rallied quickly, arcing his hand axe down in a quick swing aimed at Guinevere's head. Instinctively, she stepped back, just out of his reach, and the blade whistled past her nose.

This did not improve his demeanour. He attacked again, sweeping a horizontal slash at her midsection. Guinevere jumped, turning sideways and feeling the air shift above her as the axe cut through it. Despite the situation, she was feeling nimbler than she had in years. Whatever the wizard had done to her leg had put quite the spring in her step.

In the other corner, the scrawny Saxon was turning red in a fury. He began to swing the hand axe wildly, and each miss markedly increased his frustration. Guinevere kept jinking aside, backing away and circling around him. His pattern of attack was clear – repeated heavy, committed strikes followed by brief moments of vulnerability after missing.

He was adequate with his axe, at best. It made sense he would be on cripple-carrying duty. She let him keep swinging wildly, waiting for . . .

Yep. Here we go.

Guinevere ducked and let him bury his axe into a tree and then attacked. He swore as she struck his wrist but managed to hold on to the handle of his weapon. She hit it again. And then again. Lacing her fingers together for a double-handed, downward blow. Three of those and his grip faltered, and the axe clattered to the ground.

She drew up a leg and kicked the Saxon in the chest, pushing him back for space more than trying to hurt him. Then she dipped down to collect the axe. Its weight was unfamiliar, unbalanced, in her hand, but she adjusted quickly. She'd trained with worse.

He didn't waste any time and just charged straight at her. Guinevere sidestepped and dropped to her knees, using his momentum against him. She swung the axe at the back of his legs as he stumbled past.

It wasn't a deep cut. But every little helped.

They circled each other; Guinevere's breaths came steadily, whereas the Saxon's were increasingly laboured. She feigned a high strike; he flinched, and she crashed the axe down on his shoulder.

After that, he did his best to keep it going, but the end was a foregone conclusion. She hid the body under her pile of leaves and went to where the wizard was lying.

"Thank you. For the healing."

"No thanks needed. I have debts to pay."

She didn't know what to say to that. "Can you walk?"

"No."

She tried to pick him up, but as scrawny as the now-slain Saxon had been, he had about fifty pounds of muscle on her. "I can't carry you."

"No."

"What do you want me to do?"

He turned his face so that his ruined eye sockets seemed to look at her. "Living is better than dying. Fighting is better than giving up."

She could hear voices closing in on their position. They weren't sounding too urgent at the moment, but she imagined that would come.

"Wizard, what do you want me to do?"

"Run."

She stood, looking down at him and then around. "I can't. They'll kill you."

"They haven't done so yet."

She started to back away from the direction of the voices. "I'll come back for you. I'll bring men."

"No rush. As I said, I have debts to pay."

She just made out the first shout of alarm as she crashed through the undergrowth.

CHAPTER 20 - IN WHICH THE PURSUIT OF GOOD MANNERS INEXPLICABLY BECOMES THE CENTRE OF MY UNIVERSE

"Melehan saved my life. If he's still alive, and we know where he is, we are absolutely going to go in there and get him out."

I mean, I don't want to cast aspersions here, but Arthur seems to have strapped on his big-boy-quest-pants for a Saxon wizard he barely knows with a bit more alacrity than he summoned for his wife.

Also, for the record, I fucking saved Arthur's life. Melehan helped. A bit.

Don't get me wrong, no one is happier than me that that particular wizard is still alive - dude came through for us in a tight spot. I even named a bloody, unique healing artefact after him - but it wasn't so long ago that Arthur had me up against a wall and was choking me out. Don't remember bathing in the warm glow of any 'Morgan saved my life' chat back then.

Did someone take an overdose of her whiny bitch pills this morning?

I fear this one of those occasions where I am with the sword, my dear.

"There is literally no one in my head that I do not hate right now."

Whilst quietly seethed, I took in the sights and smells of Slaughterbridge. Forsaken marshland? Tick. Dodgy-looking rock structure that undoubtedly had a troll living under it? Tick. Picturesque, crooked stream running under it in no manner named after an even-toed ungulate in the genus *Camelus* that bears distinctive fatty deposits? Tick.

It was a lovely spot for a rescue mission.

The Saxons had set up a makeshift camp on the other side of what we shall call a 'bridge' because 'pile of stones' takes too long to keep saying, meaning we would have to go over it and through the sentries on that side if we were going to retrieve our missing wizard and princess.

If we wanted to have any chance of getting in and out alive, we needed to be able to drop the guards at just the right moment, or we were going to find ourselves taking on a couple of hundred spearmen who had already kicked our arses once.

"If we're doing something, it needs to be now," Bors' voice was a low, menacing rumble. I think he still had some tension to work out from getting his arse handed to him during the game of riddles. And the handsy Forest Guardian. Oh, and he probably still had some unresolved issue about this war party killing a bunch of his friends.

Man, these Saxons were fuuuuuuucked.

"They're getting ready for a change of sentries. If we let them have the chance to reestablish their lines, it will be hard to slip through unnoticed. I'm up for some mayhem, but we need to be realistic. Uther would have my arse for even thinking about this."

They both looked at me. "Oh, so my opinion matters now."

Whiny. Bitch.

I drew Drynwyn with a flourish and nodded. "I can lead us straight to the wizard, but this needs to be an in-and-out job. No grandstanding. No famous doomed last stands. Do we agree?"

Arthur had unslung Rhongomynyad and was already scrabbling his way down towards the first sentry.

Sure, don't worry, mate. I'm only the one with the map to the destination in my head. You go right ahead and lead.

Twat.

Bors shrugged apologetically to me, then made to quickly follow his friend, his axe held low to his side in two hands. They both started crossing, in a crouch, over the bridge towards the unsuspecting sentry. Apparently, we were really going to do this.

I tell you what, if Melehan doesn't give me the full "aren't you a little short for a stormtrooper" when we find him, I'm going on strike.

***

We were helped that what was on their side of the bridge wasn't really a proper camp. This was an army in retreat rather than a proper military set-up, so things were a bit loose at the edges. So much so that I reckoned that the first bridge sentry was looking straight at us for a good thirty seconds as we ran towards him without raising the alarm.

And then his window of opportunity to cry for help vanished as Arthur drove a spear through his throat.

He's fucking wasted carrying that spear. Man's a work of death art.

Bors darted to the left and took out the second lookout. Unlike Arthur's measured strike, Bors' axe arced through the air with raw power, removing a big, shaggy-haired head from its broad shoulders.

Then they dropped back down into crouches, as the three of us hid ourselves from any passing archers who might take offence at us straight-up murdering two of their mates.

But no flurry of arrows came our way. So far, so good.

I checked my Qi-gps, and we appeared to be much closer to Melehan's location than I had expected. He must have moved towards us. Well, that was handy.

Something's coming.

"What? What do you mean?" I looked around and couldn't see any other Saxons between us and the woods.

I don't know how to describe it, my dear. It's as if . . . you know how I visualise Qi as water?

"Dude, is this really the time? We're Magnificent Sevening a rescue operation here."

It's like we're standing on the beach, and the tide has vanished. As if all the Qi has suddenly been sucked out and away. I imagine this is how it felt to be around me.

That gave me pause. I'd doom-scrolled through many a video of approaching tsunamis, and they all started with just that phenomenon on idyllic beaches. I dropped into my Artist's Studio and could tell something was up. Although my internal reserves looked sound, I wasn't pulling in as much Qi from the wider world as I was used to. I tried to cycle things around a little faster, with little positive results. It was like trying to suck in a particularly thick milkshake.

"Any ideas what is causing it?"

Power.

"Awesome. Can you maybe work on an answer that's not wholly fucking useless and come back to me?"

Of course. I would recommend not using up any Qi right now. Keep your reserves as high as possible until I figure this out.

"Sure. It's not like we're about to do something incredibly dangerous that might need me to pull our arses out of the fire. Great timing."

"Wizard, let's go." Arthur gave me a come-hither gesture to which I was absolutely not going to respond. I tell you what, if he clicked his fingers, I was going to snap them off.

On the count of three, we cut across the open land on their side of the bridge and dashed into the woods, where we paused so I could orientate myself back to Melehan's location.

Things then started to get a little bit more difficult.

For whatever reason, whichever way we went, we kept running into little groups of Saxons who were most displeased to make our acquaintance. From their demeanour, they were obviously hunting for someone, and whoever that was, it clearly wasn't us.

Had Melehan escaped them? Guinevere?

Whatever, we were fucking these guys up and good. I wouldn't say I like to brag, but it seemed like the three of us together were a brutal team. With Rhongomynyad, Arthur kept these little pockets of twos and threes easily at bay, the spear's reach keeping them from closing in with their shorter weapons. He was a spikey line of defence that no one could cross. In the meantime, Bors acted as our battering ram. He ploughed through them, his axe smashing down any semblance of order in their defences. If Arthur was the wall, Bors was the sledgehammer.

And then there was me. Or, I guess, Drynwyn.

As you'd expect, most of the Saxons - given a choice between a giant nightmare with an axe, a whirling dervish of spear death and a twiglet with nice tits - decided I was the one they wanted to engage. So, the sword was being kept quite busy.

At some stage, I would need to take some fencing lessons. It was embarrassing to do nothing more in a fight than cling to its handle.

We'd left a trail of about fifteen corpses around us by the time horns of alarm started to be heard. At this point, I think we could safely conclude that any element of surprise we might have had was pretty much over.

"How much further, wizard?"

"Arthur, have you forgotten my name?"

"What?"

"I think you mean 'pardon,' not 'what.' After all, I'm sure we all agree it's important for the Prince of the realm to set an example regarding politeness and etiquette."

"What are you talking about? Where's the wizard?"

"Morgan . . . " Bors shook his head in my direction. "Not the time."

I don't know why I decided this was a hill I wanted to die on. "No. He knows my name. He uses it, or this quest is over."

Arthur sighed with his whole body. "Fine. Morgan, if you would be so kind? Where do we find the wizard?"

"You see, politeness costs nothing. Melehan's Qi signature is coming from just beyond the trees that smells like piss."

Arthur had taken a quarter of a step forward before I added. "Was there a 'thank you'? I'm sure there will be a 'thank you'. . ."

I'm actually embarrassed to be associated with you right now.

CHAPTER 21 - IN WHICH MORGAN GETS SNATCHED AND MELEHAN BODY-SNATCHED

"Fuck me, dude. What happened?"

I think Melehan smiled back at me. But it's hard to tell when someone has no lips. "Ah, the Celt. It's good to hear your voice again. In answer to your question, though, unfortunately, quite a lot happened."

"Fucking hell. You're an absolute wreck. How come they didn't just kill you?" Bors there, showcasing the empathy for which he is so well known.

The wizard shrugged, and tears came to my eyes at the uneven way his shoulders moved. Melehan was in unbelievably lousy shape. This wasn't just the sort of thing that happened when you pissed the wrong person off. That got you dead. This was what happened when you pissed off a complete and utter Hannibal Lector of a psychopath.

I doubt there was an inch of him that didn't carry a scar.

There was a pause as we all took in the sheer volume of suffering the man in front of us represented. Bors was the first to rally. "Well, let's not worry about that for now. Let's get you out of here." He picked Melehan up with comical ease and slung him over one shoulder.

Morgan ...

"Not right now, Big M." Judging by the lack of screams of alarm coming from the direction in which we'd come if we carefully retraced our steps, we had every chance of getting out of this alive. "Let's get Melehan somewhere safe and then review the next steps."

My dear...

"Dude, give it a rest for a second, will you? Are we all agreed? Back the way we came, stash the wizard, and then see where we are at?"

Arthur - who, like a child, was not speaking to me - turned to lead the way, followed by Bors carrying the wizard, with me covering the rear.

We'd made it about halfway back to the bridge - or nine dead Saxons if that was how you preferred to count things - when I felt the world . . . I think the only way to put it is that everything *blurred*.

One moment, we were moving reasonably stealthily through the woods, and the next, it was as if we were leaving vivid after-images all around us. Time had not slowed down - we were still travelling as quickly as we were before - but we were leaving a smeared trail of colour behind us as we went. As I watched that light became transparent and faded after a few seconds.

"Merlin? What the fuck?"

I have been trying to warn you, my dear.

"Well, less of the 'I told you so' and more of the exposition, please."

Someone is pushing on the fabric of reality around us. I do not know how better to explain it, but whatever they are doing is stretching things on this side to a breaking point.

I watched, with horrified fascination, as Bors-carrying-Melehan squashed up, then stretched out to about the length of a double-decker bus until finally resolving back to something approaching normal scale.

It was like the world had become a House of Mirrors. "Okay. So, this is creepy as fuck. What can we do about it?"

I don't even know what is causing it. I have never seen anything like that before. Someone is using colossal amounts of Qi to rupture reality, and I imagine this visual phenomenon is a side-effect of that outpouring of energy rather than the actual purpose.

Sensing I was falling behind, Bors stopped and looked around. "What's wrong, Celt?"

I nearly lost my lunch at how his face bubbled and writhed as he turned around. "Does everything look alright to you?"

He glanced around and shrugged, and if I thought the way Melehan's tortured frame moved was grotesque, then I found myself needing a whole vocabulary for body horror to describe what I was now looking at adequately. Basically, the world was increasingly looking like Dali had painted it. While drugged. And half blind. With no fingers.

The disturbance is taking place at a spiritual level. For those not sensitive to such things, I doubt they will notice anything amiss.

"Bors, mate. I'm really struggling. Merlin thinks something is going on with Qi in this area."

"People, we need to hurry up!" Arthur had returned and fuck me if he didn't look like Francis Bacon had painted him. Trust me. The 'Study of Isabel Rawsthorn.' It's worth a quick google so you understand how very close I was to losing all of my shit.

"Big M, what's my play here? Close my eyes and hope it all goes away?"

I think it might be too late for that, my dear. Oh, my word! It's coming through!

"What is? What's coming thr -"

***

Merlin felt his connection to Morgan torn away as a . . . hand reached through the boundaries of reality and snatched her away.

It was such a brutally unexpected moment that he wasted valuable seconds in outraged shock before recognising he had started to fade away. In a panic, he cast around for a Qi anchor to keep his essence from drifting into the afterlife.

There were not that many games in town.

With a grimace, he coiled himself around the shattered remains of Melehan's spirit and clung on.

These fragments I have shored against my ruins.

The wizard's body shrieked and lashed out at the unexpected invasion of his soul, causing Bors to swear, drop him, and stumble. "Will someone tell me what the fuck is going on!"

Angry Saxon shouts could be heard in the near distance, and Arthur forced the big man to his knees in silence. When they recovered their composure, the Prince hissed, "Where's the Celt gone?"

"What? What do you mean?" Bors whispered back, resettling a wriggling Melehan under his arm and peering around them. "She was just here!"

Wizard. Melehan. Listen to me. It would be best if you told them Morgan's been taken. Someone with an insane level of cultivation has just reached through the fabric of reality and plucked her from her place in the world. Tell them Merlin's talking to you.

Melehan shook his head rapidly from side to side, clearly in distress. "No. No. No. Not in my head. You can do whatever you want to my body, but you cannot have my mind. No! No! No!"

If Merlin had still had teeth, he would have ground them in intense frustration. Why could someone stolid and sensible like Bors not have just a drop of Qi? That would have made all this much easier. However, they were where they were. And he needed to get his message through. Needs must, and all that. *Wizard, I am very sorry indeed for what I am about to do. It is hugely unethical, and if the need were not quite so dire, I would not have considered it. However, it is, so I have.*

Merlin pushed Melehan's mind to one side with a shove and took the reins. Had the Saxon wizard not spent much of the last few weeks being brutally tortured, his grip on reality would never have been loose enough for Merlin to have even conceived of attempting such a thing. As it was, Melehan was just the right amount of bat-shit crazy for what Merlin attempted to come off.

So, for the first time since his death, the greatest wizard in British history opened real, physical eyes.

Well, no.

Of course, he didn't. Because someone had recently pressed the tip of a red-hot poker into both eyeballs. He/Melehan could still hear the hiss and smell the evaporating goo. But no matter.

A quick cycle of Qi - did the Saxon conceive of his Qi in terms of sand blowing on a beach? That was very strange - and the eyeballs reinflated.

In fact, while he was here, he might as well do the Saxon a few more good deeds to make up for this horrible liberty.

In a few heartbeats, Merlin had reversed all of the damage inflicted, regrowing multiple things lopped off and realigning bones.

Really, with all of this damage, it was quite a miracle the man had retained any sanity whatsoever.

Looking around the sandy beach where Melehan visualised his Qi, Merlin found the Saxon wizard sitting on the shore, staring out at the sea. Without knowing why, the sight seemed to inspire a few words of forgotten poetry—*Hieronymo's mad againe.*

Merlin moved to sit next to the hunched figure. *Look, I'm sorry about all this. I imagine it feels like an appalling violation. Especially after everything you've been through. I just need to let Bors and Arthur know what has happened to Morgan. And I don't think you are quite in the right mind to pass on the message. As soon as that's done, I'll pass the body back.*

Melehan's soul - if that's what this figure was - did not respond, pulling his knees even tighter under his arms.

Okay. Well, you should know I have fixed most of the damage, so it will be as good as new when you return to it. Better, probably. But, for now, I will just take it out for a brief spin. Back before you know it.

Merlin returned to reality in Bors' arms.

Arthur and the big man were shouting at each other. And quite a number of Saxons were closing in on their position.

"We're not going anywhere until we figure out where Morgan went!"

"And I'm telling you, as your Prince, that unless we get out of here right now, it won't matter. Because we will be dead!"

Merlin put a hand - it was good to have one of those again - on Bors' chest and tapped urgently. "I can explain everything that has happened, but you need to get to safety as soon as possible. If you can follow the Prince back over the bridge, I promise I will help you locate Morgan." A familiar face swam into Melehan's mind. That was a bit surprising. "And apparently the Princess Guinevere, too. But you must run now!"

Bors looked around wildly but, seeing no alternative, he reluctantly followed Arthur back towards the bridge and then over to the other side and cover.

He laid Merlin down and fixed him with a ferocious expression. "Now, wizard, tell me what happened!"

Merlin took a deep breath - he enjoyed being able to do that - and stood up. "I am afraid Morgan has been taken. Someone with astonishing power locked upon her position and tore a hole in reality to pull her through to their side."

"Who?" Arthur thrust his spear into the ground with frustration. "Beyond Merlin, who would have the strength to do that?"

Merlin shook Melehan's head. "That is what most troubles me, my Prince. I have no idea."

CHAPTER 22 - IN WHICH I FIND MYSELF IN MY OWN LITTLE VERSION OF SHAWSHANK

If I had a penny for every time I was torn from reality by a powerful cultivator and dragged through space and time, I'd have . . . well, I'd have two pennies.

But it's weird that it's happened twice.

The experience of being ripped out of reality and pushed into another was not unlike being rudely ejected from a club by an overly handsy bouncer. One minute, I was in the woods with my crew and the next moment, I was . . . well, I have absolutely no idea.

"Big M, what the hell just happened?"

It was then that I became aware of the legendary wizard-sized space in my consciousness.

This did very little for my mental equilibrium. Since he had returned from his banishment, I had become quite reliant on the old duffer. Sure, we had our moments, but there was something comforting in having him in my corner.

Seeking to quell my growing sense of panic, I peered around, trying to get a sense of my new surroundings. It was hard to see too clearly in the dim light, but it was pretty obvious I was in a prison cell of some kind.

Now, in the grand scheme of celestial adventures, suddenly finding oneself transported to a dark and dingy cell that could generously be described as "intimate" was not quite how I saw my day developing.

The place was a kaleidoscope of dank charm and rustic despair, with the walls channelling their "indoor rainforest" vibe. It was like they couldn't quite decide if they wanted to be solid or a liquid but were willing to give both a good old-fashioned try. It was all very avant-garde.

I don't want to give you the impression it was all doom and gloom, though. Not at all. I had a window. Right up there, just higher than I could reach, was a lofty little thing that offered a tiny, tantalising glimpse of freedom and, presumably, the sky.

I had a mate who did quite well in the marriage stakes and netted herself an architect. He'd designed and built his own house and seeing that window up there reminded me of all the skylights he'd dotted around the place. It was like the dude had something personal against windows. And - if memory serves - the whole 'forsaking all others' thing. When push came to shove, she got the house, and he shuffled away back to his parents in Pontypridd with chlamydia. I mean, he had chlamydia. Not his parents. From all the dicking around, you get me. Now, I'm not saying being anti-window and having the clap are related, but . . . I'm rambling, aren't I?

Yes.

Never have I been happier to hear from a psychotic sword.

"Drynwyn! Good to know you're here. Do you know what's happening?"

No idea. Is this a fucking prison?

"I think so."

Well, there's no sense getting all hyped up about it. Someone put you here. Someone will come and let you out. We'll fucking kill them when they do and take it from there. No bother.

I don't want to overstress how discombobulated I was feeling, but that plan actually made me feel quite a bit better.

I took a deep breath to try to get my levels of zen rising.

This turned out to be a mistake.

The air in my cell had a particular... character. Something like a blend of eau de dungeon with a hint of mossy overtones. It was the sort of scent that you'd expect to find bottled and sold in the backstreets of Brownhills, labelled "Essence of Ancient Enigma".

Not having anything better to do with my time, I sat myself down on the stone floor. Now, the straw down here is a nice touch. It added a certain rustic panache to the place. As I shuffled my arse around to try and get comfy, the movement was accompanied by a symphony of crunches, like I was laying an egg on a carpet of autumn leaves.

I can't hear Merlin. What the fuck happened to him?

"He was telling me that someone was channelling shedloads of Qi to try to break through to our side of reality and then . . . well, I guess that happened."

I don't want to be rude, but life was much fucking simpler with Rhyddrech Hael.

"I can imagine."

None of this Qi fuckery with him. Nope. The worst thing that was likely to happen with him was getting a spot of baby oil on my blade. No one ever ripped a hole in reality to drag him into a dingy prison cell. No sir. Although to be fair, we tended to visit Monsieur Whip's Dungeon a few times a month...

"And to think I was glad to hear from you."

What?

"Doesn't matter."

My eyes had adjusted to the gloom now, and I could see that the iron door in the centre of the wall opposite was the true pièce de résistance of the cell. It looked like it had seen better days, and in that, I felt we shared the beginning of a close bond. The door had character etched into every rusty groove and dent.

I could have done without the bloody handprints, though, to be honest.

The interior designer of the whole cell was clearly a fan of the "less is more" philosophy and had decided that anything more than four walls, a window, and a door was extravagant. Perhaps they were making a bold statement about the futility of material possessions. I could dig that.

Or maybe they just ran out of budget.

Although, to tell a lie, there was a bucket in the corner to my left. It was a classic piece that highlighted the room's aesthetic. I named it Bob. Bob the Bucket. He didn't say much, but I could tell he had a certain depth to him. I felt we were going to be great friends.

Are you okay? Your breathing has gone all funny.

Surprisingly, someone pointing out you are hyperventilating does little to calm you down. The problem was I wouldn't say I liked enclosed spaces. I didn't have claustrophobia or anything like that. It was just being locked in here, all alone, reminded me of some really bad times.

"I'm okay, Drynwyn. Just get yourself ready for some fiery death when we get the chance."

I don't know how long I sat there.

It's funny how easy it is to lose track of time in a dark room with just your thoughts and a mad sword for company. At some point, I became aware of the distant sounds of dripping water. It was oddly rhythmic, a sort of plip-plop symphony that provided a soothing backdrop to my less-than-ideal situation.

It was either that or the world's saddest water feature.

After a while of no one coming to let me out, I dropped into my Artist's Studio to try to meditate. I hoped that if I could reach out with my senses beyond the confining walls, I'd start to feel a little better. But it's hard to achieve enlightenment when you're constantly being distracted by the artistic splattering of greenish mould on the wall that looked suspiciously like your father's disapproving face.

Seriously, you keep fucking breathing like that, and we're going to run out of oxygen.

Time rolled by with all the grace of a one-legged turtle. I tried to amuse myself by counting the drips from the ceiling, imagining them as a sort of watery metronome ticking away the seconds of my captivity. It was like nature's own version of water torture, except less torture and more just really, really annoying.

Then, as night fell, the cell took on a whole new persona. The sunlight from my skylight began to fade, and shadows danced along the walls, thrown by the flickering torchlight from somewhere outside my little abode. It was like being in a low-budget production of "Hyperventilating Cultivator in a Cell: The Musical," except there was no music, no chorus line, and definitely no fucking applause.

I wondered what Bors and Arthur were doing at that moment. Probably something heroic and awe-inspiring, like running away from Saxons in the woods and bitching about it. Meanwhile, here I was, engaging in a staring contest with 'I'm not mad, just disappointed' mould daddy.

Sleep was elusive, like a shy nymph in a forest of dreams.

Where the fuck did that simile come from?

"What can I say, Drynwyn? Incarceration brings out my poetic side." Especially as the straw was less "bed of comfort" and more "bed of 'why is this poking me in the ribs like it wants to get intimate?'"

However, as hours drifted by, eventually, emotional exhaustion took over, and I felt myself drifting off into a fitful sleep filled with dreams of white coats and pills that made me feel dead inside.

When I woke, Bob the Bucket and Mould Father were still both there, silently judging me.

But there was still no sight or sound of my captors.

CHAPTER 23 - IN WHICH I START TO GO OUT OF MY TINY LITTLE MIND

Is this a fucking prison?

"Seriously, dude, on top of everything else, I can't be doing with deja vu today. Just can it for a little while, please."

By my reckoning, I'd been awake for a few hours of Day Two of my captivity. It was becoming quite concerning that there was still no sight nor sound of whoever had used so much Qi to grab me that fucking Merlin had fangirled over it.

As a cultivator, I knew I was unlikely to need food or drink in the near future, but the very idea that this might become a factor was disturbing.

It wasn't helping me stay calm that I kept remembering a school trip to Warwick Castle when Mr Haines spent quite some time explaining the whys and the wherefores of oubliettes.

To quote the Bearded Wonder - to be fair, I quite enjoyed his lessons. And he never set homework - the name comes from the French, *oublier*, meaning 'to forget.' We were touring Caesar's Tower, and he'd pointed out a grill on the ground, which covered a hole into which prisoners were apparently thrown and forgotten about.

I could really do without that memory right now.

Look, there's no sense getting all hyped up about it. Someone put you here. Someone will come and let you out. We'll fucking kill them when they do and take it from there. No bother.

"Mate, and I say this with all love, if you've got some sort of sword-dementia thing going on, can we deal with it another day?"

What the fuck are you talking about?

I ignored him.

I needed a plan. I didn't know where I was. I didn't know who had taken me. I didn't know what they wanted with me.

By my reckoning, I'd been in here for a whole day, and no one had bothered to check on me, so I had to assume whoever had me knew I wasn't going to die of thirst in the near future. Maybe the rules over the captivity of cultivators were different? Like, no rush. We'll get to her in a few weeks.

Fuck. That would be brutal.

I can't hear Merlin. What the fuck happened to him?

"Fucking hell, Drynwyn. I can't be doing with this right now. We talked about this yesterday."

No, we fucking didn't. Why would we? He was in here yesterday. Remember, the whole Trial of Honour, Strength and Thought?

"Mate, I'm sorry to break it to you, but we've been in here for at least a day."

Have you had a blow to the head? We were just in the forest, then something grabbed you, and now we're here. I don't want to be rude, but life was much fucking simpler with Rhyddrech Hael.

"If you're about to reminisce about your time in Monsieur Whip's Dungeon, I will absolutely lose my shit."

There was a pause. **How do you know about that?**

"Because you told me. Yesterday. When we woke up here."

And I told you we've only just fucking got here!

And that was when the penny that had been falling for the last few minutes finally dropped.

"Oh, fucking hell."

And an evil cackle boomed through the cell.

***

I don't know how often the day was reset before my contact with my captor was upgraded from an occasional evil cackle to an actual conversation.

Once I realised what was going on, I'd got my short-hand explanation for Drynwyn down to a solid few words - "Stuck in a time loop. Losing my goddam mind. Don't be a dick" - and to be fair, he was more or less rolling with it.

But then again, why wouldn't he? He couldn't remember the eight million times we'd had the same conversation. I saw a play once by some French dude or another, and the key line was that 'hell is other people."

I'm happy to confirm.

Although, the only thing that would have been worse than an eternity stuck with Drynwyn was the prospect of the same amount of time on my own.

So, it was swings and roundabouts.

"Look, this isn't the first time you've been through this. Don't be such a wetwipe. It's no different from when Merlin shut you away in a cave. Just do what you did then."

But even as I said it - yes, I've started talking to myself - I knew I was lying. This was nowhere close to what I'd been through before. Back then, I had Merlin talking me through what was going on and a proper training regime. Here, I was basically rotting away in a void.

By far, the biggest problem was that I was in such a state I couldn't settle down to do any proper meditation. Every time I tried to clear my mind, the crushing weight of being stuck in this cell settled upon me, and I was kicked straight out of my Artist's Studio.

Have I told you the story of Rhydrech Hael against the cannibals?

"Yes. You have literally told me every single story about Rhydrech Hael in existence."

Well, sorry, I'm sure. Some of us have only been here a few hours.

"And some of us have been here for what feels like most of our adult life. So, I'm sorry if I'm a touch grouchy."

You should try cultivating. I'm sure that would pass the time.

"Really? You think so, do you? Why hadn't I thought of that?"

I'm just trying to help.

***

Eeons past.

Stars formed and fell apart.

Keith Richards started to feel he was a bit past it all.

99

Drynwyn carried on telling me the same stories.

Eventually, though, it reached the stage that his voice became just so much background noise - like having the washing machine on when you were trying to get to sleep - and I was able to start to find some chill.

I inhaled deeply and tried to let my panic wash away. Drynwyn's voice was there, a steady drone that let other intrusive thoughts fade into the backwards if I focused on it.

Just when the story of Rhydrech Hael and the busty washerwoman, her husband and their four donkeys reached its climax - a real romantic tale, this one - I dropped inward to my Artist's Studio. For the first time in forever, I wasn't immediately kicked out. However, my Qi was a sorry sight. It lay dormant, thick, and unyielding, all my purple paint long dried up upon an abandoned palette.

I focused, trying to get some life into this stagnant energy. To start with, though, it was akin to pushing against a stone wall. My Qi was immovable and, and this was the scariest thing, completely cold. Each effort completely drained me, and every attempt to get it moving left me more and more weary.

Oddly, though, the more exhausted I was, the easier I could let go of my terror. Basically, it seemed like I had only so much mental energy available at any one time. I could be tired, I could be horny, or I could be scared. But I couldn't manage all three.

And then, after an especially strong push, I felt the faintest quiver, a teasing promise of movement that vanished as quickly as it came. That livened me up, and I redoubled my efforts over the next few days.

It was hard work, this struggle to awaken something that seemed determined to remain asleep. My Qi was essentially me as a teenager.

I could almost hear the echo of Merlin in my head, mocking my frailty.

I wish.

I don't know how many days reset while I struggled with something that had come to me so easily before. However, I persisted - what else was I going to do? - driven by a flicker of hope that just refused to be extinguished. I'd been able to do this. I would again. And then I would free myself.

Then, during the preamble of how Rhyddrech Hael found himself naked in a bed with a Duke, a Baron, a Princess, and a strategically shaved bear, I felt a subtle shift, and then, just like that, I was able to push my Qi around my channels again.

I don't mind telling you that I wept tears of relief. I'd been worried that if I had not done so for so long, the paint would have permanently dried out. Things were sludgy, for sure, but slowly but surely, I could push things around again.

I was just starting to get excited about the giant fireball I would be putting through that fucking iron door when ...

"Well, well, well. I was not sure you were ever going to crack that. What on earth is Merlin teaching his apprentices nowadays? So, let's have a look at what you've got going on."

I felt my eyes roll back in my head as something sharp and icy started rummaging around in my brain.

"What a bizarre collection of talents. No. We can't be having this. Some sort of weird version of the Dark Kestrel Strike? Useless." I gagged in pain as something was ripped out of my soul. Then vomited when the same thing happened again and then again. "I'll leave you <Personal Space Invader> as that has some merit. But the rest of your foundation is simply trashy, unearned silliness. Really, I am so disappointed in this. I expected to see so much better. Perhaps it would be best to leave you a bit more time to reflect on some of your choices."

The voice retreated, leaving me in a pool of sick - that was surely biologically impossible considering the lack of food and drink - and several yawning open wounds in my spirit where skills used to reside.

Is this a fucking prison?

CHAPTER 24 – IN WHICH MERLIN GETS HIS GROOVE BACK

Merlin was quietly impressed by the range of techniques this body had at its command.

In fact, after being stuck in Morgan's mind, it was rather refreshing to be connected to the spirit of someone who had clearly put a lot of time and even greater effort into building up their cultivation. Considering that most of this groundwork must have been undertaken when Merlin had been hoovering up the majority of the available Qi, this was no small feat for the Saxon to have achieved.

The self-discipline such a thing would have achieved . . . well, it was rather staggering.

Nodding appreciatively, Merlin's respect for Melehan ratcheted up quite a few notches. Entirely through his own diligent efforts, this man had easily surpassed the level of a **Harry**. Why, he was probably only a decade or two from crossing the threshold into **Hermione** . . .

At that thought, Merlin's nose - it was so good to have one of those again - wrinkled in distaste. When had he started to entertain such silliness? Cultivating was a serious process, not something that should be reduced to silly, simplified labels. He needed to get back to remembering that.

He would need to impress that on Morgan when he got her back.

Continuing his tour of the Saxon wizard's inner spiritual landscape, his initial appreciation increased. Visualising Qi as sand and then being able to command it to move was an almost masochistic endeavour. Morgan had been largely on the right track in choosing to view her Qi as paint. It was not as sensible as, say, conceptualising the whole process as water, but at least Morgan had made life relatively easy for herself by visualising a moveable liquid.

But sand? This wizard was hardcore. With that sort of willpower, imagine what he could have achieved with Merlin as his mentor!

Of course, there were innumerable improvements that a cultivator of his vast skill and millennia of experience could make to these foundations - he quietly redirected and refocused the flow of Saxon's channels to improve their long-term efficiency - but all in all, he was pretty satisfied with his new 'home'. He finally appeared to be in the body of an entirely satisfactory cultivator.

Why, if he had stumbled across this Melehan character a little earlier in things, he would not have needed to bother with Morgan at all . . .

Well, now.

Wasn't that an interesting thought?

"Archers!" Arthur shouted, suddenly ducking down behind the stone abutment of the bridge. Swearing, Bors barely hit the ground in time to avoid a flurry of arrows that would have put somewhat of a dent in his day.

The howls of humans committing to their role as wolves filled the woods as the two Britons took up defensive positions. "I've heard this song before," Bors said, spitting out a mouthful of dirt, "it didn't work out too well for us that time either."

"Forgive me if my memory of that confrontation is a little indistinct. I was a bit busy being burned alive. Fuck!" Arthur raised a hand to his forehead, which came away bloody. Some bright spark had found a sling and was adding a volley of stones to the wider bombardment. "We're not going to be able to hang around here. Let's get ourselves some distance and have another look."

Bors shook his head. "We can't. The Saxon said Guinevere is still somewhere over that side."

Arthur turned to glare at Melehan, whose eyes seemed oddly unfocused as if he was deep in contemplative thought. Then he took another look because, apparently, the man had eyes again.

That was some quick healing.

In fact, considering the state they had found him in, the Saxon wizard looked pretty much to have pulled himself back into one piece. "What's the story? Did you truly see my wife over that side of the river?"

The wizard smiled - but, in some indefinable way, the grin did not quite reach his eyes - "I did indeed, my dear. I mean, my lord. She was entirely well and gave a good accounting of herself. With a Saxon dead at her feet, she retreated over yonder to avoid further confrontation." He raised an arm and pointed haphazardly in any number of directions on the other side of the bridge. "I would anticipate, from what I saw, she will be very difficult for them to capture."

Bors grabbed hold of Melehan's tunic and pulled him in close. "And Morgan? What about her? How are we going to get her back? You said a great power stole her!"

Before answering, Merlin took a quick glance at Melehan's spirit. The Saxon had not moved from his previous position on the shore and seemed to be humming quietly to himself. All things considered - and even Merlin could sense he was probably reaching a little here - the man appeared quite content with his current lot.

In many ways, the wrong thing to do would be to disturb him, wouldn't it? After everything the poor man had been through, he deserved a break to gather his thoughts. Didn't he? Indeed, looking at this broken shell of a man, he was clearly in no shape to help Arthur and Bors right now. It would be cruel to put him in the position of needing to be an active player in the drama when what he really needed was a good rest.

In fact - now he thought about it properly - it went much further than that. Merlin would actually be in dereliction of his duty to the realm if he did not take the opportunity to step up and fill the void in the absence of the last remaining of Britain's mages.

That was a sound order of business. Once Arthur had Guinevere back, Merlin had made sure the Saxons were properly on the run, and he'd caught up on his correspondence, he'd turn this body back over to Melehan.

First chance he got.

Then, with all that settled, he'd look to track down Morgan and get back on with training her up to support Arthur's rise to power.

Absolutely.

No flaws in that plan at all.

His teeth cracked together as Bors shook him rather more roughly than was strictly necessary. "I asked you a question, wizard!"

Merlin pulsed out a small blast of lightning - nothing lethal, of course. He'd long ago learned that it was polite to give a warning first - and dropped to the floor when a shocked, in more ways than one, Bors let him go.

"Could you please remember that wizard is my title rather than my name, Sir Bors? It would be best if you addressed me as Mer . . . Melehan. I will also answer to M. Or, if you wish to be more informal, I do quite like being referred to as the Big M." He felt a little spike of residual sorrow at that, but quickly squashed it down. He'd be bringing her back as soon as everything else was under control. Then everything would go back to normal.

And not a minute sooner. No. That wasn't right. He meant 'later'.

Not a moment later.

However, first, the immediate issue. Merlin activated the strongest shield technique Melehan had learned. <Iron Dome> shimmered into life around the three men, deflecting stones, arrows, and several javelins away.

"Now," Merlin continued, "I am afraid that I have no idea what has taken Morgan. There was a breach to the walls of reality, and someone reached through and pulled her to their side of that rip. The wound in space and time remains, so, given time, it should not be too difficult to trace her destination. Although, dealing with a cultivator strong enough to make that technique work will be extremely challenging and will need careful planning. However, to be able to save her, we need to first get out of this little predicament alive. I would also suggest that the Princess Guinevere, whilst no doubt spunkfilled, is probably more in need of our help right now than a reasonably powerful cultivator. . ."

He paused, aware that Bors and Arthur were staring at him. "What?"

Bors cleared his throat. "Spunky. I think you meant 'spunky.'"

"Why, what did I say?"

"Something quite different." Arthur could not help but flinch as another arrow pinged off the shield. "Okay, wizard . . . I mean, Melehan. We achieve our own safety first, then locate and secure Guinevere. Once those two things are achieved, we will discuss how best to help Morgan."

Bors growled at that but did not offer any further comments.

Arthur turned to face the wizard, who seemed an awful lot more confident in himself than the man the prince remembered. Perhaps he was the sort who grew into a crisis? "It seems as if we are in your hands. So, what's the plan?"

Merlin moved Melehan's lips into a smile.

He really had missed this.

CHAPTER 25 - IN WHICH UTHER OVERPLAYS HIS HAND

Uther pinched the bridge of his nose and took a deep breath.

"And at what stage did you begin to recognise that none of this had ever really been a good idea?"

Igraine began to shrug, then sensing that was not entirely appropriate to the fairly dire atmosphere in the throne room, dipped further into her deep curtsey. "It would be fair to say, Your Highness, that in retrospect, more detailed planning would have been sensible."

"In retrospect?"

Igraine nodded, frowning at Uther's tone. She accepted that there was probably a certain amount of humble pie that would need to be consumed here. She had, after all, managed to lose track of both the Prince and Princess, as well as their sole remaining wizard and their most competent warrior.

For a realm teetering somewhat on the precipice, she understood that the plan she had endorsed to help bring Arthur back to himself could be considered a little injudicious.

Thus, she could accept that Uther had the right to be a little pissy in public about it.

However, a big fat black line would need to be drawn at extensive humiliation. There were far too many members of the minor nobility in the room for her liking. Speaking of which . . .

"Your Highness, on behalf of the men of Cardigan, I offer my sincere condolences for the challenges that once again beset the British people. It would be an immense honour should you allow me to lead my brave countrymen on an immediate rescue mission. No mere Saxon will prevent me from delivering Prince Arthur and Princess Guinevere safely back to you." Gwynllyw's men roared their approval at his words.

Uther studiously ignored the man.

He had been doing a lot of that ever since the arrival of that long streak of piss at Tintagel a few days earlier. News of the near-total annihilation of Arthur's Marghekyon had brought every lunatic with a sword to court to try to get in on the action, and it was becoming a touch wearing.

Despite his irritation, though, Uther understood the impulse. Saxon incursions, the length and breadth of the country were increasingly putting pressure on the native, petty kingdoms. Alongside Gwynllyw of Cardigan, he also was having to put up with various princelings and would-be warlords from Dyfed, Powys and Gwynned.

It was encouraging that there seemed to be an impulse to throw their lot in with the Britons to meet the growing threat. He just would have preferred to have their support in the form of spears on the battlefield, rather than loud, virile young men hanging around his throne room and propositioning his servants.

He already had a son who fulfilled that criterion nicely.

The tall, earnest-looking man from Cardigan might not be the most annoying of those seeking to join Arthur's band, but he seemed the least responsive to rejection.

However, Uther was far more focused on his wife for the moment. It was a rare day indeed that he could actually have something tangible to hold over her, and he intended to exploit this for its maximum enjoyment value.

Truth be told, he was not too concerned about Arthur and the rest.

For all his son's many faults, there were very few scrapes into which the lad could get himself that he could not find a way to escape: that had been true his whole life. He had been - by all accounts - burned to death not that long ago, and he'd walked away from it largely unscathed.

When you threw Bors, Morgan and Guinevere into the mix, he rather pitied whoever had waylaid them. It was likely to be a choice they would come to regret most sincerely.

Nevertheless, he did not need to tell Igraine that. At least not right now. She was looking somewhat flustered. "Retrospect, my dear? We need retrospect to identify that, having encouraged the Prince and Princess of Britain to wander alone around the Saxon-infested countryside, tighter security arrangements would be sensible. It needs hindsight, doesn't it? That seems rather interesting."

"Allow the brave men of Cardigan the opportunity to cleanse your land, Your Highness! No Saxon shall stand against the might of our blades!"

Uther fixed his eyes on his increasingly red-faced wife, ignoring the loud chorus of cheers from around the room.

Igraine cleared her throat. There would be a reckoning for this little mummer's show. Maybe not today. Maybe not tomorrow. But soon. And Uther would sincerely regret the smug smirk on his face. With great difficulty, she kept her voice neutral. "The Princess Guinevere believed she had a solution to her marital difficulties. We have discussed the importance of assisting Arthur and his wife to reach a more . . . stable relationship. I thought it apt to support her in this. Morgan agreed, and - following discussion - we put in place what I considered to be fairly robust safeguards to avoid any issues. I do not believe it could have been foreseen that the men following Guinevere would be slain nor that those tracking the prince would be accosted by a purple stallion."

"Perhaps. But, of course, we will never know what might have been achieved had the circle of those planning such things been a touch wider. The product of the collective brainpower of three women does not seem to have worked out too well for us, does it?"

There was a sharp intake of breath from those in earshot, and Igraine immediately straightened up. "I do beg your pardon?"

Uther was a veteran of countless battles. He had brought the various warring tribes of Dumnonia under his rule by strength, might and a bloody-mindedness that would put a charging boar to shame. He had personally slain ten Champions - including his own brother - in violent duels and had never backed down from any challenge. Few things in this world, or indeed the next, could cause a moment of fear to flutter in his heart.

But he was also not an idiot.

He knew that glint in his wife's eye and recognised that boded ill for his immediate well-being. "What I mean, of course, my dear, is that it may have been sensible to include a wider range of advisors in planning how to ensure this unfortunate outcome was avoided."

"I speak for the men of Cardigan when I say we would be honoured to be so included in any such discussions. We have experience in strategic, long-term thinking."

"And just so I am clear, my lord, is your opinion that those advisors should have been men? To, I don't know, dilute the volume of silly, feminine thinking that has occurred? Was that your point? I'm sorry, I may have misunderstood. Sometimes, my fragile women's ears get quite overwhelmed by all the long words."

"No, what I'm saying is . . . Hang on. Let me gather my thoughts. What I am trying to outline is that, perhaps, you, Guinevere and Morgan might not have been the ideal people to plan out a complex military operation with any number of variables."

"Because we're women?"

"No, it's not that -"

"Because you are worried our periods may all have synched, leading to vapidity and emotional instability?

"Dear gods. No. What I mean is that because you're not, and never have been soldiers, you may have underestimated the challenges."

"The men - and women - of Cardigan have a long and proud history of soldiery and would be pleased to offer our expertise in the upcoming rescue mission."

"Will you shut the fuck up!" Both Uther and Igraine bellowed at the tall man at the same time.

Grasping at the distraction to escape his wife's ire, Uther quickly sought to press onwards. "Prince Gwynllyw, my apologies. The stress of the situation, after all."

The tall man smiled back. If he had been offended by the raised voices, he did not show it. "Not at all, my lord."

"My son and his wife are beyond these walls. I would be grateful for your help in bringing them back home."

Gwynllyw's eyes shone with barely restrained fervour. He had a quest! And a quest from King Uther Pendragon, no less! This was a moment for which he had waited his entire life.

The other nobles in the throne room barely got out of his men's way as they stormed through the doors, running to the stables.

Uther shook his head. The fool. If those missing truly needed help, it would take much more than Gwynllyw and his band of merry men to make a difference. Indeed, he doubted he'd see that man alive again. He had better send to King Glwys to let him know the imminent fate of his middle son.

However, if it worked for the men of Cardigan. . .

Ignoring the continued frosty glare of his wife, Uther stood and addressed the rest of the court. "Let Prince Gwynllyw be your example. You wish to attach yourself to the court of Tintagel? Well, I shall not be ungrateful to whoever ensures Arthur and Guinevere return to us safely. Our success against the Saxons depends on them being brought home unharmed."

There was a murmur of approval in the room. Uther's generosity concerning his son was legendary. Did not most households in the room care for at least one of Arthur's bastards?

With a little more circumspection than Prince Gwynllyw managed, the room slowly began to empty of people eager to take to the countryside and locate the missing   royalty.

Uther moved to follow to see them on their way when a bony finger pocked the middle of his back. "Not so fast, my dear. I do not believe we quite finished our discussion."

Uther Pendragon, the man who single-handedly broke the Saxon shield-wall at Mount Damen, took one look at his wife's face and hurried for the door.

CHAPTER 26 - IN WHICH IT IS BIG GIRL PANTS TIME

"You're better than this."

I tried my hardest to ignore the soft voice from down by my feet. I was feeling like absolute shit and honestly wasn't in the mood for company.

The small room was filled with the smell of vomit and . . . other liquid things. While that wasn't exactly ideal in terms of my personal living situation, the bonus was that, in my vast experience, most people didn't tend to want to hang around too long if I simply denied their existence for long enough.

"No matter how bad things feel right now, tomorrow can be better."

Well, I apparently had the Spirit of Fortune Cookie Wisdom visiting with me today. Wasn't that a delight? I turned my head to spit out some sort of accumulated fluid from my mouth. Then, reconsidering, I swallowed it down. Saved me having to get up to find a glass of water.

The body was efficient like that.

I felt movement. Then whoever it was decided my personal space was optional and sat right beside me, planting a cool hand on my forehead.

I'm not going to lie—whatever complaints I might've had about boundaries evaporated right there. It felt nice. Like, *genuinely* nice.

"Why do you do this to yourself, lovely?"

Now, that felt kind of a low blow. At worst, I could be considered tangentially responsible for my current plight.

"When I called yesterday afternoon, you promised you weren't going out."

Hang on a minute.

I half-cracked an eye open.

The sun was doing its best impersonation of a judgmental parent, streaming through my bedroom curtains to spotlight the chaos I called 'home.' Cups and plates teetered in precarious towers, daring gravity to do its worst. Clothes—clean, dirty, and somewhere in a morally ambiguous grey zone—had claimed every surface.

The scent hit next, a symphony of rotting food and sour milk with top notes of regret. If there was a perfume called *Rock Bottom*, this room would've been the factory.

I also seemed to be only half-dressed, which was momentarily a worry. Bad things happened to shitty people, after all. But then I remembered this was actually the outfit I had gone out in. So, that was kind of a good news, bad news thing. Presumably, I had been in such a state even the most predatory of souls had not been able to bring themselves to do any more than stick me in a taxi.

"Are you listening, lovely?"

"Fuck off, Zizzie. I'm not in the mood."

In my memory, this was the part where my sister sighed the sigh of the righteous, slipped a tenner into my hand, and let herself out without another word.

No lecture, no sarcastic quip. Just the silent, soul-crushing weight of her *disappointed younger sibling energy*. Honestly, the ten quid felt less like help and more like hush money.

"No, not this time. We need to talk."

In surprise, I opened my eyes and looked up at her. Her voice had a firm edge to it, something sharp and unfamiliar, like someone had swapped out her usual playlist of exasperated patience for a single track titled *Not Today Satan*.

Elizabeth—though she'd been "Zizzie" ever since my four-year-old self mangled her name beyond recognition—stood there exactly as she always did, a walking indictment of my genetic potential. She looked like me if you ran me through Instagram's *Ultimate Glow-Up* filter and then added a touch of *mysteriously always put-together*.

Even her hair seemed competent.

Funnily enough, though, I'd never been able to bring myself to be jealous of her. She was just too nice.

If there had been just one moment when we were growing up where she'd acted superior - a single example of screwing me over so she could get ahead - I'd have been all over that as an excuse for some epic sibling chicanery.

But no. There'd been nothing. Zizzie had shared. She'd included. She'd rejected every opportunity my parents gave her to leave me floundering in her wake. And that attitude had carried on when she'd joined me at school. If you wanted to be her friend - and, my word, didn't everyone? - then they needed to be mine, too.

I'd fucking hated it.

I remember feeling an almost spiritual kinship with Elizabeth Bennet when I first read *Pride and Prejudice*. How, I ask you, are you supposed to find space to function—much less thrive—when you're sharing air with someone as kind, optimistic, and absurdly beautiful as Jane?

Preach, sister. I feel you. But let's be honest, you could've done a hell of a lot better than Darcy. Brooding entitlement isn't a personality trait, no matter how many wet shirts he wears.

I'd developed a whole stream of coping strategies for all the dicks and bitches in the world. I could give as good as I got in any situation, except when someone took me as they found me.

A therapist had said they felt the root of my problems was that I had never felt unconditional positive regard from anyone in my life.

I'd nodded fiercely - yeah, fuck all those guys who let me down! - whilst all the time trying to keep Zizzie's open, calm, understanding face out of my mind.

"This isn't how it happened."

"No," Zizzie took one of my hands in hers, "it isn't."

"So, you're not really here?"

"No, I'm afraid not."

The image of my bedroom shifted, and I was back in my prison cell.

There was no telling how long it had been since the voice had ripped the techniques from my mind. Days? Weeks? Time had turned into an abstract concept—just a sequence of agony interrupted by whimpers and the occasional scream. At first, pain had been my entire universe, a relentless tide I was drowning in.

Then I'd emerged, or what passes for "emerged" when you're more wreckage than person. Since then, the days had blurred together, indistinguishable except for the overwhelming sense that I was still breathing and still very much wishing I wasn't.

I'd thought of keeping an old-fashioned tally chart scratched into the wall to keep some measure of time, but when the day restarted, it was wiped away. Of course, it was.

Cycling my Qi was absolute agony with the enormous gaps that had been torn in my foundation, but I'd done my best to stick at it.

What else was there to do?

I'd even tried to put in place some of the lessons Merlin had nagged and nagged at me to try out to maximise my efficiency, but I'd never had the time to roll out. Now I had nothing but.

Don't get me wrong, the isolation had absolutely driven me out of my gourd—case in point, the sudden appearance of my darling sister in all her imaginary glory. But, let's be real, I'd spent the bulk of my adult life ping-ponging between various addled states. This wasn't exactly uncharted territory for me.

If anything, I suspect the mental fallout was significantly less catastrophic than it might've been for someone who started off with their head screwed on properly. Who knew being batshit crazy would end up as my superpower?

Somewhere out there, a therapist is weeping into their ethically sourced herbal tea. "You need to stop thinking about yourself in such a negative way."

"Sure, Ghost Zizzie. Lay your wisdom on me. I'm down for it."

It was a bit of a surprise when she slapped me.

"Stop it," she hissed.

The physical impact of the blow was pretty insignificant. Regardless of what had been done to my techniques, I still had the body of a cultivator of no little power. Zizzie'd have needed a sledgehammer to have as much as make me blink.

My shock was more that my sister had never so much as said 'boo' to a goose in her whole life. She'd once cried for an entire morning after realising she'd shut a fly in her doll's house overnight, and it had been away from its family until she released it. She'd been thirteen.

Thus, the idea she'd just straight up clocked me one - all the time gritting her teeth in a rictus of fury - was a bit beyond my lived experience.

"No one is coming to save you."

I shrugged at that. "Sorry to break it to you, Z, but that's been the story of my whole life."

Zizzie shook her head, her face returning to its standard overflowing compassion mask. "No, it isn't. No matter what you did, what you took or what you needed, there was always someone in the wings waiting to sort it out for you. Did you know Dad paid your rent for years?"

"Did he fuck!"

"He did. Why else do you think you were never evicted?"

I knew exactly what Bryan, my previous landlord, had been getting in lieu of his monthly rent. So, Zizzie's news came as a bit of a blow. In more than one way, if you get what I'm saying.

"Jace watched out for you, even after you broke up with him. He went as far as to open an account with the local cab firm to ensure you got home from whatever place you passed out in."

The image of a kind, bearded face behind the wheel of a car swam into my vision. "Mr Khan?"

"You think it was a coincidence the same guy picked you up, night after night. And he never wanted to be paid?"

To be honest, I'd never really thought about it. That was the beautiful thing about being solipsistic. You didn't need to worry about others.

"And how do you think you kept getting all those job offers? You must have known someone was pulling strings. How many times do you reckon someone can be fired before they get blocked!"

Zizzie worked in recruitment. I'd guessed she must have had the odd word, but the way she was saying it was like she was my own personal employment consultant.

"Just fuck off, Z. Being on my own is how I like it. I can take care of myself."

The second slap had more welly in it, and I saw stars. Good for you, Zizzie.

"No, you can't. You've never been able to. You make this big song and dance about being independent and not wanting anything to do with anyone, but you've never been able to achieve anything off your own back. Even here, where the whole world is literally set up to allow you to work and graft and to grow into something extraordinary, you still have needed it all put on a plate for you."

"Don't hold back, Zizzie; say what you really think."

And then my sister's face blurred just slightly, and I realised I was talking to a simulacrum of myself.

"You need to understand that unless you get up off your arse, this is it," said Tough Love Me. "This is where you will stay until you go completely off your rocker." It was obviously disconcerting to hear that advice from yourself. "No one is coming to save you. No one is even really missing you yet. For them, you've barely been missing a few hours. You can't just do as you always do, wallow in your own shit, and wait for someone to come along and clean it up. That's not going to happen this time."

"Good talk. Cheery. Proper Invictus stuff."

"You're smart. You're capable. You're tougher than you know. And the world needs you to step up." The face blurred again, and it was back to Zizzie. "If you don't get out of here, my timeline doesn't exist. I need your help, lovely. It's Big Girl Pants time."

My eyes filled with tears.

That was what we used to say to each other when something truly shitty had happened, but we needed to step up. It was the phrase we used every time Mum went awol for weeks on end. It was what I told her when that massive cock, David Johnson, broke her heart. And it was what she said to me after I lost the baby.

Is this a fucking prison?

I blinked, clearing my eyes of tears, and as quickly as she had appeared, Zizzie was gone.

With a pulse, I blasted Qi around my channels and pulled it to the surface of my skin, instantly burning off what felt like decades of grime.

Fucking hell, love. Calm down. There's no sense getting all hyped up about it. Someone put you here. Someone will come and...

"Nope. Not this time."

What the fuck are you talking about?

"I'll explain as we go. But we're not hanging around here for a minute longer than we need to. Now, just how hot can your flame become?"

Oh, baby. Thought you'd never ask.

CHAPTER 27 - IN WHICH I MAKE A SURPRISING NEW ACQUAINTANCE

You know right at the start of The Phantom Menace when Obi-Wan and Qui-Gon are kicking ass and taking names on the droid ship? Cool scene, right?

Well, there's this really weird bit when they suddenly move really, really quickly. Like, they become The Flash for a couple of seconds.

There's no real plot reason for it - it's not like it's a life-or-death situation or anything like that - and they never actually do it again. It bugs the hell out of me when, at the end of the movie, they're chasing Darth Maul and the two of them manage to get separated. And, lo and behold, Obi-Wan never tries to use this fantastic capacity for superspeed to catch up with his mate.

Ultimately, Liam Neeson gets shish kebabbed because his Padawan appears to forget he has this massively helpful and extremely handy situational skill. I always thought his final words should have been something a touch more aggrieved than 'train him ...' More like, 'What happened, dude? You stopped for a snack or something?"

Why on earth am I telling you this . . .

Honestly, I have no idea.

I guess other than the sight of Drynwyn carving through my cell door like an oxyacetylene torch through ice cream, reminded me of earlier in that opening scene when Qui-Gon used his lightsabre to slice through the blast doors.

I guess, if we're really lucky, uninvited monologues on the vagaries of popular culture will be the only consequence of my isolated imprisonment.

I fear there might be a bit more to it than that, though . . .

Anyhow . . .

So, it turns out 'Drynwyn versus Cell-Door' is somewhat of a one-sided deal. In about three minutes, he's through, and I'm out into a dark corridor that stretches left and right in an unbroken straight line without apparent end. I can make out similar doors to mine on both walls where, presumably, a bunch of people are also experiencing their own private time loop hell.

"Good job," I said, re-slinging the sword into its scabbard on my back.

Cheers. You feeling up for some bad news?

While it was cutting, I'd filled the sword in on the little time-loop-Morgan-going-crazy-Big-Bad-ripping-out-all-my-techniques thing that had been going on.

It had proved to be a surprisingly good listener.

I imagine Rhydrech Hael had probably needed to unburden himself reasonably regularly.

"How bad?"

I mean, it's not 'that succubus has poisoned you, and there's no antidote ' bad. But neither is it 'there's too many cocks in this room to adequately give them all equal attention' bad either.

"Those are two strangely specific examples."

Long and traumatic history, my friend. Long and fucking traumatic history.

I tried to take the temperature of my internal resources. I'm not going to lie, I was in quite a state. If I kept everything tightly buttoned up, I hoped I had a decent chance of getting out of here before crumbling into tiny little pieces. But I wasn't sure I had much more 'bounce back' left to take on board any bad news.

"Can you try to sugarcoat it?"

Sure. There was a pause. **You know the time loop?**

"Pretty intimately at this stage."

There's a chance - and probably not a big one. In fact, it is so unlikely I don't know why I'm fucking mentioning it. But, you know, I'm a full-service sword, and I like to explore all possibilities - so there's a tiny, slight, little chance that...

"For the love of God, spit it out!"

As the succubus said to Rhyddrech Hael. Sorry, that was inappropriate. What I'm getting at is what do you think the chances are the time-loop might not have just been localised within the cell . . .

"Fuck's sake, Drynwyn."

Sorry.

I was letting the delightful weight of that little revelation settle on me like a lead blanket when something snapped me right back to the present.

"Is there someone out there?"

I froze, pressing myself against the wall as if that would magically make me invisible. The voice—husky, female, and dripping with the smoky charm of Stifler's Mom: Post-Pack-a-Day Edition—came from behind one of the cell doors a little way down on my left.

"What do you think?" I whispered to Drynwyn. "Do I answer? Or do I pretend I'm the figment of her nicotine-stained imagination?"

The voice continued, unfazed by my existential debate. "Because if there is, dearie, and you've managed to get yourself free, I'd be ever so grateful if you could see your way clear to doing the same for me! Honestly, I'd owe you a favour. A big one. The sort you tell people about over drinks."

I glanced down at the sword. "She's laying it on a bit thick, right? Or is that just me? Do I answer her?"

I don't know. A problem shared is a problem fucking cut in half and all that. Anyway, if you let her out - and you are still in the time loop - and it all goes to shit, you'll know not to do it next time.

Sound as that advice was, I didn't want to deal with a reality in which there was a chance the day was going to reset again. I wasn't sure I could cope with that right now.

"Hello? Look, I don't want to sound clingy," the voice pressed on, "not on such a short acquaintance, but it's been quite some time since I heard another human, and I would like to make the most of this opportunity. Even if you're planning on leaving me to rot in here, I'd appreciate a few words?"

You know, there's something about that voice that sounds familiar.

"Good familiar or Rhyddrech Hael's archnemesis familiar?"

No idea.

"I sense your level of 'help' might have peaked earlier today, right?"

I approached the cell with all the caution of someone poking a bear to see if it's really asleep. "Hello!" I called, trying for cheery and landing somewhere around nervous chipmunk. "Sorry, just weighing up the pros and cons of letting you out. Look, I get the hypocrisy of me asking this, but... was there a good reason you were locked up?"

"Oh, undoubtedly," she replied breezily. "I left the High King with absolutely no choice in the matter. To be clear, that's not to say I'm *happy* about being here. Quite the opposite. But in the spirit of trust-building, I freely admit it—he had me bang to rights."

The sheer confidence of her confession made me pause. I mean, she could've lied, right? Spun me some sob story about wrongful imprisonment? Instead, she owned up like someone proud of their rap sheet.

There was an obvious follow-up question dangling in the air, waiting to be asked, but for the life of me, I couldn't quite pin it down. My brain scratched at the itch of it, like a word stuck on the tip of my tongue, teasing and out of reach.

"Right," I said eventually, mostly to fill the awkward silence. "That's... refreshingly honest."

I have definitely heard that voice before . . .

"And are you stuck in a time loop, too?"

"A time loop. Goodness me, no. That would be insane cruelty. I'm just your common-or-garden 'stick them in a cell and throw away the key' type. Time is passing entirely normally for me in here."

I drew Drynwyn and pressed it against the door. "Look, I have no idea whether this is a good idea or not. But you've asked nicely, and I could do with someone to talk to who doesn't want to kill everything we come across."

"Much obliged; I am sure this will be the start of a beautiful friendship."

There was still that strange itch in my head distracting me away from . . . something. What was it?

Drynwyn caught fire and began carving its way through. **Where do I know this voice from? It's on the tip of my blade.**

As it cut, I tried to fill the silence. I wasn't sure about jailbreak small-talk etiquette, but it seemed sensible to keep the chat going. "So, how long have you been locked up?"

"Best part of ten years, as well as I can figure it, dearie."

That little itch flared again, an insistent, nagging thing in the back of my skull. There were questions lurking there, perfectly formed and just out of reach, like dreams that evaporate when you wake up. I pushed through it. "And you say you haven't spoken to anyone else in all that time?"

"Not a soul," she replied. "Haven't seen sight nor sound of a living person. And I don't mind telling you, dearie, that sort of isolation can *do* things to you. It leaves its marks. I'd wager I'm not entirely in my right mind anymore, if truth be told."

"Preach, sister," I said, dragging Drynwyn through the last of the rusted bolts on one side of the door.

The blade hummed faintly. **This voice. So familiar.**

I moved to the other side of the door. It was bad enough dealing with an imprisoned maybe-crazy, but now I had an opinionated sword with short-term memory issues trying to play voice-recognition software. "But you're exaggerating slightly, right? Because if you're not being kept in the same type of time loop prison as me, someone must have been popping into feed and water you."

"No," the voice sounded bemused. "Why would they need to do something like that? I doubt the High King would want anyone dropping by to see me. Chance would be a fine thing. I'd have been out of here like a shot."

That itch was getting bigger.

"Well, to keep you alive. Surely, someone's been bringing you things to eat and drink over the last ten years!"

Drynwyn completed that extended cut and started to sweep across the final line to join everything up.

"Ha. It's been a long time since I've needed food or drink. What self-respecting cultivator needs such things? Especially at my time of life."

That gave me pause, and I tried - at the last minute - to pull Drynwyn free from its cut, but it was too late. The door crashed inwards, narrowly missing hitting a short, plump-looking woman in the face.

Ah, I knew it! Could recognise those dulcet tones anywhere. Morgan, nice to see you again!

Because, of course, the cultivator I'd just freed from her prison was the original Morgan Le Fay.

CHAPTER 28 - IN WHICH YOU WILL SEE DRYNWYN'S PANDORA'S BOX GAG COMING FROM A MILE OFF

Well, this has the potential to be awkward . . .

There are many and variously different ways in which Morgan Le Fey is depicted throughout the Arthurian mythos. Most often, she's related to Arthur in some way. Sometimes, she's even his half-sister, like in Malory's *Le Morte d'Arthur*. In those versions, she tends to be a witch of no little power who's an absolute ballache to deal with. She fucks anything that moves - often including Merlin - hates Guinevere and can pretty much be summed up as a Big Bad.

There are versions where she's cast as some kind of avatar of the Morrígan, the Irish goddess of war, death, and unapologetic batshit craziness. And yes, she's exactly as much fun as that sounds—think ominous cackling, crows everywhere, and a distinct *might shiv you just to see what happens* energy.

In more modern retellings, though, writers love to get *creative*, mashing her up with her sister—who, by the way, is the one who supposedly has that awkward fling with Arthur, resulting in Mordred and the entire *mess* that follows. Because, you know, nothing screams high fantasy like sibling drama, bad life choices, and catastrophic consequences for the realm.

Basically, though, I'm not sure there are many versions of Morgan Le Fey where she looks somewhat like my Great-Grandmother Ethel.

"Well done, dearie. Now, if you could just do something about the chains, that would be lovely?"

I stood, mouth agape, in the doorway, looking down at - arguably - one of my greatest childhood heroes.

Growing up in a rather chaotic household, Zizzie and I tended to retreat to my bedroom and read when all the shouting got too much. Well, at least Zizzie used to read aloud while I lay back, pretending to smoke and looking ever so cool in my caked-on stolen eyeliner and goth get-up.

It should hardly be surprising, therefore, that we tended to latch on to characters - particularly female ones - who took very little shit indeed.

Some of the earliest art I can remember painting was of a tall lady in a pretty dress fireballing groups of knights to death.

As the faces of the knights tended to be dad, boys at school and pretty much every authority figure that tried to enforce their will on me, I felt the metaphor was pretty clear.

I imagine a large part of me picking this name for myself back in the village was that, in many ways, Morgan Le Fey represented the version of myself I would quite like to have been.

Morgan farted and rattled the chains attached to her stumpy arms and legs. "Any time, dearie. I feel another big one rumbling around down there."

Never meet your heroes.

I stepped into the cell and grabbed one of the chains. As I did so, Morgan tried to pull back and just started to say, "Don't touch . . . " when it all became relatively too late.

The moment my hand connected with the cold iron, all of my Qi was sucked out of my body. Literally. I watched as it poured out of my hands into the chains, which gulped it all down greedily. It only took a few moments for my Artist's studio to be absolutely bone dry,

"Well, that was fucking stupid, wasn't it, dearie? Obviously, the only way in which someone of my power was going to be restrained in this cell for a decade was because my Qi was being restricted. How else did it look like it would be done other than through chains with a basic Leach Technique? Didn't you notice?"

Don't be too hard on her, Morgan. I think being stuck in a time loop has royally fucked up her brain.

I don't know what was worse. The lack of Qi, that Morgan Le FUCKING Fey was looking at me with an expression of epic disappointment or that Drynwyn was going in to bat for me.

I staggered and sat down. In doing so, I released my hold on the chains, and I felt little spots of paint start to reappear in my channels.

"Well, time loops will do that to you. Do you remember when Rhyddrech Hael got a bit too familiar, and I had him falling down that well for a few weeks? Thought he'd never stop crying. Good times."

Good times.

"Fuck me," I said, getting to my feet, "every last one of you is a certifiable lunatic." I nudged the chains with the toe of my boot. "So, if I can't touch them, how am I supposed to get you free?"

"I don't know, dearie. I suppose you would need access to some sort of magical sword that could cut through the metal without tripping the Qi leaching technique. To make doubly sure, it might be best if said sword had some sort of elemental affinity - like fire, for instance. But I don't know where you could possibly WELL, WHAT DO YOU KNOW! DRYNWYN, THE SWORD OF RHYDDRECH HAEL! WHAT A COINCIDENCE!"

It was dawning on me that I didn't much like Morgan.

It wasn't just that she looked like a relative of whom the only real memory I had was of her smelling overpoweringly like bleach when I went to hug her. It wasn't even the attitude of smug superiority that reminded me a little of the Big M but without his affability.

No, there was something in her eyes that unsettled me.

I might have liked her chaotic stick-it-to-the-man, 'let's have the orgy right' here energy when I was younger - younger? Who was I kidding? There's a giant picture of a very nubile Morgan currently in my empty flat that I'm sure whoever is tasked with clearing it out after my untimely death-by-truck is already whacking off to - but I'd like to think I'd developed a bit since being stuck in the Dark Ages.

If even half of the things that legendary Morgan was reported to get up to had happened in this timeline, I'd be better leaving her in chains.

I stepped backwards and out of the cell before Drynwyn got it into its head to be 'helpful'.

"Where are you going, dearie?"

"Just getting some fresh air. I'm feeling a little light-headed. What with the loss of all my Qi and the time-loop and all. I'm probably on my period, too. Just be a second."

What the fuck are you doing?

I put my fingers to my lips and then realised the redundancy of doing this to a magical-speaking sword. "Speak into my head for a moment; I know you can."

What's up?

It didn't sound all that much different, but I presumed at least Morgan couldn't hear us anymore.

"I'm not sure we should let her out. The stories of Morgan Le Fey are pretty . . . terrifying."

Oh, absolutely. She's a fucking nightmare. The best thing that ever happened to the realm was that she went awol all those years back. It would be completely irresponsible to let her out.

I paused. "So, we agree. We don't unchain her?"

Cool your coals for a minute. I didn't say that. Look, think about it like this. The enemy of your enemy is someone you can fucking use as a human shield. Whoever locked you up in here obviously did the same to her. I don't know about you, but having a serious cultivator at our back would be comforting.

"Even if that cultivator is likely to stab us in the back, the first chance she gets?"

If we know she's going to screw us over, then we can prepare for it, right? This would only be a ridiculously stupid thing to do if we thought she was actually on our side. She's obviously going to fuck us over.

"I'm not sure this is as winning an argument as you seem to think it is?"

Look, as far as we know, you are still stuck in a time loop. Until we get that clear, we might as well progress with the idea any fuck ups you make, you get a do-over for. If it turns out badly, you'll know.

"And if we're out of the time loop and we're about to open Pandora's box, then what?"

Rhyddrech Hael liked a good rummage in Pandora's box.

I shouldn't have needed to be in a time loop to see that anecdote coming.

"Is everything alright out there, dearie?"

"Yes or no, Drynwyn. What do you think?"

We don't know where we are or who took us. Or how to get out. I don't see leaving someone who could actually fucking help us escape chained up is a viable strategy.

I was torn. On one hand, nothing mattered more to me right now than getting the hell out of Dodge. Freedom was calling, and it sounded a lot like *not dying in a damp cell*. On the other hand, this woman could be—depending on which dead white guy's version you believed—a horny little minx, an unnervingly powerful healer, or the living embodiment of cosmic evil. The odds of this ending well felt... slim. Like, my time in an anorexia self-help group, slim.

"If you're not going to free me," Morgan's voice drifted out again, managing to sound both pitiful and smug, "any chance you could push the door to, dearie? It's awfully drafty in here."

"Fuck it," I said, the cosmic scale in my head tipping from *pragmatic cowardice* to *why not, let's roll the dice on catastrophe*. With a resigned sigh, I stomped back to the cell and set Drynwyn against the rusted bars.

"Go on then," I said to the blade. "Do your thing."

Drynwyn hummed with what I could only describe as glee. If swords had tails, it'd be wagging.I'm not saying this was the wrong decision, I just think if the little old woman with the epic dimples could have avoided cackling like a pantomime villain the second she was free, it would have eased my mind somewhat.

"Thank you, dearie. Now, let's fuck shit up."

CHAPTER 29 - IN WHICH A NARRATIVE ROADBLOCK REQUIRES THE COMPOSITION OF A FUCKING POEM TO UNCLOG.

"First things first," Morgan announced. "Can someone please explain to me where all this *lovely, lovely* Qi has suddenly come from?"

She inhaled sharply, as though sniffing out a particularly decadent meal, then took a few theatrical deep breaths, as if sheer lung power could somehow accelerate her absorption. "It was never like this before. Used to be like drinking a wyvern through a straw."

Curiosity—and a mild sense of impending doom—got the better of me. I engaged my Magic Eyes, and what I saw nearly knocked me off my feet. A tornado of sickly green energy spiralled from Morgan's chest, writhing and twisting like it had a life of its own.

It wasn't just flowing—it was *slurping*. There's no other word for it. It was the grotesque, wet sound you get from a straw scraping the dregs of a milkshake. Except the milkshake was the air around us, and the straw was her entire aura.

"Uh, Morgan?" I ventured cautiously. "Is it supposed to look like that?"

She gave me a wicked grin. "Oh, *absolutely not*. Isn't it thrilling? So, spill. Where is all the Qi coming from?"

Merlin only went and fucking died, didn't he!

The tornado abruptly stopped, and the woman turned to stare at Drynwyn, mouth wide open. "Merlin's dead?"

I sensed Drynwyn was likely to be about to go off on a monologue of metaphors that was destined to cause a copyright infringement claim from purveyors of deceased parrots.

I chose to intercede.

It took a depressingly short amount of time to fill Morgan in on the series of unfortunate, ridiculous, and occasionally gruesome events that had somehow dumped me into the Dark Ages. My exploits, grand as they had seemed in the moment, boiled down to a surprisingly uninspiring summary: stumble, survive, repeat.

I mean, I wasn't expecting an epic on par with Don Quixote, but when you lay it all out like that, it's hard not to feel a bit underwhelmed. Honestly, it sounded less like a heroic tale and more like the ramblings of someone who'd gotten lost in the woods and refused to ask for directions.

Actually... isn't that sort of the point of Don Quixote?

Great. Now I'm analysing 17th-century literature while trying to survive the 6th century. This feels like peak *me*.

I shook my head, trying to drag my focus back to Morgan, who was staring at me with a mix of amusement and barely concealed impatience. "Sorry," I said, "got distracted again."

"So, what you are telling me, dearie, is that there have been months and months of all this wonderful Qi swirling around just waiting to be gobbled up, and I missed it?!"

I couldn't help but feel that Morgan had slightly missed the point of my narrative. "Well, I guess, tangentially, that has been the case. But did you miss the bit about the Saxon invasion and . . . "

Morgan waved a hand dismissively. "Saxons being Saxons is hardly news. You know as well as I do," her eyes were suddenly fixed on mine, "how all of these little genocides shake out. Merlin is not the only one to get visions of the future, don't you know?"

With that, her eyes unfocused, and her voice took on an odd, declaiming tone.

In the realm of mist and stone, where ancient Britons thrived,
By sacred hill and henge, their earthen homes derived.
Their chants, like wind through druid oaks, in mystic harmony,
In lands of myth and ancient lore, their spirits roamed free.

Then came the Angles, Saxon kin, with iron, flame, and sail,
Their longships parted morning mist, a stark, foreboding gale.
They carved their runes, imposed their will on British shores so fair,
In mead halls filled with warrior songs, they spoke of conquests rare.

The Jutes joined in, from distant lands, a lesser known but fierce band,
Together with the Angles and the Saxons, they reshaped the British land.
A trinity of Northern might, they forged a new domain,
Their legacies intertwined in history's grand refrain.

Vikings next, with dragon prows, from icy fjords they came,
With axe and shield, in longboats fierce, they sought to claim their fame.
They stormed the isles with ruthless will, their sagas sung with pride,
In halls of mead, their stories told, of seas they'd conquered wide.

At last, the Normans, regal, stern, across the Channel's broad expanse,
With cavaliers in gleaming mail, they sought to enhance.
Their castles rose, a symbol strong, of a new era's birth,
Their legacy in stone and song, a testament to their worth.

Through time's grand march, these cultures merged, a tapestry so vast,
Briton, Angle, Saxon, Jute, Viking, Norman, cast.
In every stone, in every stream, these stories are enshrined,
A chronicle of many races, in England's heart entwined.

I mean, apart from the shitty rhyme scheme - expanse/enhance, really? - I did rather have to take issue with Morgan's 'vision' suggesting the make-up of 'England' ended in 1066.

She'd be advocating for Brexit next.

"So, you can see," her voice returned to his normal, "why I never had any truck with Merlin and his 'Once and Future King bullshit."

Her Qi tornado cranked up again, a vortex greedily slurping in energy like a cosmic black hole with no off switch. It was unsettling, to say the least, and I switched off my Magic Eyes before my brain decided to throw in the towel. The image lingered, though, crawling at the edges of my mind. Did Morgan conceptualise her Qi as wind? That might explain the whole *Wizard of Oz* tornado aesthetic.

Morgan, however, seemed unfazed. She was already launching into what I could only describe as a rant worthy of a frustrated history professor. "The old fool can prattle on all he likes about a 'golden age of Britain' and 'peace in our time,' but that isn't going to stop the Saxons stomping all over Tintagel when their moment comes. Nor the Normans—whoever the fuck they are—showing up to stick it to those smug blonde bastards later. And when I say 'stick it,' I mean break it off and leave us all holding the splinters."

She paused, tapping a finger against her chin in a manner that suggested she was just warming up. "Normans. Where are they even from, anyway? Normannia? Normville? A colony of particularly insufferable Scandinavians who decided France needed spice?"

"Erm," I cast my mind back to try to remember what the French were called around this time. "Frankia, I think?"

Fucking hell. Melt me down for slag and pour me in the lake. The Franks end up top dogs on this island? Bloody fucking bollocking hell.

I couldn't help but feel I'd lost control of the general thrust of this conversation.

"So, what's the plan?" I asked, gamely trying to wrestle the conversation back into some sort of order. "Can you get us out of here?"

Morgan didn't seem to hear me, so I tried again. After she ignored my question for the third time, I was starting to get peeved.

"Morgan," I reached out to put my hand on her wrist, "I asked. 'Can you get us out of here?'"

The second I contacted her, I felt myself being pulled down into a raging storm.

I found myself in what was apparently Morgan's equivalent of my Artist's Studio. However, to try to draw comparisons would have been facile. Whereas I had a blank canvas on which to paint my Qi, Morgan seemed to have a craggy rock around which roared a hurricane.

I don't know if this was reflective of how much more power, she had than me or whether it was the difference in our temperaments, but as I clung desperately to the rough rock to keep from being buffeted out into oblivion, it was clear that OG Morgan and I were not especially alike.

"How did you find your way in here, dearie?"

A hand reached out towards me, and I grabbed it gratefully. I was hauled like a sack of potatoes upwards and deposited on a flat stone surface, making it slightly easier to cope with the ongoing buffeting torrent.

I glanced over to say 'thank you' to Morgan and was somewhat astonished to see the change in her physical being. Gone was the endearing, slightly grouchy grandmother figure, to be replaced by someone who would have made Maleficient and Hela look at each other and say, 'Nah, I think that's pushed the S&M-Bitch-Queen-from-Hell thing a little far. Let's dial it back. Smaller horns. Go easier on the leather.'

She absolutely towered above me, with eyes the colour of the sickly green tornado I had seen earlier.

"I don't know. Happy to be sent back if you know how?"

"Of course I do. But let's chat for a moment. So, with Merlin gone, you're the head cultivator honcho in Tintagel?"

"Well, I wouldn't quite put it like that . . ."

"How would you put it? There's no other cultivator of substance in the court of Uther, is there?"

"No. Well, then, yes. If you express it in those terms, I probably am Top Dog cultivator."

Funnily enough, barely able to stand in the middle of a colossal maelstrom, at the mercy of a legendarily capricious Witch and still reeling from the effects of the time loop on my fragile mental state, I wasn't sure this was much of a recommendation.

Morgan made a gesture, and the swirling winds subsided significantly. I realised I had been shouting. She looked at me silently for a few moments, her head cocked to the side. It felt scarily like she was an enormous bird, considering whether it was worth her while consuming a particularly unappetising-looking worm.

"You have extremely deep wounds," Morgan said, her demeanour not changing.

"I know. The dickhead who brought me here tore out all my techniques -" but Morgan was shaking her head as I spoke - "What?"

"Those are not the wounds of which I speak. Techniques come and go. What you had once, you can have again, should you think those skills were valuable." She frowned for a moment as if reading something. "I would, for example, suggest there are better uses of your time than giving tree spirits little blue pills." I may have blushed. "No, not the gaps where your techniques were. I allude to different wounds."

Images from the time loop flashed through my mind, and I felt the blood run from my face. "Morgan, to be honest, I think I've spent long enough wrestling with my demons. If it's all the same to you, I'm trying to put it all behind me."

The wind shifted in direction and began swirling the other way as she smiled a somewhat rueful grin. "But that is not what being a cultivator means, dearie. It's not all about power, saving the world and -" that frown had returned, "did you use a Dark Kelstrel's Strike to rip the head off Voltigern's Dragon?"

"Kind of. But only once. And I also inhaled."

"You are a funny little thing. I am not quite sure what Merlin thinks he was playing at trying to turn you into another version of him. You simply do not have the foundation for it."

I opened my mouth to protest, but a gentle tap of wind closed it, clattering my teeth together.

"I do not say this is a bad thing. Merlin was . . . unusual. Those who see their journey to the heavens in terms of water are often single-minded. Relentless. And yet also prone to predictability. Merlin, though? He did something unexpected. He stole a march on the rest of us, and by the time we even realised we were in a race, he had won, and his great need for Qi left us all fighting for scraps."

Morgan flexed her arms, and the wind picked up, the hurricane around us lifting her into the air. "But it seems that time is over. With the old goat gone, there is, for the first time in generations, Qi to spare on this island for the rest of us. That puts me in an uncommonly good mood. And that is before remembering the gratitude I should feel towards you for freeing me, dearie."

"If this is the moment when you give me all manner of powers, weapons and supernatural goodies, I am absolutely here for it."

Morgan looked down at me and smiled. The bird/worm analogy suddenly upgraded to a sabretooth tiger and a very small rodent.

"Cultivators should never be 'given' anything, dearie. You take what you can through the strength of your own power. You never surrender. You never accept defeat. And you never, ever say sorry for tearing your due out of the flesh of the world."

Well, that didn't sound remotely sinister at all. It struck me that if Merlin was a crotchety old Jedi Master, Morgan was a hot Sith Edge-Lord.

"However," she continued, "I will choose to reward you with several things."

I kind of think we were playing a bit with semantics here - Gifts. Rewards. You know what I'm saying?

"Firstly, I will break the time loop around your mind."

A weight I did not know was still settled upon my chest suddenly lifted. From the moment Drynwyn mentioned it, I knew it could not be as simple as breaking free from the cell. To have that appalling horror behind me felt wonderful.

"This is not a wholly altruistic act. Should your loop remain unbroken, I fear I will find myself back in my cell tomorrow morning, and we will have to go through all this again."

"I don't care whether what scratches my back also tickles your fancy. That's the best news I've ever had. Thank you!" The rushing air pulled the streaming tears off my face.

"Secondly, I will allow you to continue to use my name."

I'm not going to lie, that felt like a bit of an anti-climax. "Thanks, I guess?"

"Again, this is not an entirely selfless gift. If what you say is true, then there are those of us who have had some time to plan their next steps once Merlin was removed. It serves my purpose for my re-emergence in the world to remain obscured. Word of Tintagel's new Cultivator will doubtless already have spread. Should people come looking for me but find you . . . well, there are benefits to me in that."

This second gift felt like less of a reward than becoming the goat at the start of Jurassic Park. "You know, I'm quite happy with picking another name. I've always thought that Æthelflæd was pretty kick-ass, I don't mind -."

The wind picked up again. "I have spoken!" Fuck me, this broad was touchy. Then she continued as if she hadn't just channelled every ineffective Supply Teacher trying to bring order to 3:00pm on a Friday afternoon. "When our business here is done, I will retreat from the world for a time to attempt to catch up with the power of the others. My name is yours until my return."

It seemed unwise to press the issue. "Peachy."

"Two more rewards. The first, I hope, will be helpful to you in healing your wounds. You already bear one of the thirteen treasures of Britain: Drynwyn, the sword of Rhydderch Hael. I shall gift you a second, the Cauldron of Dyrnwch the Giant."

A bronze pot about the size of a bucket appeared in my hand. It smelt distinctly of sulphur.

"This Cauldron increases the potency of anything created within it. Food will be more nourishing, drink will be more refreshing, and -" I think her eyebrows waggled here - "the quality of elixirs, pills and potions brewed within will be improved immeasurably. I am sure Merlin has the necessary scrolls squirrelled away somewhere to explain further."

Okay, so that was actually reasonably useful. But only if, you know, I could actually get back home to use it.

"And for my final reward -"

"You'll teleport me back to my friends?"

A sad smile crossed Morgan's face, and I began to feel her pushing me out of her internal realm. "You must start thinking more like a cultivator, dearie. To get home, you must develop the power to do it under your own steam. No, what I will give you is far more valuable. I will tell you the name of which of us imprisoned you."

"Bit of a shit sandwich situation there, but if a portal home wasn't on offer, I'd take a bead on whose arse I'd be ripping a new hole into."

I could barely hear her now as the wind noise raised, and I became increasingly insubstantial. "Who, who did it?"

"Why, the same man who captured me. The man who, after torturing me to share all my secrets, threw me in a dungeon and left me to rot for ten years. I understand he now calls himself the Bretwalda, but I know him by another name."

This felt like an unnecessarily pantomime-esque build-up to the big reveal, but I guessed she was owed a little drama.

"Which is?"

There was a pause where I am sure, in her own mind, there were three chords of organ music.

"Aurelius Ambrosius."

CHAPTER 30 - IN WHICH WE MEET A GOOD OLD-FASHIONED REVENGE DRIVEN VILLAIN

Aurelius closed the door behind him and made his way over to his favourite chair. On some level, he recognised that having such things as a 'favourite chair' was beneath a man of his age and station in life. But on another, more profound level, he understood that when you were as powerful as he was, you could indulge pretty much whatever whim you fucking wanted.

As he sat, he selected a glass vial - one of the blue ones this time - from a leather pouch on the chair's armrest and popped its cork.

As it always did with the blue ones, his nose wrinkled in distaste at the acrid, metallic smell, but he tossed it down his throat anyway.

'No pain, no gain,' as he always said.

Actually, thinking on it, he had never verbalised those words before in his life. However, as it felt like an appropriately sage piece of advice, he resolved to use it more in conversation.

Cricking his neck and wincing at the resulting sound, Aurelius Ambrosius - brother to Uther Pendragon, uncle to Prince Arthur, and long, long presumed dead and gone - closed his eyes and settled into his daily ritual of cycling poison through his veins.

***

"Give it up, Lis!" the younger man called over the rim of his shield, shuffling a little to the right to prepare a new point of attack.

Aurelius rolled his shoulders and stayed silent, circling to mirror his brother's steps. Sweat streaked down his face in a river, and he shook his head to disperse the droplets.

He was getting tired. He knew it. And Uther knew it.

He couldn't keep this intensity up much longer.

Then, without warning, Aurelius let loose a series of swift spear thrusts, each aimed to strike the centre of Uther's shield. The expected counter came swiftly, the clash of metal drowning out the shouts and jeers from those surrounding them in a tight circle.

"Brother, we don't need to do this!" Uther's voice, so annoyingly filled with confidence, rang out towards him again.

Aurelius did not answer. Of course, they needed to do this. Uther had been sniping at him for weeks, and everyone knew this was a boil which needed to be lanced once and for all. If the Saxons' advance was to be halted and then pushed back, then that could only be achieved under the arm of a single Pendragon.

While both brothers agreed with that assessment, there was undoubtedly some sibling disagreement over which of them it should be.

With a sudden surge of energy, Aurelius sought to overpower Uther with a barrage of strikes - high, low, then high again. Uther's shield absorbed each blow as if nothing more substantial than a straw was assailing him, then responded with a flurry of short jabs with his own short spear that forced Aurelius to retreat in an ungainly manner.

He did not miss the laughter in the crowd at his missteps and felt his heart sink. A leader could survive many slips on the road to victory. But mockery was not one of them.

Shaking his long hair again to clear the sweat, Aurelius resettled himself behind his shield, needing to regain his wind. The two now moved in a tense rhythm, each step measured, each attack deliberate.

Sensing the tiredness creeping into his elder brother's legs, Uther suddenly leapt forward, his spear darting towards Aurelius's head, but the thrust was deflected onto his shield, with a swift counterthrust snaking towards Uther's midsection. The latter was quick to react, sidestepping and bringing his shield across in a firm block.

This caused a few shouts of derision as the watching thegns grew restless. If there was one thing you were not looking for in a duel for leadership on the eve of a battle, it was a long, drawn-out bloodbath that left both participants good for nothing.

To tell the truth, not one of them really cared whether it was Uther or Aurelius who sat on an imaginary throne and called themselves the Pendragon. The Saxon invasion was a blight on the land of the Britons, and they were all - well, most of them - reconciled to the need to band together to meet that threat.

It had seemed like Aurelius would be the man to play the unifier role, but a year of reversals and losses in the north had led to Uther's name being very loudly championed as an alternative. During the latest retreat, it had become plain the brothers could no longer work with each other, and therefore, in time-honoured tradition, a circle had been formed under the evening sun to decide the matter.

Growing more desperate, Aurelius feigned a retreat, luring Uther forward, only to pivot and launch a sudden attack. Sparks flew as the shields crashed together, and Uther narrowly avoided a spearhead to the throat. He retaliated with a powerful sweep of his own, aimed at Aurelius's legs, which forced him to jump back for a moment. However, he was soon back on the offensive, cutting at Uther's arms and legs as he scurried backwards.

***

Aurelius intensified his attacks, his spear a whirlwind. He pressed Uther, aiming a rapid succession of thrusts, each one parried but inching closer to their mark. Uther's shield work was impeccable, yet the relentless assault from Aurelius was starting to wear him down.

Indeed, for the first time in the confrontation, Uther felt himself needing to concentrate. He was bigger than his brother. Stronger. Whereas Aurelius was more comfortable addressing a crowd, Uther was at home in the shield wall. He loved the press, the push, the feeling of matching your raw power against an enemy.

He knew the longer this bout went on, the more certainty there was for his victory. And that was without his trump card needing to become involved. Uther adopted a more defensive stance - absorbing a flurry of impacts on his shield - and took the opportunity to glance at the tall, gaunt figure that stood a little way back from the ring of thegns.

Uther wasn't sure what to make of that man - *cultivator* is what he called himself, wasn't it? However, if a quarter of what Merlin had promised him came true, he would indeed be a very happy man indeed. After all, was he not to be the father of the greatest of all British Kings?!

And that, he supposed, was where he was so different from his big brother.

He watched Aurelius over the rim of his shield, sensing his efforts to sneak any advantage. He watched as his brother made a number of feints to the left, followed by a forceful jab rattling Uther's shield. Seizing the moment, Aurelius aimed for Uther's exposed side, but with a grunt of effort, he managed a last-second parry.

No, Aurelius would not be satisfied in preparing the way for his son to be king. He would need to be the one to do it himself.

Merlin had explained that unless Uther was the one to lead the assault on Salisbury on the morrow, the future he had prophesied would never come into being. He had gone to his brother, asking for the command, but he had been refused.

And now, here they were, locked in a fight to the death. Worryingly, Uther thought that their parents would be very proud.

The sun was falling low, and they both knew the duel was nearing its climax. Seeing Aurelius' shield droop slightly, Uther found a reserve of strength and surged forward, his spear leading in a series of unpredictable thrusts. Aurelius, caught off-guard, scrambled to defend, and nearly disengaged effectively. Uther, however, feigned a strike to Aurelius's head, then, in a swift change of direction, aimed a low thrust towards Aurelius's legs, momentarily throwing him off balance.

Aurelius struggled to keep up with the attacks and parried a high strike but missed the follow-up at his midsection.

Uther's spear found its way past Aurelius's guard, and the final blow was delivered.

Uther would have liked to have felt more sorrow. However, in the end, it was mostly a sort of hollow triumph.

As Aurelius fell to his knees, blood gushing from the wound, the thing he thought hurt the most was the cheers from those he had sought to lead.

✳✳✳

"Bastards. Fucking ungrateful bastards." Aurelius' eyes snapped open, and the memory faded away.

After all he had done for them, they'd left him there to bleed out.

If the retreating Saxons hadn't stumbled upon him the following morning - because, of course, Uther led the Britons to victory, didn't he! - he'd have died of that wound.

But no.

He wasn't destined to be that lucky.

Years of torture and imprisonment followed. Aurelius's eyes flashed as those memories flared to life. But he'd shown them, in the end. Hadn't he? My word, he had.

Aurelius selected another vial from the leather pouch and - without bothering to check the colour - uncorked it and drank it down.

129

It hadn't been easy, but thirty-five years - almost exactly to the day, now he thought about it - later, and he was poised to complete his revenge on his brother,

He'd taken Merlin from him. He'd destroyed the mind of his latest wizard. And now - and was this not the cherry on the cake? - he was going to kill his precious son.

The acid - it must have been a green vial - burned through Aurelius' cheek and dribbled through the hole to fall down his neck. He dabbed at it ineffectively, burning his fingers as he did so.

Uther may have become the Pendragon.

But the Bretwalda would soon have Arthur's head.

And then there would be a reckoning.

CHAPTER 31 - IN WHICH ESCHER WOULD BE PROUD

Where the fuck did she go?

Opening my eyes, I was suddenly very aware I was on my lonesome in the prison corridor. It seemed OG Morgan had been as good as her word and had fucked off to spend some quality time with her Qi.

While I was happy for her - and pleased not to need to come up with a new name. Think of my monogrammed night linen! - I couldn't help but feel she could have waited until I'd escaped.

Even apart from having her as backup - after what felt like aeons in the time loop with Drynwyn - I'd quite enjoyed having someone to talk to who had access to a greater range of verbs and adjectives.

She was standing here one moment, and the next . . . poof. Fuck me, why can't you do actually useful cultivation shit like that?

Ignoring the sword, I instead took a good look left and right. The corridor of cells continued to stretch out in an endless line, but it didn't fill me with such a sense of despair as it did previously. Now that I was sure the day wouldn't reset again, I could feel my naturally sunny and optimistic personality return.

Are you fucking high or something? You're giving off the weirdest aura.

Gritting my teeth, I repeated to Drynwyn what Morgan had told me about who was responsible for our transportation to this little bit of paradise.

Fucking hell. Aurelius Ambrosius?! What's with all the old crew coming out of the woodwork? Next thing you'll be telling me is that you have Constantine the Great tucked under your left tit.

I was happy to clarify I wasn't breast-smuggling Roman Emperors.

So, this was all well and good but standing around gossiping like a couple of fishwives wasn't going to get us out of here.

That was an odd simile. It's one my mum said all the time about me and my sister. I used to think there were women whose role in life was to seek out and marry cod.

Fuck me, where did *that* come from . . .

I need to get a grip. I vigorously shook my head back and forth as if that could shake some of the loose screws out. Not sure it helped over much.

"So, left, or right?"

Instinctively, I felt myself turning towards the right as the most likely way out. Even without most of my techniques, I was still a cultivator, and thus, my initial gut instinct must count for something. Right? But then I remembered reading something somewhere that because we have better control of our dominant hands, we unconsciously associate good things with our "fluent side of space." So, it might not be so much that I was experiencing a Qi-informed instinct here, but that it was more likely just because my right hand got more of the action.

Although not recently.

Perhaps I could equate some of my woolly-headedness to an unprecedentedly epic dry spell.

Goodness, I couldn't keep myself focused.

"Left or right, Drynwyn?"

What?

"We need to get out of here before someone realises, I'm no longer stuck in a time loop. Both ways look the same to me and, I'm not going to lie, I'm starting to worry I'm not quite all here. Left, or right?"

Rhyddrech Hael always used to say that if you worry, even for a moment, that you might be mad, then you definitely aren't. Of course, he also practised his deep-throating technique with frozen weasels, so take that fucking advice as you find it. Come on then, let's have a look at the options.

Feeling oddly self-conscious, I held Drynwyn at full-length, pointing down towards the left-hand side of the corridor, whilst it 'hemmed' and 'huhhed' and made various cryptic comments for a bit. Then I did the same for it on the right-hand side, and he went through the same rigmarole.

After a good few minutes of earnest muttering, I couldn't take it anymore. "Well? Which way do you think we go?"

No fucking clue.

"Fucking A. Okay, let's think about this logically." I have a lifetime of experience making truly bad decisions based on my gut. Or at least an organ in the general vicinity of my gut. Therefore, it stood to reason that if I was slightly inclined to take the right-hand corridor, it was just good sense to play the odds and stride confidently to the left.

If all else fails, do the absolute opposite of your instincts. Job done.

As we walked past rows and rows of identical-looking cell doors, I was happy to let Drynwyn regal me with story after story of the legend of Aurelius Ambrosius.

I had a very - very - vague memory of his appearance in the books about Camelot I loved when I was younger. If he ever made an appearance in my favourites - 'The Mists of Avalon' and 'The Once and Future King' - then I couldn't remember much about him. He was, now I think on it, a pretty important warlord in a book I enjoyed called 'The Crystal Cave' - but that was more about the life of Merlin than anything else.

And I genuinely didn't think either of the big beasts - Malory or De Troyes - mentioned him at all. Or at least, much more than just one of Arthur's ancestors.

Drynwyn, though, in its own unique way, was filling in the gap in my education.

The way the sword told it, Aurelius and Uther were very much the Cain and Abel of the Dark Ages. The Thor and Loki. Maybe even the Beyoncé and the Solange. Although that last might be overstating the levels of duplicity, violence, and general skulduggery.

From all the tales, I was developing a very clear picture in my head of a giant slab of muscle with exceptionally thin skin who just couldn't get enough of showing the world how big his cock was and - in particular - how much bigger it was than his younger brother's.

By the fiftieth time I heard about a raid, or a shield wall, or a siege where Aurelius went out of his way to rub his little bro's face in just how awesome the big dog was, I felt I knew him pretty well.

Basically, as far as I could tell, Aurelius Ambrosius was a dick who should count himself very lucky it took Uther so long to decide to drive a spear through his heart.

The more I heard about some of the things Aurelius got up to in his youth, the more I felt myself re-evaluating my feelings about the Pendragon.

With such a colossal douche as a brother, he must have had an absolute clusterfuck of an upbringing. If the only model of affection he had was someone who seemed to delight in demonstrating how much weaker and more pathetic he was, it was hardly surprising he wasn't exactly Mr. Available Dad to Arthur.

When I got back, I was giving Uther the number for my therapist.

However - and this felt pretty important considering the whole 'ripped me out of reality and stuck me in a time loop' thing - at no stage, in any of the stories, did Drynwyn mention Aurelius was a cultivator.

Nah, that sort of shit was all Merlin. I felt Drynwyn shudder a little in its scabbard as if reliving a bad memory. **It wasn't until a bit after Uther shish kabobed Aurelius that any of those cultivating bollocks began. Merlin was absolutely the first of them I heard about. But OG Morgan, Nimue, Mim the Bitch Witch and Taliesin all rocked up in short order after that. Aurelius was dead and gone by then.**

"Apparently not."

I couldn't help but notice we didn't seem to be getting anywhere during our Great Escape. We'd been walking for a good ten minutes, and as far ahead as I looked, the corridor stretched on and on.

Although . . .

I squinted and peered forward. It looked like one of the cell doors was open a little way ahead.

Drawing Drynwyn, I quickened my pace into a run, closing the gap much quicker than expected. I still sometimes forgot that, since getting more serious about my cultivating, I was a fucking ripped athlete. This was a whole new world for someone who had gotten out of breath looking for the remote.

I drew up a little short of the door and began approaching it cautiously. Oddly, after rows and rows of locked doors, it appeared that a second door hung open not that much further up the corridor.

It was all very strange.

It wasn't until I dipped my head into the first of the rooms that I realised what was going on. I confirmed it by looking into the second, where a broken set of chains lay on the floor.

Fuck me, we've walked around in a circle!

I stood back and looked left and right again. This wasn't just a really long corridor. It was presumably one long corridor in a fucking massive circular tower. It must be big enough that it looked like we were walking in a straight line when, in fact, we were - ever so slightly - curving around.

But if this was a tower, we'd walked the entire circumference without seeing a way up or down to other floors.

And that was fucking worrying.

CHAPTER 32 - IN WHICH GUINEVERE REFLECTS ON A MAN'S LOVE FOR HIS THICK WOODEN SHAFT

"Just like choking a chicken," Guinevere reminded herself, stepping up behind the oblivious Saxon.

In one fluid motion, she was into his blind spot, reaching around to cover his mouth. At the same time, her right arm snaked over the Saxon's right shoulder, her right hand grasping her left wrist to secure a firm hold.

As he began to react, Guinevere squashed her chest against his back - right arm braced across his throat - and shifted her weight to her right leg, preparing to apply the necessary force. With a vicious jerk, she pulled her right arm back while pushing forward with her left.

She could hear her old trainer's words as she did so, his soft lisp oddly emphasising his words.

"If completed correctly, this movement will target the cervical vertebrae, where the spinal cord connects to the brain. The correct application of sudden torque, combined with the forward pressure, will thus disrupt the spinal cord's function. It's a manoeuvre which requires both strength - hence your morning press-ups - and precision and will dislocate the cervical vertebrae, resulting in immediate cessation of neurological functions and collapse. Now, select your chicken."

As she knew it would, there was a loud crack, the Saxon's body went limp, and Guinevere gently lowered him to the ground.

Checking his body, she once again cursed at the complete lack of any helpful gear these odd wolf-clad spearmen carried. Just on the law of averages, she'd have assumed she would have come across at least one with a bow and arrow.

But no. It was all spears, spears, spears. Men and their enduring relationship with big pointy sticks.

Following her encounter with the maimed wizard, Guinevere had largely stayed ahead of a rather haphazard hunt for her. Something seemed to be up in the Saxon camp as - on more occasions than she'd have liked to think - a bit more thoroughness would have completely closed down her avenues for escape.

It was all the more odd as these Saxons in wolf furs were handy. Certainly, leagues more capable than those waifs and strays whose pursuit of her had been the initial cause of her quest plan for Arthur to unwind. That made their suddenly chaotic behaviour all the more noteworthy.

At the sound of horns blowing - and the responding howls of wolf calls - Guinevere pressed herself low over the body of her latest victim. Had they seen her?

But no. The sudden crashing noise of lots of running feet was going in the opposite direction.

However, it was more than just her relief at remaining unspotted that caused a smile to spread on Guinevere's face. A little band of three spearmen had just run past her hiding place, and she was sure she heard one of them say the words 'Bryttisc wīgend'. While Saxon might not be one of her stronger languages, she knew enough to make out these men were hurrying to face "warriors from Britain."

Slipping into their wake, Guinevere hurried towards what she hoped would be a sizeable British warband with whom she could link up.

****

"For fuck's sake! Where are they all coming from!"

Bors, Arthur and Merlin's-spirit-in-Melehan's-body had fallen back from Slaughterbridge to a small copse of trees. The Saxons had swarmed over the river to follow them and, annoyingly, had done so in such numbers that their intended routes for further retreat were largely cut off.

Arthur reversed his spear and smashed it into the forehead of a Saxon who'd misjudged how much cover his mates were willing to offer with Bors kicking ass and taking names on their other flank.

"Just keep pulling back!" Bors bellowed in reply, picking up the man opposite him and hurling him at the next approaching group.

"Wizard?!" Arthur shouted, "We could do with some help here!"

Merlin obliged with a fireball that initially burned a hole through the shield of an onrushing Saxon and then carried on straight through that somewhat surprised - if only briefly - man and then into and through his two fellows behind.

"Thank you!" Arthur spun Rhongomyniad in a wide arc and continued to step backwards slowly. He had no real sense of the end goal here, but - for the first time in a while - he was comfortable with that.

For now, there was just the pure joy of the battle.

He had forgotten what this felt like. Ever since his injury, he had been unable to reach this state - neither with weapons nor a pair of tits in his hands - and it was astonishing to him how he had survived so long without it.

With a foe in front of him and Bors to his side, both under the watchful eye of a capable wizard, what more could he look for in life?

"Do not mention it, my dear, erm, my Lord," Merlin replied, sweat running down his face in rivers.

To his chagrin, the wizard was rapidly discovering the considerable difference between having a bottomless supply of Qi and being an ordinary cultivator. It had been so long since he had needed to ration his use of power that he had entirely forgotten that it was a thing.

When piggybacking on Morgan's supply, he had been limited to a minimal range of actions. The nature of his connection to her had been fragile and largely internal. However, since seizing control of Melehan's body, he had access to lots more goodies.

It turned out, though, that it might have been wise to have gone a bit easier on sampling from the candy store. He wasn't quite completely out of Qi - even habits long forgotten died hard - but he was starting to scrape the bottom of the barrel. As Melehan visualised his Qi as sand, this was a particularly uncomfortable experience.

And then they were out of the trees and in the open. Which meant the arrows started falling again.

"You see that?" Bors was pointing to something on their left.

135

Arthur quickly glanced that way, receiving a stinging blow that removed his helm for his moment's inattention. He drove his spear through the chest of the offender and flung him aside. "Fuck off, you twat! What is it, Bors?"

The big man had more immediate space than Arthur, all of the pursuing Saxons having decided that someone else could have the honour of engaging that particular deathtrap. "Looks like an old stone cottage."

Merlin shook his head, droplets of sweat going flying. "Dead end. We'd just get surrounded and trapped in there."

Bors took an arrow to the shoulder, swore, tore it out and impaled it in the face of a braver-than-average spearman who'd made a dash for him. This object lesson did little to encourage anyone else to try the same. "Better in there than out here."

Arthur nodded his agreement. He didn't miss that the magical shield protecting them from projectiles looked decidedly patchwork. The wizard was getting tired. "Look, let's not borrow trouble from the future. We can't keep this up much longer. We need somewhere to take a breather, and that place looks as good as any. On my mark, we leg it. Wizard, once we run, put everything you've got to buy us some space."

Although Merlin nodded Melehan's head enthusiastically, his stomach churned. There was barely enough sand on the beach to keep his weak barrier up, let alone anything else. But then he rallied. He was Merlin. He lived to do the impossible.

As Bors and Arthur broke into a run towards the cottage, he filled his hands with what little Qi he had left and brought them together in an almighty 'bang'. The explosion caused a blast of air to surge out, knocking all the Saxons who had emerged from the copse flat on their backs and flinging the others who had moved around to encircle them up and away.

Not stopping to watch the aftermath of the spell further, Merlin turned and ran after the rest of the group.

Although nowhere near having the athletic capabilities of a cultivator, Arthur and Bors had really shifted, and it took the wizard longer than he would have expected to catch up. They were just beginning to barricade the solitary window of the cottage when he arrived.

The tiny building's stone walls were weathered, colours blending with the earth. Its sod roof had seen better days but looked like it might keep the rain off in a pinch. Besides the window, the heavy timber door was the only way in or out. Bors had put his foot through it to get in but had propped it back in the gap. As he moved past, Merlin pushed the last drop of his available Qi to the door, wedging it in place.

Inside, the single room was almost entirely bare, with any hints of its past life fading. Merlin assumed it had once been a shepherd's hut, but any sign of occupancy was long gone. The fireplace, stone like the walls, was cold and clearly unused for some time.

There was not much spare room with the three of them inside, but it would serve as a last-stand foxhole.

"Not sure I'm seeing this as an upgrade on our situation," the wizard said through pain-gritted teeth. Sand as Qi. What sort of masochist did that?

"Look, we're in here, and they're out there," Bors said. "It'll take more than just a few arrows to get through the walls, and if the door is secure," he raised his eyes at Merlin, who paused and then nodded, "then we've bought ourselves some time. Just need to tighten up on the window."

Arthur was trying to squeeze the remains of a broken cot bed into the small gap when a long-haired figure came crashing through, diving full length through with a spear in hand.

That form of suicidal attack took them so by surprise that none of them immediately reacted. Bors was the first, reaching down and pulling the figure to their feet. His fist had pulled back to launch a brutal punch when he stopped, his mouth falling open.

"Gwin?"

Guinevere smiled sheepishly and blew her hair out of her face. She nodded to each of the group in turn. "Bors. Improbably healed wizard," - there was a moment's pause and a change of tone - "Husband."

CHAPTER 33 - IN WHICH BORS AND CEDRIC RENEW THEIR ACQUAINTANCE.

"Sorry to break up this touching reunion," Bors said, picking up the broken cot bed and forcing it back into the window space, "but we're about to have a lot of company."

Arthur tore his eyes away from his wife - filthy, covered in blood and sweat and looking more pleased with herself than ever - and peered through the gaps in the makeshift window protector. A good fifty Saxons were cautiously moving to surround the cottage.

"Okay, I'm open to ideas. What do we do?"

The answering silence was not all that he could have hoped for.

"How far away is the army?" Guinevere finally asked.

"What army?" Arthur and Bors said at the same time.

"Well, it obviously isn't just the two of you out here, is it? That would be ridiculously irresponsible. Even for you two."

"To be fair, we have gained a wizard. And Morgan was with us back when this all started." Bors rumbled.

"And Morgan is where?"

"We're not sure. We think someone very powerful stole her." Arthur recognised this was not a helpful response. "Look, we were going to rescue her once we'd recovered you. Now that we have successfully managed that first part of the mission, we can get right back to helping Morgan."

"You're taking me finding you, evading a Saxon warband and literally landing in your lap as 'successfully recovering' me, are you?"

Merlin was about to have Melehan interrupt, but Bors tapped him on the wrist and shook his head. *Nope. Don't get in the middle of this* was the undoubted subtext.

"If you really want to pick at that scab, wife, I am sure we would all be delighted to hear the no doubt fascinating tale of your escape from captivity. By the looks of the state of you, I'm sure it will be a story filled with brio and derring-do!"

"Don't be such a colossal arse, husband."

"Maybe if you weren't showing yours to all and sundry, I wouldn't need to be!"

Guinevere blinked, then looked down at her leather hose. "Seriously? Is that at the top of your list of worries right now? We're minutes from death, and you want to waste time ragging on me for being inappropriately dressed in public? I am very sorry that during my life and death struggle to return with all haste to your loving embrace, I failed to ensure I did so while wearing a fucking dress! I bet my hair isn't all fancy and smelling like flowers like you like either, is it? You are such a fucking man-baby!"

It was at this moment the Princess of the Britons would have liked to be able to make a dramatic exit. Turning and finding herself wedged face-to-face with a Saxon wizard somewhat thwarted that plan.

There was a tense silence, and then Bors sighed and then cleared his throat. "Well, I bet we're all glad we got that out of systems, aren't we? Now, to bring us back to the matter at hand. No, we don't have an army nearby. No, we don't know where Morgan is. Yes, we seem to have gained a wizard who, by the colour of him, is one fart away from Qi exhaustion. Yes, we are currently surrounded. No, I have absolutely no plans about what to do next."

Guinevere nodded. "Okay. So, no fast travel out?"

Melehan's head shook regretfully. "Not for at least an hour. And then, I couldn't tell how far I'd be able to take us." The wizard's eyes closed and adopted what - as understood by the other three - was 'a cultivating face.'

Bors brightened up at that news. "An hour? No worries. We know the ones in the wolf-furs don't like wizards," he grimaced and nodded at Melehan, "well, obviously, he knows that. The torture and what have you. Sorry about that, by the way. Glad you got over it. Where was I? Yes, these guys will have to get in here the old-fashioned way. If we can't keep them out for an hour, we're honestly not trying."

"I literally broke in here not five minutes ago with nothing more complex than a good run-up."

Bors stuck his tongue out at her. "Yes, but you're a fucking bad-ass bitch, and we weren't quite ready." He reddened slightly. "Begging your pardon and with all due respect and all that."

"No, that's fine. I've been called worse. Regularly." Guinevere pointedly didn't look towards Arthur.

And then a difficult situation became an awful lot worse.

Because Cedric of the West Saxons arrived.

***

"Hello in there?" Cedric called out to the cottage in his odd Kentish dialect.

Silence.

"I am not sure keeping quiet and hoping we go away will likely be a particularly successful strategy."

Silence.

"My men tell me there are four of you in there. I imagine it must be very snug. By the description of your leader, am I to take it that I have - once again - stumbled upon a meeting of the Dumnonia Scroll Club? Who would have thought it? Of all the places my warband could look to lay our weary heads, it once again seems to be right in the middle of a literary festival."

A deep voice bellowed out from the cottage. "Coincidences are a bitch, aren't they?"

Cedric gave a smile that had nothing of humour about it.

The High King had - repeatedly - made clear his displeasure at the slow nature of the retreat of the West Saxons. Most of the warbands that had made up the defeated army had already returned to Wintanceaster. And thus, he and his men were rather conspicuous by their absence.

But Cedric was nothing if not single-minded. That old fool in his giant tower could rail as much as he wanted, but he had unfinished business with the Britons. Once he was back under the High King's eye, he would have another cultivator foisted on him and would lose the element of freedom he so craved.

139

He was not so insane as to think he and the eighty spears he had left could capture Tintagel. However, he was certain he could bathe some of his frustrations in enough British blood to take the sting away from his defeat. More than anything, he did not intend to return home with his tail between his legs.

"Speaking of bitches, I think a member of your little club has been the cause of some disquiet amongst my men. Many, I think, would like to discuss the deaths of several of their friends with her."

"I doubt she'll be keen on a group hook-up, but I'll ask. You never know with her."

The silence stretched out. A few of Cedric's men started to cough and shuffle around.

"Briton?"

"She says thank you very much, but-" the voice paused as if checking for the correct wording - "she's too engrossed in this latest translation of the deeds of Beowulf to fuck any of your men right now. She wonders if there are any passing doves with sufficiently small vaginas available. You know, the rarer sort? She doesn't recommend trying it with a common-or-garden bird because your tiny Saxon cocks would be too intimidated by their cavernous openings. Not that we think doves have massive vaginas, I want you to understand. More than in relation to your men's tiny little dicks they would seem so. Contextually."

"Are you trying to make me angry, Briton?"

"Is it working?"

Cedric nodded to one of his men.

Those of his spearmen who also carried bows, lit an arrow on fire and launched them at the roof of the cottage.

"You know the roof is made out of sod, right?" The voice from inside the cottage had an amused tone. "That famously not very flammable substance. The very nature of soil and vegetation serves as a natural barrier against fire's wrath. But good for you for trying. Looking forward to seeing what you try next."

Cedric ground his teeth.

***

"Are we pissing off the man with the army for any particular reason?" Guinevere asked, peering through the gap in the window.

"The more time he wants to spend chatting shit with me, the better. By the way, did you hear how they assumed I was the leader? That's my star quality shining through, that is."

"It's certainly something," Arthur muttered.

"Speaking of pissing off the man with an army, my Lady, what have you done to rub them up the wrong way? Was it rubbing them up the wrong way if you know what I'm saying?" Bors waggled his eyebrows theatrically and then stopped, blushing again. "Sorry. I get cruder in pre-battle mode."

"Doesn't bother me," Guinevere replied, "Who doesn't enjoy a good rubbing?"

"How long, wizard?" Arthur was doing his best to tune out the voice in his head asking why his best friend and his wife appeared to be flirting.

Merlin cracked Melehan's eye open slightly. "An awful lot longer if you keep interrupting me, my de - my Lord. The amount of Qi I will need to fast-travel us to a distance that would be helpful is not insubstantial. I really do need to concentrate."

"They're coming," Bors growled.

"How many?" Arthur tried and failed to push his way to the window. Guinevere grimaced. "All of them."

CHAPTER 34 – IN WHICH CEDRIC GETS HIS HANDS DIRTY.

"You've got to admire their pluck," Bors huffed, pressing his back to the door. "Is that what we have to do? "Arthur grabbed hold of one of the spears pressing through the window, yanked it, and pulled its owner into range for Guinevere to run them through. "Can we not just tell them to fuck off and be done with it?"

"I mean, if you think it would do some good",… Bors stuck his head through the now largely totalled cot bed, which was stuck in the window gap. "Fuck Off." He jerked back in time to avoid a flurry of arrows. "Nope, they're still pretty motivated to get in here."

Guinevere finished with the spearman Arthur had tugged towards him and stepped back, running a hand through her hair. This was not quite the most desperate situation she'd ever been in, but it was pretty hot work. Her arms ached with the spear's weight and the effort of keeping so many frenzied souls at bay.

"Wizard, how long," Arthur shouted, half dragging a Saxon into the window space whilst simultaneously beating at them with the butt of his spear.

"Honestly, every time you disturb me by asking that question, our escape time edges slightly further away. In years, I can imagine your descendants will be sitting behind their parents in a motorised conveyance chiming, 'Are we nearly there yet?' there will be a wailing and gnashing of teeth. Someone will threaten to 'turn this car around, right now', while the other will offer the ultimate threat ', don't make me come back there!' We will get there when we get there!"

Merlin let Melehan's voice trail off as he realised everybody in the cottage was staring at him. "By which, I mean, it's nearly done."

There was a large crash, and Bors was shaken momentarily away from the door. "I'm not going to lie, they're giving a pretty decent account of themselves," he said, forcing it back closed with an effort.

"Can we stop complimenting. The. People. Trying to kill us," Guinevere yelled as she stabbed through the window at two very enthusiastic Saxons who seemed inordinately keen to make her acquaintance,

"I call it as I see it—the easiest thing in the world to go half-arsed at this. Let someone else take the lead. Hang back until we're worn down. But not a bit of it. These guys are juiced for it—big thumbs up from me on that score. Hang on a minute."

Just as it seemed Bors would be pushed from the door, he yanked it open and let five or six Saxons come tumbling in. Bors stepped over them, grabbing his axe and freeing his arms to lay about him into the press outside. Arthur and Guinevere had made short work of the heaps of arms and legs trying to untangle themselves at his feet.

When all were no longer in this world, Arthur stepped behind Bors and tapped him on the shoulder. "Switch" with a smoothness born of years of practice, Bors—

sporting hundreds of minor wounds and drenched in blood—stepped to the side to let Arthur pass and then back into the cottage.

The Prince of the Britons did not leap into the middle of the fray like his friend. Instead using the greater reach of his weapon, he stayed halfway in the doorway, thrusting out anyone that came too close', "Fuck me that was glorious!" Bors picked up a dead Saxon off the floor in each hand and posted them through the window, knocking down those on the other side trying to clamber in. "We need to do this more often."

"Sure," Guinevere had hoisted a third body onto her shoulder and threw it out to follow the ones Bors had deposited. "Let's make it an annual thing. We find an isolated spot with no hope of rescue and then invite the natives."

Bors grinned massively and removed the final bodies, throwing them through the window and over Arthur's head to relieve the pressure on him. "That's what I like about you, Gwin—you're never afraid to get your hands dirty."

There was a pause as each of them watched Arthur defend the doorway.

"You know I may be out of line here, the big man rumbled, "but if seeing that man fight doesn't make you hot, 'I don't know what will."

Guinevere did not answer for a few heartbeats as her husband spun, whirled, and danced to keep at bay the collective efforts of an elite warband to get beyond him, "I guess that's the problem. Sometimes, a woman needs something more than a man who is handy with the spear."

"Actually, Mrs Bors is quite clear that…."

"I beg you not to complete that sentence."

"Fair enough." With that, Bors stepped forward and bodily yanked Arthur inside the door, slamming it shut and bracing himself against it. "Round eight it is to us, I think."

Merlin cracked open Melehan's eye, taking in one blood-soaked Bors and the strain on Arthur and Guinevere's faces and doubled his efforts to cycle his Qi.

***

"Can somebody tell me what I'm missing?" Cedric's voice was icily calm.

Those around him instinctively stepped backward. The heat of their master's rage was directly proportional to the steadiness of his tone.

"This is not a rhetorical question. Why am I not currently in possession of some new prisoners?"

When he received no answers, he pointed at Drynfol, one of his newer recruits, and said, "You. Speak!"

Drynfol might be new, but legends of what occurred when Cedric was displeased were legendary.

"We're nearly there, Sir. It can't be much longer before they are too exhausted to defend." With that, everybody took a collective step away from Drynfol. No one needed to be inside this particular splash zone.

"I am sorry. We were waiting for them to give up, were we? I had not realised this was our strategy."

Drynfol made to reply, but Cedric pressed on, reaching out and dragging the terrified man up close. "What is the delay? It is two spearmen, a bitch with claws, and a cropped Wizard.

143

"I have heard that those of the wolf are to be feared. We are a terror to run from, and our shadows are long cast upon the land. We're not a season of rain to be endured. We do not wear down those who oppose us. We take!

"And I want to take that fucking cottage!"

Of course, by then, Drynfol had very little opinion on the matter, having had Cedric's knife sheathed repeatedly into his chest.

Dropping the corpse, he grabbed the spear from his bodyguard and stalked me towards the cottage.

"Thin-looking mother fucker, has just shanked one of his men and is coming this way."

Arthur winced as his wife swore.

Guinevere turned on him with a snarl: "I'm sorry. Is there a list of words you would rather I did not use? Please furnish me with them, and I shall, of course, as a dutiful wife, comply. Or would you rather I simply remain silent?"

"If wishing made it so, "Arthur murmured.

"Fuck you, husband."

"If wishing made it so."

Bors guffawed at that, breaking the growing tension. "Ah, young love. Nothing like it. "

"Britons." A voice calls from outside.

"Shitstains?" Bors replied.

There was a beat in which the whole of the Saxon army took a step backwards from their increasingly red-faced commander. "Where is the famous honour of Uther's men to which I've heard so much? Squirrelling yourself away behind these pathetic walls. Do you not dare to face us?"

"Dude, there are about eighty of you—more like sixty since we're going through you like Arthur at a new brothel (sorry, Gwin). We'll stick to this method unless you all get in line and take a ticket. Thanks very much."

"Would you not fight me, then? One-on-one. leader to leader, I promise my men will let you go if you prevail."

"Not seeing an incentive here, mate. As far as I can tell, you've given it a good go, we've dicked all over you, and now you're scrambling around. I'm sure you're absolutely the man, but I'll wait behind my nice strong stone walls, thank you very much."

"Coward"

"Sticks and stones may break my bones, but words will never hurt me. Trust me; I experiment."

"Don't you dare fight me".

"Says the guy with sixty men - actually, it's fifty-nine. You killed your own man a little while back. Just to say - one leader to another - that does surprisingly little for morale if you are wondering. I'm more 'a carrot' than 'the pointed stick\ sort."

"When we pry you loose from your bolt hole, quivering and screaming at our victory, I will ask you again about morale. We will see which of us is laughing then."

"I'll do it!" Bors turned to the speaker, "Seriously."

Guinevere nodded. "We can't keep this up forever. He sounds like someone who likes the sound of his own voice, does all sorts of soliloquising first. It easily buys us enough time. And if not, I'll kill him."

"I'm not letting you do that, Gwin."

"Bors, I outrank you in many ways. I'm surprised you can't see me coming up from below. I tell you; I'm doing it. And there's nothing you can do about it."

Bors shifted his eyes to Arthur, who remained silent, then on to Melehan. "Wizard? Any words of wisdom?"

"Any time now, just lining up the right spot." Although he kept his voice steady, Merlin was worried.

Melehan had a rather small number of fast travel destinations available – he reminded himself that not everyone was a legendary Cultivator – and none of the ones he could see were remotely familiar to him. The last thing any of them needed was to have one frying pan exchanged for another blazing fire. "Five more minutes. Ten Tops.

"Britons! Are you shitting yourself in fear in there?"

Guinevere grabbed Arthurs's spear and yanked the door open. "More like pissing ourselves in laughter. Come on, Cedric, let's be having you".

CHAPTER 35 - IN WHICH GUINEVERE STEPS UP

"You know a lesser man would feel emasculated by his wife steeping like that. He would think that it said something negative about his manhood." Bors side-eyed Arthur as they watched Guinevere walk through a host of spitting, shouting Saxon warriors towards Cedric. "It takes a big man to let the little woman do his work for him. That is all I am saying. A big man, secure in his masculinity, not worried about how others…."

"Why don't we all just shut the fuck up for a minute" Arthur nudged Melehan's body with his foot. "Any second now, right?"

Merlin grimaced internally but kept Melehan's face still. Certainly, especially when you consider that reality is an indefinite unit of time at a 'second'. I mean, what is a 'second' when you get down to it? I will definitely be able to teleport us away momentarily.

Merlin had three fast-travel options, and he didn't like any of them. As far as he could tell, Melehan had only developed this ability since joining the Saxon army, so he had linked all his destinations to various military installations. The easiest option – Qi-wise – was to go to a small fort that he recalled sat just on the edge of Uther's territory. If he spirited them there, he would still have plenty of Qi left for some destructive spell-slinging. However, he had to be realistic. As a competent cultivator, Melehan did not have access to the required range of techniques. If he had access to even a fraction of his original Qi resources, Merlin wouldn't think twice about dropping them into the fort and "bringing the thunder", as Uther was wont to call it.

But now…

The second option wasn't much better. From the impression he could get of the place, it was over the sea in Frankia—presumably in the middle of some Saxon outpost. That hardly seemed like a sensible place to portal the Prince and the Princess of the Britons.

The Third option, though, had its drawbacks. There seemed to be some sort of tricky defences around it, and while Merlin had the knowledge to overcome them, it would leave him very short of Qi to be able to help on arrival. But more than that, he had absolutely no idea where he would be taking them.

"Anybody know anything about a massive dark tower in the middle of nowhere."

Bors shrugged "Only if you ask what Mrs Bors calls my …."

"Wizard, in a few seconds, my wife will be fighting, one-on-one, against Cedric of the West Saxons. Right now, I'd take a fucking Dark Tower."

"Funnily enough, that's what Mrs Bors said last night." Merlin quested the third destination once more. How had something like this structure been built without him knowing? It was a proper Old-fashioned Wizards Tower. He was even working through Melehan's memories. He could feel the pull of Qi being sucked into the place.

But there was something else there, wasn't there? A Presence he recognised…

Merlin's excitement made Melehan almost jump to his feet.

"Morgan. I found her."

***

Looking at her opponent, Guinevere regretted her bravado in accepting the duel. The West Saxon was tall and wiry and had the wrong amount of bellicose intensity in his eyes. A touch more, and she knew she'd be able to inflame it into rockiness; a drop less, and she'd be able to overwhelm him through her aggression.

But this guy was going to be a handful.

"Is this the best the British can offer? A whore to the slaughter?"

Cedric's men roared in coordinated approval to this insult. Guinevere chose to remain silent.

"What, too afraid to answer? Or is your mouth only good for one thing?"

Guinevere rolled her eyes and planted her spearhead down in the dirt. "Look, how much humiliation can you really take here? I'm all up for a bit of banter, but if you're already at the stage of killing your own men when they give you bad news, me ripping you a new one before literally ripping you a new one will hardly improve your reputation. You've trapped two warriors, a mouthy whore, and a crippled Wizard, and we've been ably besting you for the better part of the afternoon. Our Commander is so sure you are a limp dick that he's sent me out to deal with you because he can't be bothered to do it himself; if I were in your shoes, I'd call it quits before I bend you over my knee to receive the spanking you deserve."

Guinevere watched Cedric's eyes as she spoke, hoping to see the flame of anger ignite and roar around him. She was to be disappointed. He merely grinned back wolfishly.

"I think we would all like to see that, whore."

And without any further words, Cedric attacked.

"Wizard!" Bors and Arthur shouted in alarm at the exact moment. "I know, I know. I am working as fast as I can." A glimmering light surrounded the seated men.

"Work faster" Arthur's voice was grim, his eyes locked on the battle in front of him,

Guinevere instinctively settled into a defensive pattern. She was light of feet and found it easy enough to dance around the early exchanges. She didn't dare make any attacks of her own yet; she couldn't risk a clash of spears that would leave her unarmed.

She had fought against men her whole life. Her father was anxious enough about the marriage and forthrightness of her personality that he had allowed her to be trained as if she was the much-desired son with whom he had not been blessed.

She had always found that the trick was to weather the early storm of a much stronger opponent. Men wanted to dominate and to humiliate, and it made them cocky. Literally, her well–trodden path to victory was to be submissively on the back foot and seek to strike when he got sloppy.

But Cedric was not playing that game.

His eyes never left hers as he stalked her, his spear snaking out in a blur to test her footwork, but with no real commitment behind it. His movement was economy of movement, and carrying Arthur's heavier spear, Guinevere was worried if anyone was going to be tired, it would be her.

She lost concentration momentarily, and the tip of Cedric's spear drew a thin line down her forearm. She spun away out of range, cursing. It wasn't a nasty wound, but she suspected he hadn't intended it to be and was taunting her.

Arthur swore, seeing his wife falter. He turned to the Wizard and saw the project on the wall of the small cottage. The man was whispering, "Almost there. Almost there."

She had no choice but to change it up.

Guinevere closed the gap by spinning the spear in an expansive arc, moving from constant, cautious retreat into reckless assault. She was rewarded with a momentary flash of concern in Cedric's eyes, and it was now his turn to fall back. Years of sparing with the house earls blossomed in her mind as she drew in close and threw every dirty trick they had taught her.

Within the range of his spear. She stamped down on his feet, aimed a knee at his crotch and whipped her long hair into his face. She could not hope to hurt him seriously – he was at least twice her weight – but she needed the confusion this line of attack could cause to buy extra seconds.

But it was to no avail. She couldn't create a wide enough opening to slip her spear through his defences. And what was worse, she was passing the point of 'tired' and into exhaustion.

And Cedric knew it. The butt of his spear connected with her knee, causing her to stumble. Switching off the numbing pain, she barrelled forward to press her attack, but he slipped to the side, slashing carelessly as he moved past her, opening another wound on her back. There was a pause – it probably was barely a heartbeat, but to Guinevere, it stretched out for hours.

She was outmatched here, and every passing man in her life had always told her that her arrogance would get her into trouble. She could not get out of it someday. It seemed like today was the day. With a yell – visualising a host of condescending, paternalistic faces as she did- she sighted on the middle of Cedric's body and threw her spear with as much venom as she possessed.

Almost lazily, he knocked it aside.

"Fuck"

Bors had ripped open the door and ran towards the duellers as Guinevere threw her spear. Arthur was on his shoulder, and they crashed into the Saxons, separating them from the princess. They took countless injuries as they forced their way through, but they were never going to close the distance in time.

Cedric took a moment to glance over at the cottage. His men would soon have the two warriors subdued. It had all worked out as expected. The now unarmed woman opposite was trying to settle into a defensive crouch, offering the smallest possible target. She was a feisty one; he would give her that, and it seemed a shame to kill her.

But not that much of one.

He didn't even look her way as he thrust, keeping his eyes locked on the two men being dragged down by his war band. They seemed oddly distraught about the death of a whore.

His spear took Guinevere in the chest.

"And we are a go." Merlin put Melehan's hands together and finally triggered the technique. He vanished instantly, and the men restraining Bors and Arthur were left groping thin air. A heat beat later, Princess Guinevere dissolved into the air.

As did Cedric's Spear.

CHAPTER 36 – IN WHICH I BREAK BAD.

I'd done the circuit of the tower at least three more times. On each occasion, I hope to have spotted a hitherto unnoticed way up or down.

No dice.

I was trapped within a perfect circle, both sides of which were dotted with cell doors. The only markers I had to stop were turning into some kind of evil infinity loop with the open doors of my cell and the one the original Morgan had been trapped in.

Idly, I knocked on a few other doors as I went. It would be fair to say the quality of the results was not high. Most of the doors elicited no response at all. The occupiers, presumably dead or trapped in their own private hell, didn't have the wit to respond.

All things being equal, though, I preferred the silent ones.

On the rare occasion my knock received a response, it was of a type I had long since categorised as 'junkie in the underpass keen to drink your blood to soothe their thirst.' I'd come across that particular band of psychotic malingering far too often in my life, and well, let's say I was grateful for the doors separating us.

I eventually gave up trying. In the back of my mind, I fantasised about -maybe- uncovering a crack team of cultivators, sentenced to crimes they didn't commit, that I could buddy up with, break by the combined might of our oddly specific skill sets, and then survive as soldiers of fortune. Maybe you should hire us if no one else could help or find us.

I'm drifting again, aren't I?

You know how the real Morgan cultivated her arse out of here in about a minute? it could only really be fucking great if you could do that.

I ignored it.

I always admired the way cultivators could just 'pop' in and out of existence. Like, sure, you are mostly bloodthirsty megalomaniacs seeking power at all costs, but the fast-travelling thing was a fucking riot at parties.

I ignored it.

We'd probably be home right now if you paid more attention to Merlin's lessons.

I threw the sword as far as I could down to the far end of the corridor and set off in the other direction.

Time to count my blessings.

It took me a while to come up with some. I guess the fact that I was no longer stuck in a time- loop counted as a big one. Although, I was struggling to see the end of the upside. This might not be a temporal loop, but it was a pretty fucking physical one.

And that seems to be it. My sole blessing right now is not being trapped in a dimensional prison.

My life has really gone through some wild changes recently.

Having no other ideas, I plopped down in the middle of the corridor and pulled my knees to my chest. I traded one prison for a slightly larger one. Sure, I can get a bit more exercise out here, but at best, it was a marginal improvement, if not an active demerit.

In the distance, I could hear Drynwyn shouting for me, but it could wait. I didn't think my mood could take many more snide remarks about 'why you are such a shitty cultivator.'

I dropped into my Artist's Studio and enjoyed pushing my paint around my channels. Something soothing about the ebb and flow took the edge off my anxiety. There were only a few dealers in and out of my local area, which would have been much poorer had I known Q1 cycling was an option.

Whoever ripped out my techniques left me with <personal space invader> and nothing else. OG Morgan seemed to think that was the worst thing in the world, and I knew Merlin lamented the frivolous way in which I'd gone away building up skills.

Maybe this wasn't the absolute worst thing that happened to me. Perhaps this was the chance to build up those foundations Merlin kept going about.

I hated saying it, but I missed Merlin.

Sure, he had a wholly different repertoire of 'you're terrible at cultivating,' but at least at the end of it, he usually had some advice to offer. Having spent at least a millennium listening to Drynwyn's anecdotes of Rhyddrech Hael, I was all for a bit of patient, constructive – hypersexualised advice.

I flicked over the page and looked at my inventory. Merlin insisted on loading me up with only scrolls and ancient tomes about cultivation. I'd flicked through some of them but considering the last time I tried to follow an instruction manual, I'd nearly blown myself up trying to absorb mana stones, so I was a bit wary of them.

However, I would wander these halls for a long time unless I found a way to change things. Besides, what else was there to do?

I'm going to level with you; the difference between being stuck in an endless time loop and blitzing your way through the wisdom of hundreds of learned cultivators is not as different as you may think.

I'm not saying this stuff is dull… No, I am.

It's flocking dull, deadly dull, and watching paint dry in front of her boiling kettle while waiting for the cows to come home dull.

No matter which I tried, I didn't have enough of a foundation to make heads or tails of the instructions. Even the ones I managed to follow in broad outlines referenced techniques and steps I had no conception of. I really should have paid more attention to Merlin when I had him.

I dropped one called 'Fire Dynamics in a Stone Welding' (honestly, I had no idea whatsoever. I'd idly hoped this might explain how to rip the floor open so I could drop through to the level below, but no—at least not without decades of careful and considerate study) and picked up the next one in the row, 'Apprentice Alchemy.'

My hopes were not precisely soaring as I turned past its first page. And they hardly improved when the entirely patronising author outlined the various bits of kit required before even starting "on the hallowed and mystical journey towards the most blessed of crafts."

Not possessing anything that could be considered a mixing bowl, I was about to put it back in my inventory and move on to "Ellian's third law of ice flow" with a little itch nudged the back of my head. OG Morgan hadn't just given me a pat on the arse and wished me well when she escaped. She gave me that cauldron.

I pulled it out of my inventory and sat on the corridor floor. To be clear, if you are visualising a massive black iron pot when I say 'cauldron' you need to rationalise your expectations. What Morgan had given me was, at best, a small bowl. I could fit both in my hands comfortably around it. Neither was it metal, but rather some form of heavy stone material. I've never had that particular middle-class joy at having a kitchen with actual, you know, surfaces, but I screwed enough guys that are to recognise the material this cauldron was made out of granite.

It came with the lid and either a pestle or a mortar, but I wasn't sure which. It was a heavy stick made of granite with a phallic bulge at the end.

I watched it for a few minutes, wondering if it would be sentient. Hey, don't just judge. I didn't know that swords could talk until recently, and hating myself ever so slightly, I tapped it with my finger and said, "Hello? Can you talk?"

Nothing.

So, either it couldn't talk, or it was a dick. I wouldn't accept it if it could be both. I turned back to the scroll. So, I have a cauldron. What's next?

I perused the following three pages of info, which I could comfortably summarise as follows: "Gather some heart moss and grind it." There were a lot of flowery phrases about doing the latter under the light of Hunter's Moon and doing so while clearing my mind and spirit. But fuck it.

I looked around the corridor and saw a dark green material glowing between the stones. I don't know if this was the heart moss, but as soon as I looked at it, I did.

Merlin would have been able to explain it. Drynwyn would be able to tell me an epic fucking story about Rhyddrech Hael knowing the properties of any herb he touched, which would make him precisely the sort of guy I needed around me in my previous life. However, would that help me in my current predicament? It would not.

Anyway, I was an herb-whisperer. I grabbed a handful of the moss and dropped it into the cauldron and, using the pestle/mortar — still no fucking idea — ground it into a thick green paste.

Next, I needed to create a 'suspension.' Having had more than my fair share of 'enforced, fixed-term absences from school, ' I recognised the word but sensed it probably meant something else in this context.

So, I would have to ask Drynwyn, wouldn't I?

I'm not talking to you.

"Oh, come on. We only met a few minutes ago when I threw you away for the first time. You can't take it that personally."

You threw me to take out the fucking commander of an army. I can get on board with that. Here, you just lobbed me away. As if I was a common or garden sword! Takes the piss.

Oh my God. I'd hurt the sword's feelings. "Look, I was getting frustrated. You've got to remember I'd just escaped from a time loop. I was not quite myself. I didn't mean anything by it."

So, are you sorry? You're not just here because you need my help?

"Look, obviously, I need your help, but I'm sorry too."

I think you're just saying that.

Fuck me, I appeared to be in a dysfunctional relationship with my own weapon. I've had this conversation with every boyfriend I'd ever had in various guises: "Why don't we celebrate drawing a nice thick line under all of this by singing a suspension?"

What the fuck are you talking about?

"A Suspension. That's like a song or something, isn't it?"

A suspension isn't a song. It's a water-based liquid. You know? You are a complete fucking moron. Don't you even listen to basic information?

I chucked Drynwyn down the length of the corridor again. I was getting a nice, tight spiral on it now. I dropped into my inventory, chose one bottle of spring water, and poured it into the cauldron on top of my heart moss paste.

Nothing happened.

I picked up the scroll again. This was starting to feel like it was too much like cooking. Another skill I failed to develop. I scanned the instructions to see what I was trying to help make and ignored all sides of unnecessary self–satisfied prose. I was able to assert that this was an 'Elixir of wellness. It was the single most basic concoction a cultivator could produce and would generally improve my overwhelming well-being. Given a choice that only several things I'd rather be able to be brewing up, but beggars can't be chosen. I need this elixir as a base for anything else that appears later on in the scroll. Flicking to the back, I liked the look of 'Water of Life,' seemingly the equivalent of Adam waving his sword about and yelling about the powers of Grey Skull.

So why did I see Bupkiss? "Add a handful of Heart moss to boiling water. Cover & reduce."

Fuck, I was going to need Drynwyn's help again, wasn't I?

CHAPTER 37 IN WHICH I AM REMINDED OF THE IMPORTANCE OF JUST SAYING 'NO'.

So—and who would have believed it—it turns out I am not a natural alchemist. I'd hoped that—made it up with my sword for the millionth time—it would be a pleasant, smooth journey to the brewing of a mixture that would somehow get me out of my predicament, but I was to be disappointed.

Plans can change.

This is getting quite embarrassing now.

For what felt like the nine-zillionth time, my cauldron boiled dry, and the promise of an 'Elixir for wellness' failed to appear. "Maybe your flame is too hot?" I asked snarkily.

My flame is never anything less than completely fucking perfect, I will have you know. It is never too hot or too cold. It is always exactly as hot as it needs to be. A poor workman blames her … you know… her fucking things.

"Look, there are no other instructions. I ground up the moss." I picked another handful between the flagstones beneath me and threw it in the cauldron. I picked up the pestle (or maybe the mortar) and ended up with the same green goo I'd felt most of the afternoon.

I don't want to be that sword, but how the fuck is playing Little Miss Alchemist helping with our current predicament?

I Ignored it.

Sitting here fiddling with my cauldron—that sounds much dirtier than it was meant to be—wasn't exactly top of 'How to achieve a great escape,' but truth be told, I wasn't overburdened with ideas. I could run up and down the hall screaming and wailing, but I doubted that would be helpful.

Plus, I wouldn't say I liked cardio.

So, it may be the most effective use of my time; instead of any other - literally any other - ideas, I was happy to give it a whirl.

Come on, big man. Light it up

Drynwyn dutifully caught fire, and the water was bubbling away in no time. What was I missing? I scoured the instructions for more ideas. Moss water boil. It wasn't much more complex than that.

Just checking to see you are fucking using your QI, right?

"Of course, I am." How long a pause can I leave before asking a follow-up question? "When you say Qi . . ."

Tell me we were not trying alchemy without you putting your Qi in the fucking mix!

"It doesn't say anything about that in the instructions."

Fuck me! This is a handbook for cultivators! It doesn't tell you to make sure you are breathing and to wipe your arse after you shit either, but I imagine it's crediting you with some modicum of fucking sense. Fuck me!

I dropped into my Artist's Studio and looked at the cauldron from that perspective.

Damn it, the fucking sword was right. Just like little lines were going from my channels and off into my armour and mana stone earrings, I could sense I could make the same connection to Morgan's pot.

I pushed at this line and then a thicker one out towards it and felt something about it shift. Like, it

had stopped being a thing I possessed and moved into being part of me.

Fucking thing still didn't talk to me, though.

Prick.

I returned to reality and studiously ignored making eye contact with Drynwyn. Which considering I had no idea where its eyes were, was quite an achievement.

Well, if we've all picked our bollocks up off the floor, why don't we try this again and aim to be less utterly pathetic.

The temptation to see how far I could javelin this fucking thing down into the distance was quite overwhelming. I see it as personal growth that I merely swore under my breath.

I dumped the half-completed elixir out on the floor. If I ever lost my way inside this place, I'd

just need to follow the long line of abandoned experiments back to base camp. It looked not unlike a Shire horse with epic diarrhoea had shat its way several hundred metres down the corridor.

The moment I started to grind the next handful of heart moss, I could tell the difference. Immediately. It wasn't quite like a host of heavenly angels started singing as I mashed the damn stuff up, but it wasn't too far away.

Fucking hell! That's a bit over the top, isn't it? And I speak as the sword that accompanied Rhydrech Hael when he went undercover in a Cardigan brothel for two years. He worked his way up from the bottom to... well, the bottom. There was a pause. **Come to think of it, not sure there was a mission involved, there. I am not actually sure what the end goal was, really...**

I let Drynwyn burble away as l finished with the heart moss. It was now glowing in a very attractive manner and was warm to the touch. I popped another bottle of spring water in - there was that unnecessarily backing music again - and Drynwyn did its fiery thing.

There was a tug from the lid of the cauldron on my Qi channels, so I popped it on top.

And sat back while the most glorious smell in the world emanated from the little bowl.

After all the disappointing failures, there was something quite liberating about success. I couldn't easily remember the last one I had, purely due to my efforts. And that included both of my lifetimes.

How do you know when it is ready? I could do with some fiery flame of death downtime.

Almost the moment the sword spoke, I felt something change in the cauldron. I dropped into my Artist's Studio to see what the process looked like from there.

The cauldron was ... radiant. Like seriously, it was easily the most beautiful thing I had ever seen and was gulping down my Qi like a drain. So much so I had to tap my earrings to even myself off. But when something looked so incredible, it could do what it liked.

OG Morgan said that this was one of Britain's Thirteen Treasures. I could absolutely believe it. I popped back out and lifted the lid off. The aroma of every home-cooked meal that had ever persuaded me I'd finally found Mr Right greeted me. My mouth watered just at the thought of tasting what waited within.

I dipped my finger in and was just bringing it to my mouth, when Drynwyn made an odd noise. It
sounded like it was clearing its non-existent throat.

Look, not for nothing, but I know a little something about Elixirs of Wellness. I'm not saying you shouldn't try it. I'm just saying YOU absolutely shouldn't try it.

I paused and lowered my hand. "Why? It smells amazing."

I'm sure it does. I can read your emotions and you're basically falling in love with the fucking stuff before you've even tried it. I'm just saying, from what I know about you, I'm not convinced introducing a happy-joy substance right now is likely to speed up our escape at all.

"You're talking to me like I'm some sort of out-of-control, drug-dependent street person."

I didn't need a pregnant pause that was ready to pop to engulf the conversation. "Is it really that potent?"

It's a fucking Elixir of Wellness. Well, at best you've produced a shitty half-arsed one even using a fucking legendary cauldron. It will cure you of everything, strengthen your body and basically bliss you out until the effect wears off. Call me selfish, but I'd rather we concentrate on getting out of here rather than you get off your tits.

The rare valid point.

I flicked through the scroll. There were many things later that could help me, most of which seemed to have an Elixir of Wellness as a critical ingredient. They needed all sorts of other ingredients, and I only had the contents of one very long corridor

Oh, and the inventory of Vortigon's Dragon's Horde...

However, before I ever wanted to start thinking about skilling myself up, I needed to get the quality of this elixir to something called 'Flawless.'

"How can I work out how good an elixir I've made?"

Stick it in a bottle and store it in your inventory. That should keep it for you.

I did so and was rewarded with a little tag next to it that said **Inferior Elixir of Wellness [1]**

That seemed more than a little harsh for something that the thought of tasting made me weak at the knees. Self-control was not my defining characteristic, so I was very proud to have it in my inventory without sipping. I don't think a bottle of wine made it through the night in my flat.

Right. So, I had an unlimited amount of moss. More water bottles than I could count. And
an enchanted cauldron.

Let's get cooking.

CHAPTER 38- IN WHICH WE FIND ANOTHER POINT ON THE LOVE TRIANGLE.

Two hundred and thirty.

Two fucking hundred and thirty Inferior' Elixirs of Wellness before I managed to produce one that was labelled "Common' in my inventory. That's a lot of moss.

It's also an awful lot of Qi, and I'd tapped out most of my mana stones and was dangerously close to emptying my Artist's Studio. However, rather than feeling that sickening feeling I'd come to associate with running on fumes, I felt ... satisfied.

Like (and forgive me, I've never actually done this, so I'm extrapolating from available evidence), I'd run a marathon for which I'd been training really hard. **We're going to stop now, aren't we? I need a fucking break. I only have so much rage in my heart."**

"Yep. Let's pause there," I lifted the cauldron off Drynwyn and put it back in my inventory.

Interestingly, I had a whole new page dedicated to my alchemical efforts. The cauldron and two hundred and thirty Inferior Wellness Elixirs were in there. The scroll I was currently following was there, but — and this was particularly nice — a whole row of other scrolls (presumably sorted from my wider inventory) also about alchemy had arranged themselves.

I found I could read through them while cycling - as long as I didn't take them out of that page - so I was genuinely multitasking for the first time in my life.

That is, if you don't count snorting a line of something that was possibly washing powder whilst blowing my dealer and downing a bottle of Jack Daniels.

Are we counting on that? No, I didn't think so, either.

The first thing I realised, browsing through the material, is that ancient alchemists thought a lot of themselves. You'd have thought they'd found a cure for cancer the way they spoke about their "wondrous and prodigious art."

Okay. That's a bad example. There is a potion for the "dissolving of Unwanted Growths and Lesions" - but that could be aimed at targeting ex-boyfriends for all I knew. The list of ingredients there was so long and comprehensive that I doubted I'd be troubling the good people in Stockholm for one of their prizes any time soon.

I could probably have coped with all the self-congratulation if the prose had been better, though. At least it was easier to identify actual advice and recipes among the verbose reflections.

Walking through a "dappled wood and spying the most perfect babbling book in all creation." At art school, I ended up spending much time around boys of a certain age who fancied themselves quite the Romantic wordsmiths, so I had a reasonably high tolerance for flowery bullshit. Some of this stuff, though, was off the charts.

Nevertheless, between the "dazzling luminance of the night sky" and the "sweet aroma of freshly tilled earth"—these guys had definitely partaken of Elixirs of Wellness if you know what I'm saying—there were more than a few valuable hints.

The quality of your cauldron, for example, was directly linked to the quality and quantity of Substances you could produce. If I had any doubts whether Morgan's gift was decent, they were dispelled by the reading of a particular alchemist—he called himself Elgicaramus the Magnificent. Still, his writing absolutely reeked of being on Eric, who spent eight years researching and perfecting the art of a god-made elixir of wellness!

Suddenly, two hundred and thirty goes didn't seem too shabby.

Elgicaramus spent most of his time trying to locate a cauldron that he could force enough of his Qi into to raise the quality of the secret sauce above 'poor'. The day he found one, he could add "the merest splash of my potent juice" (I really hope he's talking about his Qi here, or I've been reading a very different book). He was so happy he nearly forgot to add unnecessary adjectives to his descriptions. Neary, but not quite.

I studied my cauldron again. Even with me full-on cycling, it was still sucking on down more Qi than I could easily produce. My armour and mana stone earrings eventually reached the point where I couldn't add any more. But the cauldron was drinking it in like a bottomless well, which, incidentally, was my nickname at my second job. People can be cruel.

Putting the scrolls to the side for a bit, I concentrated on my cycling. Not just letting it poodle around in the background but properly pushing and pulling with my breathing - the way Merlin kept moaning at me to try.

It was weird to think how difficult I'd found this to be not that long ago. My paint absolutely flew round my channels, still having that slightly sticky spot near my liver, but with each pass, that felt easier and easier. What is more, that odd water feature in the core of it all was noticeably fuller than before my kidnapping. It wasn't quite to the brim, but I didn't think it.' would take much more for it to get that way.

I needed someone to ask what would happen when it was complete.

I missed Merlin.

That thought pulled me out of my sense of calm and back into reality.

You're leaking.

Wiping my eyes, I stood up and stretched my back. "How long had I been cycling?"

Did you misunderstand my fucking job description? I'm a sword, not a fucking personal organiser. I measure time by the distance between kills."

Yep, I definitely missed Merlin.

I left my cauldron to keep guzzling down all the excess Qi I'd generated, hoping that at some stage enough would be enough, and I could test out what a fully kitted-out Treasure of Britain could really do with some heart moss and spring water.

I suspected I wouldn't be producing 'Common' elixirs for long.

Poor, Inferior, Common, Uncommon, Rare, Epic, Flawless. It would be quite a journey before I'd have the ability to make something that would help me escape— or, at least, the ingredient I needed. Presumably, it would be a similarly long journey to perfect that particular portion, too.

Anxiety bloomed in my stomach, but I pushed it down.

My entire first life had been one frantic search for the quick fix—for the thing— animal, mineral, or vegetable—that would make everything okay. That would soothe

the pain—even for a minute. And a minute would be charitable for some of the lads from Art School.

But that was the old me.

Sure, 'new' me was basically the same fucked up person, but with Magic. But I was beginning to realise that there was a whole new range of options open to me, that didn't involve the quickest possible solution.

I remembered one of my first conversations with Merlin about cultivating and how it was all about the quality, not the quantity. He'd been so worried about how quickly I was burning through techniques and progression markers. He'd obviously sensed that, given a choice, I was all about the cheat code and not the journey.

The funny thing was, when I was painting, that absolutely wasn't me.

No matter what else was going down in my life, I never rushed my art. The last time I was evicted, I'd found myself carting around pictures portraits I'd begun four or five years earlier. I'd not abandoned them- I kept going back to them again and again - but I recognised they deserved care and attention I didn't seem to afford to much else.

Fuck me; I'd been screwed up.

You're leaking again.

Smiling, I picked up the sword. "Yeah, don't worry about it."

I didn't say I was worrying about it. I don't know how you fucking things work. Rhyddrech Hael actively seemed to seek out opportunities to leak as much as he could. But I'm coming to recognise that might not have been the healthiest approach. I assume you have a fair amount of moisture you can expel? From memory, by the third time, he was just firing air."

"Mate, can we make that the last Rhyddrech Hael anecdote for a bit? Not that I don't love them, but they leave me needing to take a bath, and if you haven't noticed, they're in short supply around here."

"A shower in my cell there is."

I froze and then slowly turned towards the door from which the voice had emanated.

"Hello? Out there is anyone ? I was saying a shower in my cell there is being. Well, not a shower. More leak in the roof with all the water flowing through it. Happy to share it with you I'd be if you're interested?"

The voice was unmistakably Scandinavian. It was like someone had taken the essence of all things from that part of the world, mashed them together with added herring, meatballs and difficult-to-assemble flat-pack furniture, and released the ensuing accent on the wild.

It was like having Barry White to speak Elvish.

"It's not a bath it is being, I'm afraid. But needs must, as my dear mother says always."

I wasn't really sure how to react. Other than Morgan, there'd been no sign that anyone was alive or sane in these cells. But I hadn't tried them all, that would have taken forever.

The law of averages had to dictate that someone else would be behind one of these doors that was capable of aiding in an escape attempt.

"And whatever cooking you are out there delicious is smelling. Not that I'm not grateful for all the mushrooms growing on my walls I have, but it's good to have some variety. Hello? Are you still there?"

"Yes, I'm here."

"Glad to hear it. I was worried I'd frightened you off with my silliness about mushrooms and baths and such like. My mother always says Shordigjordsson, you speak too much. But how else can you get to know another without all the talking?"

He rambled on for quite some time. There was something incredibly soothing about the musical rumble of his voice.

"Why are you in the cell?" I realised if I didn't interrupt him, there would be no stop to the flow of his words.

"Ah, now there is a saga. It began..."

Fucking give us a precis. I'm rusting out here.

If the man was offended, it didn't show in his voice. "Certainly, brusque one. I landed with my crew after a storm, and there was – sorry, my language skills are not what I would wish. Would you call it raping and pillaging? There were more of the Saes - the Saxons - than we'd thought. I sought the leader, but he wouldn't play fair. Next thing I know, here I am.

"And your name is –", I thought back, " –Shordigjordsson?"

A laugh came from behind the door. "No, that's what mother calls me is. My name is –" and then he made a noise not unlike the ice falling from a faulty fridge ice dispenser.

"Okay, I have absolutely no chance of saying that. What did your shipmates call you?"

We then played a complicated game: "Let's find ways to describe me that you can understand." I had the best time.

Fuck's sake! Why don't you just call him "annoying twat behind the door"? I could get behind that.

"Right. One last try. Can you translate any of those nicknames for me?"

There was silence. "Thin stick with spike on the end?" he asked hesitantly. Now we were getting somewhere.

"Spear? Your mates call you 'spear'?"

"No. Not entirely - It's the ones you have on horses. It is a joke, you see? Because I'm too big to sit on a horse. They were a funny crew. Lots of japes. Always with the jokes."

My mind whirled for a moment, already seeing where this particular impending trainwreck was leading.

"A Lance? They called you Lance?"

"Yes. I was called Lance a lot."

Fuck.

CHAPTER 39 IN WHICH IT ALL STARTS TO SPICE UP A LITTLE.

It took Drynwyn far less time to cut through the door behind which waited… Look, I'm going to call him 'Lancelot' because anything else sounds stupid, okay? Anyway, Drynwyn did its thing, and there was soon a large hole in the cell door.

Although, as it turned out, not Lancelot size.

Even seated and in chains, I could tell this was a big man—maybe not Bors big—but there were not enough of these genes to go around. He had long, dark hair that was well past his shoulders yet was wholly clean-shaven. He could have been anything from twenty to forty, but his mischievous blue eyes suggested he could be even younger.

This dude was *trouble* if the fluttering in my stomach and elsewhere meant anything. I've had my fair share (and probably several other people's) of tall, dark, and handsome fellas. Most of these turned out to be mad, bad, and catastrophically dangerous to know. So, I think I'm speaking from a position of knowledge when I say nothing good will come from letting this guy out of prison.

Fifteen hundred years of Arthurian lore hit me square in the head.

Launcelot, the greatest of all Arthur's knights, embodied the "verray parfait gently knight." Launcelot who couldn't keep it in his pants. Which led to Camelot falling.

I remembered my vision of Camlyn from the Enchanted Forest. Could I avoid all that pain and heartache if I shuffled down the corridor and pretended I had never heard of him?

"It's good to see you. I have been alone for a long time. Please try out my shower." He nodded towards a stream of water pouring from a hole in the roof of his cell.

Two things struck me.

Firstly, I think Lancelot may be a touch slow. Not like a complete full-blown moron or anything. But I'd think twice about giving him any pet mice or letting him stroke my hair in a barn if you know what I'm saying?

Secondly, though, and this was a bit more critical, through the gap in the roof through which water was pouring, I could see the sky.

***

"Look, as massive, traumatic chest wounds go, I've seen worse," Bors voice was trying to project as much confidence as he could; it was failing.

Arthur kneeled by the unconscious form of his wife. They'd done what they could to stem the bleeding, and - in relative terms - she seemed stable. There just wasn't a long way to go from 'stable' to very terminal.

"There's got to be something you can do, Wizard?" the Prince asked desperately.

Merlin shook Melehan's head. "The fast travel has completely drained me. In enough time, I should be able to do something, but . . ."

The three of them looked down at the blood-soaked grass beneath Guinevere. They all knew they didn't have that sort of time.

The Dark Tower loomed above them. They'd teleported to a tiny corpse of wood just to the right of the entrance.

"My Lord," Bors said, gasping his axe, "if there is one thing I know about a building like that, it has to be crammed with healers. Just packed with them."

Arthur raised his eyes to his friend. "Along with the hundreds of warriors that they are in there to heal . . ."

"You got a better plan?"

"What? A better plan than 'take me to your healer?" He looked down at his wife. She was paler now than when they'd arrived. If that was at all possible. "To the enchanted forest, to the bridge of dreams, and finally to the Castle Perilous."

"What?"

"This quest turns out to be more accurate than we thought." Arthur shook his head. "I don't even have a weapon."

Bors nodded at the do guards at the entrance to the tower. "While we were enquiring about the whereabouts of all their healers, we could ask the way to the armoury? Or can just fuck them up as we go."

"You want to do this?"

Bors shrugged back. "You want to sit here and watch her die?"

Arthur covered one of Guinevere's hands with his and squeezed it. "No, I cannot do that," he said, standing and pointing at Melehan. "Every pinch of Qi you generate is directed at her, keeping her alive, you understand me? I don't need her healed—we'll get somebody else to do that—but you don't let her die, you hear me?"

Merlin nodded Melehan's head. "I do, my dear – my Lord, I will do my best, but her wound…"

Arthur reached forward and picked the Saxon Wizard up with one hand, raising him to within inches of his face. "Let me speak plain. Sir Bors and I are going into that fucking tower and we will be coming out with a healer. We're going to kill anybody that stands in our way, and chances are, this will get us a bit riled up. If, healer in tow, I find my way back here, and my wife is no longer with us, the trauma you received in the hands of Cedric of the West Saxons will feel like the genuine and kindest of ministrations at the hand of a lust-filled virgins compared to what I'll visit on you. And when I'm done, which will take a very long time, Sir Bors will …

Arthur looked at the big man, who added." Fuck you up the arse with my axe."

There was a pause, and then the Prince continued, "Do we have an understanding, Wizard?"

Melehan's head nodded. "I will do everything I can, my Lord."

"You better." Arthur let their wizard fall back to the floor. "Let's go."

As the two stalked off into the shadows to approach the tower, Merlin could hear the last bits of their conversation. "Fuck him up the arse with your axe? That was the best you could do?"

"I panicked. You were all over this vengeance nightmare vibe, and I didn't expect you to throw it at me. I wasn't prepared," and they were swallowed up in darkness.

***

Aurelius Ambrosius was not having a perfect day.

Of course, these things were relative. When you were the Bretwalda of the Saxon territories in Britain, even your bad days there were better than most.

He was well-fed, well fucked and had access to any number of quality-of-life benefits. Moreover, he sat in a giant, Qi-attracting tower, which ensured that even as he slept, the roaring fire of his QI was kept well-fuelled.

He was, by any measure, winning.

And that mattered more to him than anything else in the world.

So, this afternoon, little reversals were not that significant in the grand scheme of things.

Nevertheless, Merlin's apprentice wriggling free from the time-loop pit he had thrown her in was annoying. He had any number of games planned there, and it was irritating that they would go unfulfilled. He knew such things should have been beneath him - they should have crushed the life from her the moment he had her in his powers – but there are so few true pleasures left in him to live. By necessity, he hadn't been present for Merlin's last moments, although he had been responsible; so he had been looking forward to grinding the apprentice down to the dust – in proxy as it were.

And now she was out and about on the top floor and already freed that bitch Morgan Le Frey. Mind you, by his reckoning, the apprentice had been in that loop just shy of a hundred years. He doubted she'd have much sanity left to do more than wander the corridors and gibber.

And Morgan being free? He had caught her before and doubted the old witch would risk tangling with him again.

So, his day had two minor blemishes. Neither was ideal, but he would not lose any sleep.

The third issue was a bit vexatious.

Cedric hadn't managed to lose Arthur.

Of course, the West Saxon hadn't known who he had captured. Aurelius knew enough about that man's wider ambitions to never let him know the full extent of what he had in his hands.

But had him, he had. And then, somehow, he'd let him slip away.

Aurelius reached for his leather pouch and took out three vials, downing them all in one go. This was inadvisable. Even with his myriad of resistance and healing capabilities, he knew better than to do this.

But, after all, what was life without risk?

The combination of acid poison and the dragon's blood burned down his throat, destroying it and blistering as it went.

Aurelius pushed the merest spark of his QI towards it, not wanting to dull its effects, but neither was he so blasé about his life that he'd risk actual harm.

Then he felt the whisper of a presence that made his eyes wide open, and he sprayed the remaining half mouthful against the wall. Where it quickly burned a hole.

***

"You have beautiful hair,"
"Cheers."
"It's red like the sun."
"Yep,"

"My mother said women who look like you are snares for the pure of heart."

"Thanks - hang on, what?"

We are trying, unsuccessfully, I might add, to force the hole in the roof of Lancelot's cell to increase in size. Drynwyn is no fucking use, apparently; something as facile as pouring rainwater is the equivalent of an ice bath and a horny teenager.

His flame would not flicker.

The cell roof was about ten feet above the ground, so the only way we could reach it as if my hydrophobic sword wasn't an option, was for one of us to sit on the other's shoulders while the others tried to break the ceiling down.

Fun fact: apparently, being cultivated did something crazy for my mass. As well as being faster, stronger, and fitter than I've ever been, I am also—in the words of a recently released prisoner—" weigh as much as a whole whale of sperm."

So, I have insane weight gain to add to my list of anxieties.

This is why Lancelot is currently sat on my shoulders and petting me like a dog.

"Snares for the pure of heart. That is why she killed Brunhilde, Sigurd, and Valeson. She said they were trying to take me away from her. I don't think she'll like you."

"Well, she can go and join the club. We've got jackets and a theme song and everything. Are you having any luck?"

"At what?"

This dude had to have, at best, a room-temperature IQ. "You're pulling down the ceiling, remember?"

"Oh, I did that a while back. Sorry. What do you want to do next? That was fun."

With as much delicacy as I could summon, I shrugged him off my shoulders and looked upwards.

To be fair to the big lug, he'd done quite a good job. The roof of his cell is now fully opened to the sky with a hole I was confident we could fit through.

I was just starting to figure out the mechanics of achieving that when I heard a sound, I'd never thought would bring me so much pleasure.

Bor's swearing a blue streak.

"Fuck you, and you and you can for fuck off in particular."

***

Operation Find Guinevere A Healer, wasn't going as well as it could be hoped.

For a start, every Saxon they encountered appeared to be suddenly committed to the idea of murdering Arthur and Bors the moment they saw them.

Then, there was the strange configuration inside the giant tower itself. They'd been expecting some form of spiral staircase upwards opening out on chambers and rooms, preferably one that said "Here be healers" or something similar.

But no, instead of any staircase there were glowing orbs around the walls, which, presumably, portalled you to the floor you wanted. Or, as Bors put it, More fucking Cultivators bullshit."

"Any ideas?" Arthur yelled, turning a sword aside with this shaft of his 'borrowed' spear and pivoting to drive his shoulder into his opponent's face.

"Why've I always got to be the one with the plans? You're the socialite military genius. It was my idea to storm this place armed with nothing more than our swinging cocks. It's got to be your turn!"

Arthur scanned the space around the entrance to the tower. Unless they saw somebody cast a healing spell, they could not identify one to drag back to Guinevere.

They needed some form of sign there was a Cultivator about.

The moment he thought that, one of the glowing orbs suddenly increased in size, and his father walked through.

But no, it wasn't father. It was a taller, older, grimmer - if possibly – version of the man he knew. He was carrying a spear and walked with a swagger that Bors and he instantly recognised.

That of someone who had stood many a shield wall and had ever walked away on top.

"Who the fuck's this baller?" Bors whispered, withdrawing with Arthur away from the new threat.

"Fuck knows."

"Now, now, nephew. Is there any way to greet me after all this time? But we'll have plenty of opportunities to reacquaint ourselves. But first, I must turn to my most pressing question. Where is Merlin?"

CHAPTER 40 - IN WHICH WHEN THE BOUGH BREAKS AND THE CRADLE FALLS. A FUCKING LONG WAY.

"Quick, you need to be, or my back-breaking will."

"Oh, do fuck off, you fat-shaming twat."

With as little grace as I could summon, I pressed down on Lancelot's back and enacted some sort of ungainly jump, grabbing the exposed brick of the cell ceiling with my right hand.

For a horrible moment, I thought the whole thing wasn't going to hold - PTSD-style flashbacks of a particular level of the original 'Prince of Persia game came flooding back - but then I tightened my grip and was able to swing myself upwards and through the gap we had created in cell roof in a manner wholly defying the laws of physics.

Up yours, Newton. Equal and opposite reaction, my arse.

I was free.

Well, I was standing on the top of a Dark Tower, hundreds of feet in the air, with no idea where in the world I was. Oh, and a psychotic, vengeful Cultivator miles above my level was hanging around somewhere. And my only companion was so lacking in wit and intelligence, whilst also being unnaturally buff, that he was a shoo-in for the next series of Love Island.

What I'm getting at is that I wasn't exactly home and hosed, but after what I'd been through, I was feeling pretty damn chipper.

I peered down through the hole at Lancelot, reaching his arms up at me and jumping up and down with a stupid grin on his beautiful face. His whole demeanour resembled nothing so much as a really good-natured puppy wanting to play.

Not for the first time in the last few minutes, I found myself a touch baffled to reconcile my reading about Lancelot and the reality of this slab of muscle. Was this guy really going to be the catalyst for Camelot's downfall?

"Helping me up, you will? The sky I want to be seeing, pretty hair!"

Mind you, it wasn't even like the age of Arthur had even properly started yet. If it ever would.

We had no Merlin. Arthur and Guinevere hated each other's guts, and Uther was still king. This wasn't like any version of Camelot I knew. But, then again, I was still in existence, so I could presume the timeline hadn't altered significantly from what was supposed to happen.

Zizzie was still alive out there somewhere.

So, say I left Lancelot down there in his prison. Would that make things more or less likely to work out well? This lump would lay the pipe to Guinevere at some point in the not-too-distant future. As sure as eggs are eggs, it would be this which would bring about the whole 'end of the world' vibe I saw in my vision of Camlyn.

On the other hand, I knew of many stories where, without Lancelot, the whole Kingdom would fall into ruin anyway. And it couldn't possibly be a coincidence that I ran into him here, could it?

I remember what my dad used to say. "There are no coincidences. Only secret plots you haven't uncovered yet."

Yeah, cheers, Dad. I always wondered where I got my raging paranoia from.

Decisions. Decisions.

"I don't know what you're against the big guy, but if you want, I'll fucking fry him for you."

"Cheers, D. It's not that I don't appreciate your psychotic instincts, but I'm not sure that's how I want to handle this right now. If I decide a fiery demise is the only way forward, you'll be the first person I call."

I looked down again. Lancelot was still doing the odd jumping and hopping thing. Staring at him, I couldn't quite see what would appeal to Guinevere about this man.

I mean, obviously, I did.

He was the closest thing to physical perfection I'd seen outside the Elgin Marbles. And I'm including my late, lamented woodcutter in this, too.

But the Princess I'd met seemed to have a bit more about her than just swooning for all the muscles.

But then again, who was I to chat shit? If I were stuck with Arthur, I'd probably take the opportunity for an angst-free shag too.

Whichever way I looked at it, I didn't think the smart play was to leave him locked up. I leaned down through the hole, grabbed his wrist, and pulled him up with a quick jerk.

"You're crazy strong, pretty red-haired lady. Mother would cheerfully carve you up with her favourite axe."

"Thanks. Glad to be of help. Tell your friends."

Now free, we both explored the top of the Tower, seeking an appropriate way down.

Well, to be strictly accurate, I looked around, and Lancelot followed me about like a lost puppy—a big, hauntingly attractive puppy with giant muscles and eyes you could get lost in.

To be honest, I could get used to this.

My good mood lasted until I realised quite how stuck we actually were.

The Dark Tower's roof was perhaps a hundred feet square and—apart from the hole we'd battered in Lancelot's cell ceiling—was utterly devoid of any way to get down.

After jogging around it a few times, I found myself peering over the edge, trying to calculate precisely how wide my exploded corpse would spread if I jumped.

I was pretty confident it would be a job beyond all the king's horses and all the king's men.

Basically, it was a very, very long way down.

However, even from this great distance, I could make out Bors's battle cries when the wind gusted in the right way, and that got me right in the feels.

They'd come to rescue me.

I couldn't help it - call it the residue trauma of the time loop, if you like - but a lump formed in my throat, and tears streamed down my face.

Many so-called white knights had tried to swoop into my life over the years. Most wanted something- obviously- but I think a few genuinely saw what a fucking wreck I was and were motivated to do something about it.

Of course, regardless of motivation, I'd told them all to fuck off to whence they'd came. And the horse they'd rode in on.

But that was the old me.

This new girl? Well, let's just say that when a literal white knight rode into town to save her, she wouldn't be turning them away.

What are you thinking? I recognise that fucking mental glint in your eye. Not saying I don't approve - your side of this partnership could use a bit more oomph - but your plans of late have lacked a certain . . . logical coherence.

"Fuck off. At least my plans are more evolved than setting everything on fire. No, listen. I'm wondering exactly how much healing an Inferior Elixir of Wellness is capable of. Oh, and whether you'd bounce."

***

"Merlin's dead." Arthur's voice was flat, and he circled around the Tower, trying to develop an angle of attack.

Aurelius Ambrosius. Who would have thought it?

He'd heard stories of his uncle, of course. But the vast majority of them were pretty consistent with the fact that - you know- Uther killed him.

"That's what I thought," Aurelius gestured for his men surrounding Bors and Arthur to fall back slightly, "and yet why can feel him in the air?"

Bors and Arthur exchanged glances, and the big man moved forward to a defensive position. "Well, unless you think I've got him rammed up my arse, I'm not sure what more we can tell you. But while we're in a questioning mood, what the fuck's a Briton doing palling up with the Saxons?!"

Aurelius' eyes slipped to Bors, and he clenched his fist together. In moments, the big man grunted in surprise and collapsed, clutching his chest. "I've heard people live just fine with only partial heart function. Apparently, those stories are exaggerated." He turned his gaze back to Arthur. "Where is Merlin?"

Arthur licked his lips, trying hard not to panic as Bors' skin took on the colour of slightly off milk. "I'm going to guess the offer is that if I tell you, you'll let us live?"

Aurelius smiled, and Arthur noticed several of his teeth were... were they melted?

"Of course not. But if you spin me an entertaining tale, I might just kill you a hair quicker."

Arthur was about to come back with a witty, cutting remark - any second. Any second now - when he was interrupted by two loud - yet oddly soft, squelching noises from beyond the entrance.

And then a loud clang.

***

If you're interested, the sweet spot to surviving this death dive seemed to be downing ten Elixirs each—to get a good buzz on—and then cramming as many vials in our mouths as we could hold on to the way down.

The plan—and I admit, this was not one of my better ones—was that the bottles would break when we hit, and maybe—just maybe—enough liquid would get down our throats to get another round of healing rolling before we died.

Oh, and I also had my Healing Rock wedged firmly in my hand.

It would be fair to say that I still had a long way down to go before I began reconsidering the advisability of this plan.

It would have helped if I'd had anyone with a functioning brain cell to help talk me out of doing it in the first place. Lancelot, though, had been absolutely on board with Operation Jump-from-twenty-thousand-feet-without-a-parachute.

"Is that what you think is best, pretty hair? Let's do it."

Seriously, Guinevere, this guy better be dynamite in bed.

As the ground rushed up to meet me, I turned on my back, indicating to Lancelot to do the same. The last thing we needed was to spill the elixir outwards when we hit.

Fucking hell. We were going to hit . . .

Then we clamped our teeth shut and hoped for the best.

We'd been falling for longer than I would have thought possible when . . .

***

Merlin couldn't keep this up.

He pumped every grain of Melehan's Qi he generated straight into Guinevere, and it was not going to be enough.

He knew there was only so long a cultivator could operate at absolute zero, and he had already crossed that line a while back.

If Arthur didn't appear soon with a fucking amazing healer, there would be two more corpses waiting for him when he returned.

He was just giving in to the blackest pit of despair when Merlin was suddenly amazed by the appearance of not one but two rather unexpected presences.

The surge of adrenaline increased his cultivation by the slightest amount, but it was enough.

A few extra grains of sand were shot over to the Princess.

Merlin forced open Melehan's eyes, hoping to catch sight of what had grabbed his attention.

One was a welcome if rather quickly moving blur outside the Dark Tower. The other, which he could see just inside the building's entrance, was a much less pleasant acquaintance.

Especially as, the moment they made eye contact, Aurelius Ambrosius began striding towards him.

***

Arthur was thrown bodily out of the way as Aurelius stormed past him and made his way quickly outside his Tower.

It had been an awfully long time since he had been so summarily dismissed, and the injury to his pride hurt almost as much as the wall he smashed into by his uncle's shove.

Almost.

Fortunately, the rest of the Saxons who'd surrounded them had followed their master outside, so he was able to quickly run to Bors' side.

"Can you stand?"

"I doubt I could even fuck, but I never let that stop me before. Help me up." Arthur tried to ignore the paleness of the big man's skin and how heavily he appeared to need to lean on him. "It's like someone hit me in the chest with a hammer. Only not as much fun. Where did that smug bastard go?"

They slowly reached the entrance just in time to see Aurelius backhand Melehan against a tree.

***

The funny thing is, there wasn't much pain.

I doubt there was enough time.

I was me.

Then, I was roadkill.

And then I was me again.

I sat up, and - oh, excellent! There's all that pain I was missing- and quickly downed a bunch more Elixirs, crawling over the ground to pour some more down into what I thought was Lancelot's mouth. It could have been his ear, I guess.

It was hard to tell.

Say what you like about Inferior Elixirs, but they didn't fuck about. In seconds, Lancelot started reinflating. Yep, that's the best verb I have for what was occurring. Like a burst balloon, lying in a pool of its viscera, blowing itself back up.

If it weren't so sickeningly appalling, I'd have been looking for this year's Academy Awards for Special Effects.

Then something moved to my left, and I spun, seeing Bors and Arthur emerge from the entrance to the Dark Tower.

They looked like absolute shit.

"You get an Elixir of Wellness! You get an Elixir of Wellness! We ALL get an Elixir of Wellness!" I shouted, slinging little bottles everywhere.

There's a chance I may have become a little hysterical.

As the potions took effect, I quickly recovered Drynwyn, who seemed none the worse for his mid-evening flight and tried to calm myself.

"Dudes, so good to see you! You didn't need to come all this way." I went for an awkward hug, but Arthur pushed past me. Bors followed him at a run.

I turned to see what all the non-Morgan-related fuss was about and saw a wonderful visual of a slightly less attractive Uther pulling Melehan's arm free from its socket.

I winced. "Not sure an Inferior Elixir is really going to cut it there".

And l ran to join the fray.

CHAPTER 41- IN WHICH WE EXPLORE WHO HAS THE MOST ENORMOUS COCK IN TOWN

It appeared the world had gone to hell in a handcart.

Just ahead of me, Arthur and Bors were struggling with a group of Saxons, trying to get through to the newly unarmed - sorry, I couldn't resist - Melehan, and . . . fuck me, was that Guinevere at his feet? The Princess had a horrible-looking wound to her chest and was lying in a slowly widening pool of blood.

What the fuck had these guys been up to?

That felt like a question for another day - if we made it through this one alive. I targeted a line of Saxons who were trying to hold Arthur and Bors back from reaching Guinevere and triggered <Personal Space Invader>, throwing as much Qi at it as I could.

The effect was pretty damn satisfying.

The moment the technique was activated, it was like a deep trench ran itself down the middle of the pack of defenders. Blue-painted men were thrown every which way as if hit by a particularly spiteful hurricane.

Arthur and Bors burst through the middle of them, and I followed in my friends' wake, pulling an Elixir out of my inventory, ready to pour on Guinevere the moment I was close enough.

That plan became slightly derailed when the Uther lookalike suddenly let go of Melehan and pointed directed at me.

That he did so with a hand still holding the wizard's arm gave me somewhat of a vibe. Who the fuck was this guy?

"Apprentice! You will rue the day you left your cell. You will look back on your time within as a golden age."

I'd like to think I had a plan. I'd like to think that my countless hours stuck in a time loop gave me the opportunity to come up with an excellent range of solutions and plays for just this sort of situation.

I'd like to think a lot of things.

However, this felt like one of those situations where an 'old-faithful approach would be best.

I threw Drynwyn at him.

Dropping Melehan's dripping arm, whoever the fuck this was caught my sword and -as expected- went up in a very satisfying column of flame.

Ignoring the conflagration, I took the opportunity to skid to Guinevere's side and pour an Elixir down her throat, dimly aware that Arthur and Bors were doing their best to hold off a sizeable number of Saxons who had - due to the frying of their boss - become pretty damn motivated all of a sudden.

By a strange yodelling battle cry from back towards the Dark Tower, it sounded like Lancelot was also about to add considerable belligerence to proceedings.

But I didn't have time for that. I was watching for any sign the Princess was healing.

No dice. After a moment, I added a second and then a third Elixir down her throat and, this time, started to see some progress. It took two more of them before I was happy that the massive injury — had someone stabbed her with a spear? - was closing, and some colour was starting to return to her cheeks.

At that stage, I turned my attention to Melehan.

In many ways, he looked a million times better than the last time I saw him. In fact, I'd say he looked positively glowing if he weren't missing an arm.

I shuffled over to him, pressed my healing stone into his remaining hand, and went to give him an Elixir.

The wizard shook his head. *No point, my dear. This body is much too far gone.*

"Dude, a bunch of these just helped me shake off being absolutely marmalised from a great, great height. Not to brag, but I don't think a missing arm will trouble it much."

And then my brain caught up with my ears.

"Hang on..."

Yes, it's me. It's good to see you, my dear. I hope you've been using your time away profitably?

I made a noise that suggested we could talk about that another time and that he should very quickly explain what the fuck was going on. It was quite an expressive sound—one of my best.

Let me explain: I was forced to hitch a ride in this poor, unfortunate cultivator when you were ripped from the world. However, even ignoring this latest injury, I rather fear my host had entirely given up on the ghost, as it were. He's . . . well, we're in terminal Qi exhaustion, even ignoring the wound. Elixirs need the recipient to want to live, and I'm afraid he just doesn't have the will to heal. There was a brief pause, and then he asked, *How's the Princess?*

My head swan, trying to make sense of his words. "Guinevere's getting there. But, how . . . I mean, can you get back into my head?"

That should not be an issue, my dear. However, my presence in this body is the only thing keeping this particular wizard in one piece. The second I leave, he will undoubtedly pass, and I think we'll need the extra pair of hands shortly. Well, hand, at least.

"Why?"

Drynwyn thudded to the ground beside me. **Erm, we may have a fucking massive problem here...**

I looked up at a blackened, ruined skeleton of a man grinning at me. "Thank you," it said, face exploding where incinerated muscles moved. "It's been a while since I was tested in that way. Now, do remind me, where were we?"

***

Bors and Arthur were doing their best to keep the Saxons that continued to pour out of the Dark Tower from reaching the small group behind them. Morgan had helpfully cleared a path through the press, and they'd made their way through, then swung around to take up a decent defensive position.

Well, as decent a position as two guys could have against a horde.

The trees on either side of them offered just enough of a barrier that - for now - it made more sense for the attackers to go through them than waste time flanking them in the woods. The gods knew how long that situation would last, but no one ever grew poor, betting on the single-mindedness of Saxons.

A roar of boiling air and burning heat hit their backs, suggesting Morgan had gone with Plan A when dealing with his uncle. Arthur shuddered under the force of a very repressed memory of his own encounter with catching Drynwyn and concentrated on killing Saxons.

"Just like old times," Bors grunted, grabbing a fallen foe and throwing his corpse into the crowd before them.

"True. I do kind of miss the hundred elite warriors that would usually have our backs in these sorts of situations, though."

"Nah, they were just window dressing. Me and you, Arthur. We were the main event."

However, despite Bors's bravado - and their years of experience and undoubted prowess - both knew that, short of a miracle, they would soon be overwhelmed.

Numbers always would tell.

And then, just as things were looking pretty bleak, a vast, shirtless man with long glowing locks was beside them, belting out the strangest war cry either of them had ever heard.

The newcomer reached out to the nearest Saxon, disarmed him with a slap and then set about the attackers with his looted sword.

"Who ordered the barbarian?"

Arthur ignored Bor's question as he tried to comprehend the . . . beauty of this man's swordplay. Although he preferred the spear himself, he had no little training with the sword, but he had nothing - literally - on this guy.

It was like their saviour was moving through an entirely different plane of existence than any of the Saxons in front of him. They may as well just have stood still and surrendered for all the good their efforts to engage him did.

The man danced through them, hacking, slashing, and cutting as he went like death made corporeal. It was an astonishingly brutal sight.

"Don't know about you, my lord, but I'm feeling pretty fucking redundant right now." Bors was, likewise, struck by the sheer inevitability of destruction being meted out to the Saxons.

Suddenly, with time and space to share, Arthur glanced behind him and gasped at seeing the blackened form of his uncle.

Was this truly Aurelius Ambrosius looming over Morgan and his wife?

"Help him... whoever he is." And Arthur turned to run to protect the figures behind them.

"Help him? Fuck me. I guess I can hold a towel for him or something". Bors stepped to the shirtless man's flank, trying to keep out of the way of the spinning, flashing blade.

***

I froze, staring helplessly up at the sight looming above me.

As I watched, the terrible injuries from his cooking healed like they had never been there, and soon, I was again in the presence of Uther's scarier-looking double.

"Who are you?" I whispered.

173

"It doesn't matter. All you need to do is answer one important question, and then I'll probably just kill you. That sounds fair, doesn't it?"

"Depends on the question." I was feeling distinctly more terrified than my voice betrayed. This guy had just tanked Drynwyn. I didn't know what to do with that. Arthur and the combined might of every protection Merlin could load upon him hadn't been able to do that.

What the fuck was I supposed to do about him?

My head rocked back as he slapped me. A bunch of teeth flew from my mouth and instantly regrew. Hey, on the upside, this Elixir was the bomb.

"Do not be impertinent. I can always restart your time loop. Where. Is. Merlin?"

Look, I don't have much of a poker face. I'd generally found losing at strip poker tended to open more doors for me than it didn't. So, I don't think I'm entirely to blame for my eyes slipping towards the crumpled form of Melehan.

"So, it is what I thought", the scary dude turned away, seemingly dismissing me from his existence. I don't know why, but this pissed me off, but I was smart enough to know there was not a thing in the world I was going to be able to do about it.

Then Arthur was there.

I'm sure I've mentioned it before, but it is worth repeating that this guy can handle his spear.

He arrived like a giant bird of prey swooping down onto the back of the other man, spear poised to eviscerate him. I thought for sure we were in game-over territory for a moment, but then Uther's double turned and deflected the strike away with his own spear.

Arthur landed, rolled and was back on the offensive in moments, doing everything he could to turn the dude into a pincushion.

We've all seen the Viper versus the Mountain scene, right? Google it and have it playing in the background for a bit. This was just like that.

Hopefully, though, we're going to get a slightly different outcome . . .

"I need a weapon," Guinevere's voice startled me from my Season 4 reverie. I turned to see the Princess rising to stand. Her clothes made a sickening, squelching noise as she did so, the litres upon litres of blood adding quite a visual impact to her appearance.

Even then, she was still managing to be the most luminous woman I've ever seen. The bitch.

Ignoring me- I was beginning to get a bit miffed about that. What sort of rescue attempt was this? - she ran down towards the Dark Tower and liberated a spear from the cold-dead hands of one of the dozens of Saxons littering the ground.

Looking that way, I could see Lancelot and, to a lesser extent, Bors going absolutely to town on the remaining blue-painted figures. I mean, like full-on Darth Vader coming down that corridor at the end of Rogue One. These guys were going hard.

I could be wrong, but I was sure Guinevere missed a step when she glanced at Lancelot. But if she did, it was only briefly and then she was running back to help Arthur.

I watched them two-on-one the big guy for a moment, before hurrying back to Melehan's side.

Uther's double was clearly toying with them, and we needed a better plan. Don't get me wrong, they were, in this instant, the very definition of a power couple. I doubt many opponents could have stood in the way of their graceful, synchronised movements. Each seemed to know exactly where the other was, their attacks and defences in perfect unison.

I bet their sex life was amazing . . .

I shook that thought from my mind. Regardless of how utterly awesome these two were, they made no impression on the big guy whatsoever. He was barely even defending, letting both their spears trace red streaks over his body, injuries that healed immediately.

"Who the fuck is this?"

Melehan's . . . Merlin's? Who the fuck knows at this stage? voice was faint. *Aurelius Ambrosius. He's Arthur's Uncle.*

"I think he's a bit more than that! That dude tanked Drynwyn, and he's making Guinevere and Arthur look like irritating gnats at a picnic." I paused for a second. "He's the guy who tore me out of time, isn't he? He ripped out my techniques. Big M, I was in a time loop forever." I could feel tears streaming down my face again. "What do I do?"

I can get you to my tower.

There was a curse behind me, and I risked a glance back. Arthur was on one knee, his arm broken. Then it reknitted with a click - damn, it really was the little Elixir that could - and he was back in the fray.

"How? You can't fast-travel when another cultivator is about."

Melehan ... Merlin smiled. You can if you don't care about making it out in one piece. He passed me back my Curing Rock. *I need a mana store. The well is dry. Or, rather, I guess the beach is empty.*

I grabbed one from my inventory and pressed it into his hand.

"Now what?"

Now we see if I was as good as everyone said.

CHAPTER 42 - IN WHICH ALL IS FUN AND GAMES. UNTIL SOMEONE DROPS A NUKE.

Merlin dropped onto the desolate beach where he knew he would find Melehan. The Saxon wizard was still in the same position, knees drawn up, staring out into the distance. The sea did not seem to have either come in or gone out since the last time Merlin had visited his host - the waves still lapping just short of Melehan's feet. The same hazy mist hovered just above the horizon, hiding anything that may be visible.

Merlin quickly crossed over the grey sand - it would be fair to say the overall atmosphere of Depression Cove hadn't perked up much in the last few days - and sat beside him. "Hello, Melehan. How are things?"

As he'd pretty much expected, there was no response. If the Saxon even realised someone had joined him, he gave no sign.

"Look, obviously, I've not really done the right thing by you since my arrival. It would be fair to say that I got a little caught up with being alive again and haven't given you as much thought as I should have done. I've been taking advantage of you being all..." if there was a word other than 'broken' that Merlin could use in this circumstance, it eluded him for the moment. Honestly, it was hard to look at the desiccated shell that was Melehan right now and have any other word leap to mind. That doesn't matter. "What I'm trying to say is that what I have been doing was very wrong, and I'm extremely sorry. "

There was no response.

A frown creased Merlin's brow, and he felt a spike of irritation. "Not for nothing, my dear, but I can probably count on the fingers of one hand the number of people I have sincerely apologised to. I know you are not in a tremendous place - mental health-wise - but politeness costs nothing."

"What do you want, Merlin?" Melehan's voice was soft and indistinct, the gentle sound of the waves sliding up the beach almost drowning them out.

Merlin's frown vanished. Just for a moment there, he'd been worried he'd left it too late. There were countless stories of cultivators who'd slipped inside their cores when the going got tough and simply never came out again. The way time dilation worked here might have made it feel to Melehan that it was only moments since Merlin was last beside him.

Equally, though, it might have seemed like centuries.

All things being equal, then, the fact that the wizard was able to talk to him was a pretty good sign.

"Ah, hello there. You are compos mentis, after all. Excellent. Look, I'm going to level with you, things are looking pretty bad out in the real world at the moment."

Melehan carried on staring out across the sea. He did not appear to have blinked since Merlin had sat down. "I'm sorry to hear it. If you were wondering, things are looking pretty grim in here, too."

Merlin did his best not to look too carefully around the desolate beach. He did not have time to get too bummed out right now. "Yes. Yes, I can see that. Far be it from me to offer someone interior design tips on their own soul space, but you'd be amazed what a few well-chosen statement pieces can do. If you want, I could whip up a couple of nice cliff faces to jazz the landscape up a little. I don't know, but maybe an ice cream van or two? I could even encourage a few nymphs from my own internal space to pop in to keep you entertained."

"Tell me what you want or get out."

"Look, I'm trying to make amends here, Melehan. I have wronged you and want to make it up to you. Are you sure there's not anything I can offer?"

"The only thing I want, wizard, is to die."

Merlin did his absolute best to keep a grin from widening on his face. "Well, do you know what? It's funny you should say that..."

***

Aurelius was becoming bored.

The unexpected heat that had occurred when he caught Drynwyn had been mildly diverting. It had been an extremely long time since he'd held a Treasure of Britain in his hand - his Saxon hordes placed much less interest in collecting them than he could have hoped - and the remembrance of things past had put him in an uncharacteristic, good mood.

And then his nephew and - he presumed - the boy's wife had turned up to show no little skill with the spear, which also had the effect of reminding him of simpler days.

He and Uther had sparred in this way throughout their youth, and there was a pleasure in relieving, however, briefly, a period of his life where the most pressing issue of his existence was deciding which serving girl he would be fucking that evening.

But, as seemed to happen too regularly nowadays, there was no challenge to be found here, and ennui was settling in.

It was hard to take a fight seriously when, no matter how often they wounded him - and to be fair, they overcame his defences more often than he would have expected - he was never really in danger. After all, at his level of cultivation, no weapon forged by a human would ever bring him low.

Stifling a yawn, he decided to bring this diversion to a close.

With a lazy flick of his hand, he released a gust of wind - <Wind Surge> being one of his standby techniques for dismissing irritants - and slung his two attackers towards his men for them to finish off.

Hmmm.

What remained of his men.

What had happened there?

Aurelius's eyes quickly focused on a tall, beefy - why was he shirtless? - man putting the last of the Dark Tower's garrison to the sword. How had that godless barbarian got loose again? He'd been running merry hell through the town of Wansdyke when the panicked request for help had reached the Bretwalda. It had, of course, been the work of moments to transport him to one of the cells in the building above.

177

You didn't kill someone that good with a blade. Not if you might be able to make use of them in the future.

However, it looked like he was up to his same old tricks again. What good was it having Saxon minions when they could not subdue one lone barbarian? No matter how glossy his hair.

Aurelius's decent mood was quickly vanishing. He would need to deal with that one personally. Again. He did so hate repeating himself.

He spared the scene of casual destruction a few more heartbeats until his nephew and his woman crashed into a pile of corpses.

Without waiting to see if they'd survived their impromptu flight, he returned his attention to Merlin's apprentice and the Saxon wizard he now suspected was hosting some remnant of his old foe's spirit.

The apprentice was crying, which he didn't much care for.

His captors hadn't cared when he cried, had they? How could she not have learned that most basic of lessons yet? When you were a cultivator, no one cared how you felt. Tears did not mean anything. You took what you needed because there was no one to save you.

Cultivating 101.

What did she possibly have to weep about? After everything he'd done for her? Did she not understand the honour he had done her! A spark of fury ignited in his Qi, and the air around him shrieked as it evaporated in the heat of his anger.

This apprentice had been given an infinite amount of time to cultivate. He'd removed all the frivolous techniques she'd been allowed to pick up. And she'd had all the distracting demands of life withdrawn from her. She had no need to eat, to drink, to sleep. What better situation could she possibly have found herself in to grow strong?

He'd had to do it the hard way. Day by day, year by year, beating by beating. She'd had decades to develop her craft and had barely been out of the world a day!

And how was she thanking him? By sobbing like a baby.

He strode forward and grabbed her by the scruff of the neck. Merlin's apprentice hung limply in his grasp, not even bothering to fight back, which irritated him even more.

He shook her to try to get some sort of reaction. You didn't give up like this. You didn't surrender. You fought with tooth and claw. And when they ripped those out, you grew new ones and kept fighting some more.

With the girl seemingly unconscious in his hand, he looked down at - presumably - the cause of her woe. The Saxon with the missing arm was pretty much dead. Which meant if, as he suspected, this wizard was a repository for the last bit of Merlin's soul, it was just a few more moments before that wanker was finally purged from this world.

It made sense, he supposed.

For the last six months, Aurelius had always had that nagging feeling that this particular door was not quite closed. This was why he had wasted so much time and energy removing any potential from the timeline that could offer that old goat something to hold on to.

It was unpleasant work—and Aurelius was not proud of the innocent blood he bathed his hands in—but if you wanted a job done, it was better to do it once. Do it thoroughly. And salt the earth behind you.

He gave the girl a shake.

And yet, this pathetic specimen had slipped through. Looking at her, though, he could understand how he may have missed her during the slaughter. If this was all the fight of which she was capable, it was no wonder.

He kicked the broken figure at his feet. "You have Merlin inside you, don't you?" Maybe he shouldn't have pulled off his arm. But it was easy to forget how fragile people were sometimes.

To his surprise, the eyes of the wizard flicked open slowly. "Aurelius?"

"Ah! So you do recognise me. I'm glad. It has been a matter of profound sorrow that you died without knowing who was responsible. I'm glad to be here at the end to witness your final passing from the world. It does me good to feel your despair."

"You . . . always . . . were . . ." Melehan's voice was barely a whisper.

Aureus leant down towards him. The girl dangling in his grip: "What? Clever? Devious? Inevitable?"

Melehan wet his lips with a grey tongue. He clearly only had seconds to live.

"No." Another deep breath. Then, the Saxon's eyes suddenly became extraordinarily focused and filled with awareness. "A needy cunt."

And then, a series of unfortunate events took place.

***

Melehan had been sure that his weeks of torture at the hands of Cedric would have done something to cleanse his soul. To bring the scales back into balance after what he had done.

But no. He was too much in the red for that.

As soon as he had looked at his soul space, he knew there would be no way to make amends for the lives he had taken at Isca.

That awareness had broken his mind.

It had taken Merlin to show him a way to finally bring it all to an end.

His eyes narrowed on the High King. The man who had forced him onto the path his life had taken. He had never wanted to be a battle wizard. He had found such joy in his small acts of cultivation.

Well, no more of that.

He felt the Qi block fall over him, indicating he was within another wizard's aura. Fighting his every instinct, he braced himself and pressed through it.

But try as he might, he couldn't quite force the fast travel destination to connect.

"Merlin?" he shouted into the void.

***

He's too close, my dear.

"I don't know what that means!" My head was feeling crushed by a build-up of Qi in the atmosphere

It's so nearly there. We just need a bit of distance from Aureluis. Can you push him?

"I'm dangling a foot from the ground by the neck. I'm strong, but I don't think I can do much. I can try to stagger him with my wit?"

My dear, I'd forgotten what a hoot you could be. Perhaps, I don't know, use your Qi?

I fired up <Personal Space Invader> and gave it everything I'd got. I moved Aurelus, maybe three feet back. So, there was that.

179

MALORY

Hey, on the plus side, he dropped me.
"Far enough?"
The Uther lookalike was already walking back towards us, a grim expression on his gloomy face.
I wish there were another adjective, but I was shitting myself.
"Far enough," I heard Melehan murmur. "For Isca"
And everything went white. And very loud.

CHAPTER 43 – IN WHICH SOMEONE NEEDS TO PICK UP THE PIECES OF A VERY PISSED OFF BIG BAD

He did not know how long he had been unconscious.

But, then again, did it count as being 'unconscious' when your very soul had been sheared away from your body and left to find its own way home? Aurelius did not know.

He was pretty sure that, at least for a moment back there, he had actually died. He had felt everything that was 'Aurelius Ambrosius' cease to be and merge with the story of the universe. In many ways, this had not been an entirely unpleasant experience. After nurturing so much hate and anger for so long, there was the ecstasy of release to be found in suddenly not needing to be that person any longer.

But then, of course, the inevitability of death came up against the force of his implacable will, and the Grim Reaper decided he had easier targets to visit that day.

With a sharp intake of breath, therefore, consciousness returned to the Bretwalda. What had been dead was now alive. However, whether that would turn out to be any sort of blessing remained to be seen.

His eyes started to pull the world around him into focus, and he recognised that there was a human-shaped form peering over him.

Well, his right eye did, anyway.

He did not appear to possess a left one anymore.

That was an unwelcome, if not wholly surprising, development.

The intensity of the torches in the tent he found himself in caused him to wince in agony, and he raised a hand to shield his face. Well, he would have done if he'd had a hand to raise. Or an arm.

Or a . . .

To be fair, he'd had less traumatic wake-ups in his time.

He could not seem to remember what had caused this level of catastrophic damage. Had he been training his resistances and, somehow, completely underestimated the dosages of his potions? That seemed spectacularly unlikely, but then again, so did his finding himself in such an appalling state. All things needed to be considered. Even his own fallibility.

Memories slowly began filtering back to the forefront of his mind, jostling the overwhelming pain out of the way as he sought to make sense of what had occurred.

Something had exploded. He could remember that vividly. And, unusually enough, he did not feel that he had been the one to cause it.

Which was odd because if there had been an explosion strong enough to put him flat on his back, with body parts missing, he would have expected he must have been the one to cause it.

No. Not *something* had exploded. *Someone.*

He had been moving towards a figure. Whoever it had been had seemed very important at the time. He could still taste the residue of his rage towards that person at the back of what remained of his throat.

He had been seconds from killing them, and then . . . this had happened.

Whatever 'this' was.

Knowing that the quickest journey towards answers was going to be getting some healing on board, Aurelius tried to move himself into his soul space. However, in a further unwelcome development, he found he did not even have enough Qi to perform even that most basic of cultivation techniques.

He couldn't remember the last time such a thing had happened. He always had enough Qi. That was kind of his thing.

The whole situation was baffling him and, what is more, he was feeling desperately dehydrated,

As he no longer appeared to have a tongue, it took him longer than he would have liked to be able to croak out, "Water!"

The terrified-looking Saxon in his eye-line, looked down when Aurelius made this request with an expression that was one-part relieved, two-parts disappointed, and - he was glad to see - all parts terrified.

The man withdrew and reappeared with a cup he pressed to the High King's lips. Or where his lips would have been in a less brutally judgmental universe. As it was, the cup's rim rested against the exposed bone of Aurelius' lower skull.

"Are . . . quite well, my lord?"

"Perfectly fine, you fucking moron. I find I am always at my best when the skin has been flayed from my bones…" was what he would have liked to have said. But you needed more vocal apparatus than the explosion seemed to have left him right now for that sort of snark.

He settled for making some sort of non-descript groaning noise instead. Fortunately, though, the water that was being poured down into his gullet had just enough residue Qi for the most minor of repairs to begin.

It was true what they said. Every little bit helps. Although he assumed that the purveyors of that little aphorism didn't have this sort of situation in mind. He still couldn't prise open his soul space, though.

Aurelius' attention returned to the man above him, who was still wittering on. "We were initially concerned that you had passed. However, after careful examination, it seemed that there was still a spark of life within you. I do not mind sharing, my lord, that we feared . . ."

"Yes, I can smell it."

Aurelius's mind tried to access the fragments of memories he still possessed. He found that if he moved backwards away from the moment of the devastating conflagration, things were a little clearer. "The captives? What had become of the Britons?"

There was a longer pause than suggested he was about to be presented with good news. "The explosion, my lord, it was utterly overwhelming. Indeed, we witnessed it all the way from Halwell Fort, where we were stationed. It was like the world was ending - the noise and brightness dwarfed even the sun. As soon as we saw it coming from the direction of the Dark Tower, I knew it was crucial to investigate. We made good time - it was only a week to get here - our wizard said there was something preventing her from fast-travelling. When we arrived . . . well, we found you and nothing else."

Aurelius ground his teeth, or he would have done if he had any left. He crunched bone together in a significant show of irritation. "No bodies?"

"No anything, my lord. I should be clear, our scouts have reported that there is not *anything* for about three miles in every direction. Even the soil has been reduced to a colourless nothingness. It is as if the landscape has been wholly scrubbed of life."

Aurelius let that news settle for a moment. Whatever had occurred was unlike any offensive Qi technique he had ever encountered. That sort of leaching of life was almost counter to the very nature of Qi. What on earth had happened. "And my tower?"

"We have summoned slaves to begin the process of rebuilding."

Well, that was the final turd on a monumentally appalling morning. Quite apart from losing the perfect place to cycle Qi - and all the advantages that had given him - there was the loss of all those prisoners for whom he had such exotic plans. That hurt almost as much as the actual exquisite agony his wounds were causing him.

"Bring me your company's wizard. Immediately."

The anxious face above him became even more concerned. If that was possible. "That . . . I mean to say, I cannot, my lord. We were still a day away when she suddenly cried out in agony, holding her heart, and then dissolved into ash."

Aurelius cursed, but he supposed that made a sort of perverted sense. Whatever had happened had drained all the Qi in the surrounding area - which explained why he was still in such a state a week after the event. Even debilitated, he should have been able to regen enough Qi to rebuild his ruined body. However, if this part of the world had been transformed in a Qi vortex - which he feared it might - then things began to make a bit more sense. Anyone unfortunate enough to wander into such a dead zone would suffer a catastrophic loss of atomic cohesion pretty damn quickly. Those with Qi would succumb first - it was a testament to his epic levels of resilience that he was still in one piece - but normal humans would not be far behind on the death train.

"I would guess your war band are all becoming sick?" Aurelius hazarded.

The man nodded, brightening now the Bretwalda had given voice to their plight. Half of the spears under his command had already taken to their beds - from how they looked, he did not think they had long left before they went the way of the unfortunate wizard. "Yes, my lord. It would be excellent if you were able to -"

Aurelius ignored him and tried to roll his torso to the side to sit up. He had minimal success in this endeavour. As he was missing all his arms and legs and, thus, lacked some fairly significant appendages for such a movement, this was not much of a surprise.

Merlin had paid him back, after all.

That thought, appearing unbidden in his mind, dragged him back to what had happened in those last few moments he could remember. However, no matter how he thought about it, his brain rebelled at the very concept of another cultivator having access to that sort of ability.

The power it must have taken . . .

"I'm sorry, my lord. I missed that?" The anxious man was not especially keen to get too close to the ruined remains of the High King. You never knew when dead could be catching.

"I said, 'Merlin's back.' And we will need to address that."

Aurelius closed his eye. Nope. Needed an eyelid for that. This whole situation was becoming quite unbearable.

"Pluck out my eye."

"My lord?"

"I don't have any eyelids. So I can't blink. So, my eyeball is tinder dry, and it hurts. Pluck it out. Now."

"I don't think that is a good idea, my lord."

"You truly do not wish to know all the things that are good ideas to me right now. If you do not wish my next mission in this world to be removing you and your entire bloodline from existence, you will do exactly as I say. Remove my fucking eye."

In the darkness that enveloped him, Aurelius found himself - bizarrely - realising he was not too displeased by things.

It felt pretty counterintuitive, but it was just possible this was not the terrible event he had initially thought. After all, in the six months since the 'death' of Merlin, it had been challenging to find things to motivate him.

It was true that Uther's surprising success in repelling the Saxon invasion had been mildly diverting. But now it seemed that Merlin was not quite so dead as had been advertised, and juices were flowing anew—or they would have been if he still retained any juices. That would come with time and distance from ground zero— that he had not realised he had missed.

He had killed the old goat once before, and he could absolutely do it again. Whenever he wanted.

The pleasure, after all, was in the expectation.

But first, he needed to get out of this Qi dead zone before this sorry little warband turned to dust and left him all alone again.

He gave orders for a litter to be constructed, for messengers to be sent far and wide to alert the rest of his people to his plight, and for him to be carried as fast as possible, towards home.

He assumed this first group—and potentially even a second—would perish before he was far enough out of the toxic air where his Dark Tower had stood to heal himself. However, provided the willing sacrifices kept on coming, things would work out okay.

And once he was back to normal?

Well, then there would be quite a reckoning for Uther, for Arthur, for Merlin and for his blasted apprentice.

CHAPTER 44 – IN WHICH THERE IS CONSIDERABLE EFFORT TO FIND THE UPSIDE

We tumbled out onto the ground floor of Merlin's tower. Once I had my bearings, I performed a quick head count, and - somewhat shockingly - we all seemed to be there.

Minus Melehan, anyway.

That 'all' was a bit insensitive, wasn't it?

That was the second time the Saxon wizard had saved my life. I didn't think there would be a third.

It turns out that the whole 'cultivators cannot fast travel within the aura of other cultivators' was less an immutable law of the universe and more like some pretty helpful health and safety advice.

Kind of like not allowing a toddler under the influence of top-quality LSD to drive a tank through a tea shop during a Women's Institute bake sale. I mean, sure, you can do it if you want, but the outcome is likely to be reasonably sub-optimal for all concerned.

Unlike when he'd saved Arthur and me from Cedric at the end of that disastrous battle, the act of pushing a bit of group fast travelling through Aurelius's aura had caused some spectacular - if brief - consequences for everyone left behind.

He had a choice to make, my dear, and he made it without fear. Without pain. He only was holding on to a great determination to make amends as he passed. He was relieved, if anything.

"Yeah, I'm afraid that doesn't help at all, Big M. But thanks for making the effort."

"Everyone okay?" Bors was the first of us up on his feet. "Arthur? Gwin? Strange man I never, ever, ever want to face in a duel?"

Various groans indicated the little party was, if not positively chipper, then alive and kicking.

"I'm fine too, by the way!"

Bots looked at me and grinned massively. "Of course you are, you little chaos monkey. You don't think I missed you jumping off a tower five hundred feet in the air, shaking that off, bulldozing your way through a war band, and then going *mano a mano* with Aurelius fucking Ambrosius." He clapped me on my back, fracturing at least three of my ribs. "If I had a hat - which I don't as they make my ears look too big according to Mrs. Bors - but if I did, I'd tip it to you. That shit was tight."

He appeared to be holding on to a very different memory of recent events than I did, but as I opened my mouth to disagree, he'd already moved on to grab Lancelot in a big bear hug. "And you, you big loveable ball of certain death? You are my new best friend in the whole world."

Lancelot laughed and hugged him back. "Ah, thanking you, 1 am!"

But I couldn't help but notice that the barbarian's attention wasn't on the hairy colossus squeezing his life out like the last smidgen of toothpaste.

It was on the woman slowly getting to her feet, helped by her husband.

"She has pretty hair," I heard him murmur.

Fuck. What had I done?

****

After tanking my way through insane amounts of damage in and around the Dark Tower, it was thus a bit humiliating to spend the next four weeks in bed.

While my alchemy scrolls were long on that science's wonders, they were a touch shorter on the epic effect side aspects.

Apparently, one Elixir of Wellness would land you on your arse for a few hours when its effects wore off. In the volumes I had downed them . . . well, as the Big M put it, this was one of those very limited set of circumstances where a decade-plus of massive substance misuse stood me in good stead.

Actually, what I said was that all the parts of you the toxic build-up should have scoured away were already gone. Basically, the only way I can make sense of you still being alive following such frivolous use of massively powerful chemicals is that you should already be dead.

Potato, potahto.

I still felt like absolute shit, though.

If you're worried about Lancelot? Don't be. From what I am told, he woke up the next day with a "pain in my belly", drank a few gallons of mead, and the wanker was out bear hunting with Arthur and Bors in the afternoon.

I don't want to give you the impression I was feeling a little pushed out by that ungodly sausage fest, but I was. I absolutely was.

And I wasn't the only one feeling down about recent events.

I'm sorry I let you down, Morgan.

"I've repeatedly told you, mate, that you didn't. If you couldn't turn that guy into charcoal, then what sword in the world could."

You needed me to come through for you, and I didn't. I'm not sure I can ever forgive myself. You might as well melt me down and start again.

I don't know what was worse: having Drynwyn with performance anxiety or that he had stopped swearing.

Both were pretty weird.

I'd spent most of my convalescence trying to make up for lost learning time with Merlin.

If my interminable span in the Dark Tower's time loop had taught me anything, it was that I simply did not know enough about what I was doing. Although Merlin had been going on and on about my lack of proper foundations, I hadn't come across a problem in the Dark Ages I hadn't been able to blag my way through.

My encounter with the Bretwalda changed that, and I had promised myself that I would never be in that situation again.

If the Big M was impressed by my newfound determination to be top of the cultivation class, he was good enough not to make too much about it.

It turned out I could do an awful lot of remedial cultivation during a month of bed rest.

My alchemy improved a fair bit during this time, too. As I'd thought, brewing up in a Treasure of Britain significantly upped my game, and I was starting to learn some pretty interesting things.

I never really saw the point in alchemy, Merlin said sniffily. *There are natural treasures in the world that do everything you can dream of. It has always been my opinion that spending your time looking for them is better than trying to make inferior versions of your own.*

"You're just bitter because no one liked you enough to give you a magic Cauldron as a 'thank you', aren't you?"

Am I jealous that Morgan Le Fey - the original Morgan Le Fey; that wild cat from the nether pit of hell that once tried to raise the seas to swallow the world - never felt the need to show me some gratitude? No. No, I am not.

"You know, in most of the stories I've read, you are quite the hot and heavy couple over the years?"

Don't believe everything you read.

"What, so you never were tempted to dip your wick? Play Find the Wand? Delve the Qi? Butter some parsnips. Plunge the-"

I think I preferred it when I was in Melehan's head. He had a nice line in moody silences that you could learn quite a lot from. Are you ever planning on stopping?

"Probably. I wasn't sure where that one was going, to be honest. But seriously, did you know her way back when?"

There was a pause.

I wasn't always the most powerful Cultivator in the land.

"Stop!"

Do you want the story, or do you want to be . . . you?

"You know, I'd love it if I could do both."

Well, tough. It is not a long story, but it is probably instructive for you to know it. There were a number of us who all came into our power at the same time. Morgana was one; I was another. It was long ago and a very different time. I may not have been the righteous man who - well, not stands before you today, but you know what I'm getting at. Essentially, my dear, if you think I am difficult now, you should have seen what I was like end before a millennia or so smoothed out my edges.

There was a tone to his voice that encouraged me not to interrupt.

Cultivators are encouraged to fight to test themselves against others. Mostly, this can be done in a spirit of learning. However, occasionally, accidents happen. And when they do, the spoils go to the victor.

I took a moment to think through his words. "I envisage a Highlander, 'There Can Be Only One' situation here."

Then you wouldn't be too far from the truth.

"So, you became the biggest, baddest spellcaster by, what, murdering all your friends?"

There was another long pause.

There are certainly some versions of what happened back then that would not argue against that being the truth.

"What about your version?"

Merlin sighed with lungs he no longer had.

I was young and powerful, and I did not trust anyone. Least of all, Morgana. I don't think either of us would come out too well from a detailed examination of our actions back then. But, my dear, it is not ancient history that needs to concern us.

I sat up a little in my bed, knocking alchemy scrolls to the floor. "Aurelius?"

Indeed. He was no cultivator when I knew him. It is not unheard of for traumatic events to unlock latent potential, but there is no way he could have reached - he paused - I'm going to say the words 'Bellatrix Lestrange' for the sake of speeding things up, and I hope we all understand what I mean and that no more needs to be said about it.

"My lips are sealed, Big M."

Good. Well, there is simply no version of linear progression by which he could have reached the level of cultivation required to challenge me.

"Dude, he didn't challenge you. He killed you. Without you knowing. My man got himself some skills."

The point still holds, my dear. The man has clearly used every trick in the cultivating handbook to reach his current cultivation level. And he has had years and years to do so.

I let that thought percolate through my mind for a moment. "So, what do we do?"

As recent events have made abundantly clear, you cannot hope to challenge him yet. But, and this is where we have some good news, he will be experiencing the same issue that plagued me in my later years—progression at the higher levels is complex. He is probably as strong as he will be for hundreds of years. You've got a wide-open future of development ahead of you.

"Am I understanding that the 'good news' take here is that our opponent is so far advanced compared to us that he can't actually get all that much stronger?"

If you put it like that, it sounds so much bleaker, right? But for clarity, he absolutely can get stronger. Insanely so. But the more important question is whether he will do so in our timespan to do something about him before he kills us all? No, probably not.

"Can't imagine why I thought things were bleak. I am going to need to put in insane amounts of hard work here, aren't I, Big M?"

You absolutely are, Little M.

"Nah, I don't think that's going to stick."

I'll see how it goes.

I missed the opportunity to argue because a servant had appeared at my door.

I had an audience with King Uther ahead of me.

CHAPTER 45 – IN WHICH ARTHUR AND I BURY THE HATCHET

King Uther looked like he'd aged about fifty years.

I guess finding out the brother you had killed during a duel decades ago was not only not dead, but an insanely powerful cultivator in charge of the Saxon population of the British Isles will do that to you.

To be fair, Queen Igraine didn't look much better, but I think that had more to do with her worry about her husband. Considering the generally antagonistic nature of their relationship - at least as far as I had witnessed it - it was really disconcerting to see the depth of the concern on her face when she looked at him.

"And you're sure it was Aurelius?" Uther asked me for the hundredth time.

"Your majesty, I can only tell you what Merlin said. To me, he was just this big, powerful wizard who looked spookily like you."

Although I reflected, not so much at the moment. Even coming out from under a Drynwyn special, Aurelius still had a bit more about him than the Pendragon. Uther looked awful . . . "However, the Big M had no doubt. The dude with the scary Dark Tower was Aurelius Ambrosius."

Uther shook his head and gazed down at his hands. Which he was wringing. Like a bearded Lady Macbeth without access to some really decent Lush consumables. "To think he was alive all this time! The years that he has been lost to me."

I exchanged a furtive glance with Bors, who had the same look of deep disconcertion on his face as I presumably did.

I was definitely missing good old kill-them-all-and-burn-their-corpses Uther. This sad sack with the worried eyes was not inspiring me with confidence that we would come out swinging at the Saxons. I decided to try some of my legendary wit and charm. "With all due respect, Your Majesty, I don't really think the issue here is him being lost to you. There's not a tearful sibling reunion coming in your near future. The guy's Dr. Doom, mixed with the Emperor, with extra sprinklings of Sauron on top. Merlin is pretty sure he would have been able to tank the explosion we left behind, so we really do need to, you know, start suiting up before he kicks off Round Three."

"Perhaps," the King sighed, "but we must not give up hope."

Fuck me.

The last thing I expected from him was to deflate this badly. We had a serious issue here. Apparently, the Prince of the Britons was feeling the same concern.

Arthur, standing at the back of the chamber, cleared his throat. "Hope, father? Have you entirely taken leave of your senses? We have a Saxon warband camped on the banks of the Kammel. Their Bretwalda is a cultivator to which we have no match, and our greatest fortress is no more. I think we are beyond the stage where we 'hope'. You need to call the witan, gather the kingdoms to your banner and put together a plan that puts us on the offensive."

I braced myself for another explosive chorus of 'Go fuck your wife,' but Uther merely nodded and sighed. "Perhaps you are right. I just am not sure whether this would not be too aggressive a move."

Seriously, we were in trouble here.

Arthur must have sensed the same, and he pushed off the wall to stride forward. Obviously, there were more significant problems right now, but I still couldn't help but wonder what Guinevere and Lancelot were up to at this moment. "Father, we cannot just sit here and hope the Saxons will leave us alone. You are the Pendragon. With the combined might of the kingdoms, we can put enough men in the field to push them all the way over the river and some distance back beside. But we must do it soon. I beg you to give me leave to . . ."

"Granted." Uther's voice was soft. "Prince Arthur, you have my complete confidence in this matter." And with that, he gathered up his furs and made his way, tottering much more than I remembered, from the room. Fucking hell, he'd lost a lot of weight since I'd last seen him.

Igraine looked at him, appalled, and then hurried after him, shaking her head toward her son.

That left just the two of us in the throne room. We were silent for a minute, and Arthur turned to face me, scratching his beard thoughtfully. He remained as bald as a coot. "Did that sound to you like I've just been put in charge of leading a counter-offensive?"

"Dude, that sounded like an abdication."

"None of that," he snapped, his face suddenly grim. "I don't have the support amongst the other kingdoms. Sure, they'll stand for me leading their armies. But they won't accept me as the Pendragon. Not yet. That will all change if I can throw the Saxons back onto their own territories.

Arthur was talking a good game, but I couldn't shake the image of Uther stumbling from the throne room, a broken version of the imposing figure I had met with before the wholly disastrous "Quest for Guinevere." I mean, I had gone through some spectacular shit in the last month or so - including the fact that the month had lasted centuries. And I'd spent most of that time being tortured - and of the two of us, I was the one in the better shape. It kind of looked to me that Uther might be done.

I decided Arthur needed a bit of tough love. "Look, mate, I don't want to piss on anyone's chips, but you're going to need to get those other kings on board pretty quickly with you being the way forward. Your dad looks like he is one disappointing pudding away from a full-blown breakdown. We're talking King Theoden at the start of the Two Towers here. And I'm not sure he's pulling out of his funk."

Arthur's hand clanked against my breastplate. "You will speak of my father with respect!"

"And. lest we forget, you absolutely do not put your fucking hands on me."

To his credit, he apologised immediately.

Of course, that might have had something to do with Drynwyn growling softly at my side, but I'm going to choose to believe he simply remembered his manners.

Nevertheless, it was a good reminder that our relationship wasn't as stable as we might have hoped, especially given what was probably coming our way.

Arthur moved to sit on Uther's throne. I'd seen him do this countless times before - the action didn't seem to have any metaphorical importance to the Britons - but it still made me realise how close we were to Camelot becoming a thing.

And how far away we were from how it all felt in the Lore.

"Does Merlin have any words of advice?" Arthur asked.

Oh, boy, did he…

Most of what the Big M seemed to want to do next involved me brewing up some sort of epic-tier poison and then dumping it in every water source in Saxon-held lands. I'd tried to explain the concepts of collateral damage, war crimes and unacceptable civilian losses, but these seemed quite alien to him. In fact, he appeared to have priced them into his great strategic plan.

Eventually, though, he did have a couple of suggestions that didn't promote genocide.

"He says you need some big victories. It would be best if you won and were seen to win. Nothing builds on alliance faster than a big swinging cock to get behind."

"Merlin said that?"

"I extrapolated from, you know, the general gist."

There was a pause, and then, "What do you think of Lancelot?"

What did I think of him? No way was I walking into that bear trap. "What do you think of him, my lord?"

Arthur's face lit up like a child who'd been told not only was school closed for a snow day, but most of the teachers had been trapped inside and would likely freeze to death in the coming days.

My word, that was a dark simile. I really need to find a way to chill out.

"I like him. I think he'll be a massive boon for our chances of turning the tide. Did you see the man fight?"

"I imagine he is quite the swordsman. Experienced. Thorough. Probably gets the job done and more."

My dear… Merlin said warningly.

"Yes, he is very impressive, isn't he! He's already defeated everyone in the castle. I can just about beat him with a spear or a quarterstaff, but with a sword in his hand, there is simply no one to touch him."

The sheer joy on the man's face when he said this nearly made me weep.

The eventual betrayal will not define their relationship. Arthur and Lancelot are destined to be the closest friends before that turns to dust. Even then, at the very end, there will be forgiveness.

Somehow, that didn't quite settle the issue for me. I wondered how much strife I could help avoid now if I said the right words.

And how many years of laughter and joy would you forestall, too? Life is not about the avoidance of all pain. I would have thought you, of everyone, would understand that.

Hmmm. The rare valid point. While wondering how best to demolish that line of argument, I realised Arthur had spoken again. "Sorry, my Lord. Irritating wizard buzzing in my ear."

Arthur looked both slightly put out and also somewhat cowed. "You can hear him now?"

"Mate, he never shuts up."

"Okay." I thought he wanted to say something else but stopped himself. "Have you seen much of Guinevere?"

I hadn't. Like me, she'd had to deal with the after-effects of an overdose of Elixirs of Wellness and had been confined to her rooms.

"Not much. How is she since her injury?"

"She's well, thank you. Down to you, of course. I never really had the chance to thank you for everything you've done for us."

I opened my mouth to speak, but he pressed on. "Seeing my father... like that has brought home the precarious nature of the situation. I need to grow up, don't I?"

"No arguments from me on that score, mate."

My dear, he's trying to build bridges with you. Have a care. You don't need to burn them all down on the principal.

If Arthur had noted my tone, he didn't say anything. "I've asked her if we can try to start over. To put our recent past behind us."

"You mean all the epic fuckwittery?"

Arthur winced. "Yes. Although I did not put it like that, of course. I have promised to close that chapter of my life."

I was not able to restrain myself from shrugging. "What do you want, a round of applause?"

My dear...

Arthur slipped from the throne to stand directly in front of me. "I would like to try to make the same offer to you. There have been... incidents in our history that I regret. It had seemed to me that you were a poor version of someone I had cared a great deal for. But I now recognise that it is not your fault, and I should have treated you more respectfully. Can we wipe the slate clean and start again?

He held out his hand for me to shake.

Stability.

That seemed more important right now than holding on to grudges. He'd said all the right words, and if I wanted Camelot to actually become a thing, I needed to give peace a chance.

I took his hand - but squeezed it a little harder than I needed to. "I can get on board with that, my prince. But it needs to be all of it, you understand me. No fucking around on Guinevere, and you need to lean into the whole Once and Future King thing."

His nose screwed up at that. "You know, I fucking hate that title."

"Hey, I was voted 'Most Likely to be an Easy Lay' at secondary school. You got off easy."

EPILOGUE – IN WHICH WE BRING THE SECOND BOOK TO A CLOSE

Tintagel.

Where the Atlantic's finest attempts at erosion meet architectural optimism.

Where those who live within dare the elements to do their worst, while quietly acknowledging that they probably will.

Where history hangs as heavily as the fog, and the line between legend and reality is as blurry as the view on a typical Cornish day.

The fortress itself is perched atop a cliff that seems to sulk into the ocean and is a testament to what humans can achieve if they take in the weather, transport links, and essential comfort, then just go, 'fuck it, we're here now. Start building.'

Even by the mid-fifth century, Tintagel's stone walls were already heavily streaked with the residue of countless salty onslaughts, looking like they'd been doused in giant tears.

That's pathetic fallacy, that is.

As the Saxons became the most recent invaders to discover, the only way to reach the castle's entrance is a masterclass in the traditionally warm, friendly British welcome: a narrow, dangerous path above the sea that dares any visitor to slip and add their bones to the surf below. Then, at the end of this cheerful route stands the main gate, an intimidating mix of iron and oak that suggests a greeting more akin to "get the fuck out of here" than "please come on in, weary traveller. Would you like a cup of mead?"

Tintagel's towers rise above the walls, their tops shrouded in mist, of which Merlin's tower gives the best impression of disappearing off into another dimension—a dimension where upkeep isn't a priority.

Meanwhile, ravens, those cheerful symbols of impending doom, nest in the eaves, their caws blending with the wind's lament to create a soundtrack of perpetual melancholy.

Seriously, is it any wonder Uther was feeling a touch down about things?

Beyond the walls, the landscape continues with the theme. Windswept moors stretch out in all directions, dotted with shrubs that look like they've seen better days and trees that have lost the will to stand straight. And that ignored the destruction wrought by the Saxon army that had so recently squatted out there, like a malevolent toad, 'living off the land' as the popular euphemism for rape and pillage would have it.

So had it been, and so, for just a little longer would it have been.

For, just off the edge of the coast on which Tintagel stood, there was a ripple on the still surface of the ocean.

An observer may have thought a seal was just about to pop up for air, but only briefly as a mass of blonde hair breached the surface.

It was a woman, and she was strangely beautiful. As in, she had all the features that popular consciousness would recognise as attractive - giant, blue eyes, generous lips, a perfectly proportioned nose - but there was something ethereally odd about how they all sat together on her face.

Whilst she may have, superficially, looked human, the overall impression was more like she'd killed and skinned the most perfect woman in the world and was now wearing her like a slightly ill-fitting costume.

Let that description settle in for a moment.

Treading water, the woman looked around in confusion and the rising and falling surf for a few minutes, before blowing strands of hair from her face.

"Fucking hell. How many times? I told them that any old body of water won't do. This is the middle of the bloody ocean."

With a reasonably spectacular show of petulance, she started skulling towards the shore, hampered somewhat by only having one hand available to swim. In the other, she trailed a long, black blade behind her, which left sparks in the water its wake.

Before long - she swam with the speed of a cresting shark (a simile that has an awful lot more that is accurate about it, rather than just being a clever arrangement of words) - she reached a depth where she could walk and lifted the sword out of the water.

It was then that an interested observer would realise that the strange bubbling sound that had accompanied this woman's appearance was, in fact, the sound of the sword talking. Now free of the sea, it was possible to make out what it was saying.

"Shambles. That's what this is—a shambles. I'm surprised they didn't just plop me in the middle of a massive rock and get done with it. Seriously, I don't know why I bother."

The woman reached the shore and shook herself, the water evaporating off her clothes. She was tall and dressed in glowing blue robes. Her entire look was so fragile that the massive, black iron broadsword she was carrying was somewhat incongruous. However, it was as if it were nothing but a feather in her grip.

She paused, looking up at Tintagel's looming, boxy shape for a moment, then pressed on up the beach and towards the woods, following the mouth of the river.

There had to be a decent body of water she could find somewhere nearby.

And from there, she could finally be rid of this damned prima donna of a sword and get back home.

For the Lady in the… to be confirmed span of water had arrived in the world of Tintagel.

And she was bearing Excalibur.

<u>THANK YOU</u>

Hi everyone! I hope you enjoyed the broadening of the cast in Book 2. There's still a few more key Arthurian figures to show up. You'll have to see if they make an appearance in Book 3.

Arthur's needing to get his hand on a certain sword in the stone before the Saxons rock up for a rematch. So, there's a whole quest chain upcoming packed with goblins, dragons, goblins, the Fae, giant sea beasts and more goblins. There's a lot of goblins. Like . . . a lot.

If you've enjoyed the ride so far, I'd love for you to leave a review or spread the word. It's one of the best ways to keep this circus rolling, and it means a lot. Plus, it lets me know you're out there, as unhinged as the rest of us.

Thanks again for sticking with it. There's plenty more madness where this came from, and I can't wait to share it.

Cheers,

Malory
28/12/2024

QUEST FOR THE DARK BLADE

Book 3

By Malory

When the kingdom wobbles, there's only one way to steady it—grab a legendary sword. Simple, right? Wrong.

King Arthur's sitting on the British throne, but not everyone's buying the whole "Once and Future King" schtick. Apparently, what he needs to shut up the doubters is the Dark Blade. You know, the one. Massive sword which is oddly stuck in a rock, guarded by a soggy woman handing out weaponry like it's the prize in a raffle. (Seriously, who came up with this system?)

Enter me—baby Cultivator, reluctant hero, and professional screw-up. Now I'm stuck leading yet another merry band of misfits, this time into the Land of the Fae. Spoiler: it's less "fairy tale" and more "acid trip with a murder problem." The locals don't like us, the rules of reality are up for debate, and the sword? Let's just say it's playing hard to get.

Between Fae politics, magical prophecies, and Merlin's ghost reminding me how much more work I have to do before I'm actually any good at this, this is quite the road trip.

Welcome to the Dark Blade—where the magic's weird, the dangers are weirder, and betrayal is just a stab in the back away.

Coming Soon!

RISE OF MANKIND 6: AGE OF GLASS

By Jez Cajiao

The Age of Glass dawns, a fragile era balanced on the edge of oblivion. Will it shatter beneath the relentless hammer of fate?

From the depths of despair to the pinnacle of power, Matt's ascension to Dungeon Lord has been a crucible of blood and terror. But the higher he climbs, the more precarious his perch becomes. As winter's icy fingers close around his hard-won domain, Matt and his beleaguered allies yearn for respite. Instead, they face a nightmare beyond imagining.
The Coronaught infection sweeps through the land like wildfire, twisting human flesh into abominations that defy sanity. Grotesque mutations stalk the shadows, their hunger insatiable. In this maelstrom of horror, Matt must be more than a leader – he must become a legend.

With each agonizing decision, the weight of command threatens to crush his spirit. Can he salvage the humanity of the infected, or will the price of compassion be too steep? Nuclear fire looms on the horizon, a cleansing inferno that promises annihilation. How much of his soul will Matt sacrifice to shield his people from the coming storm?

In the bowels of the earth, Matt labors to transform his dungeon into an impregnable fortress. But in a world where loyalty shatters like spun sugar, yesterday's allies may become tomorrow's executioners. Survival exacts a terrible toll, paid in blood and betrayal.

Step carefully into the Age of Glass, where every triumph balances on a knife's edge, and a single misstep can leave you bleeding in the dark.

Preorder Now!

__THEFT OF DECKS__

By Lars Machmüller

When the deck is stacked against you? Change the game!

In the frontier town of Isarn, Chase will never be more than the lowly Darkborn thief he is. Banned from training, banned from acquiring better cards, if the Lightborn had their way, he'd be banned from life itself.

He's not alone though, and the one thing he and his friends have is determination. Losing a hand to a brutal punishment only fueled his obsession to get access to his own amazing, reality-bending cards.

That is the path to power and a future for them all. Nobody cares where you came from when you're rich enough. For now, though, they're facing both established powers, churches and age-old prejudices. It's time to get to work, and if the Lightborn won't share and play nice?

Sometimes the only way to get dealt a better hand is to steal the whole damn deck!

__Buy on Amazon__

QUEST ACADEMY

By Brian J. Nordon

A world infested by demons.
An Academy designed to train Heroes to save humanity from annihilation.
A new student's power could make all the difference.

Humans have been pushed to the brink of extinction by an ever-evolving demonic threat. Portals are opening faster than ever, Towers bursting into the skies and Dungeons being mined below the last safe havens of society. The demons are winning.

Quest Academy stands defiantly against them, as a place to train the next generation of Heroes. The Guild Association is holding the line, but are in dire need of new blood and the powerful abilities they could bring to the battlefront. To be the saviors that humanity needs, they need to surpass the limits of those that came before them.

In a war with everything on the line, every power matters. With an adaptive enemy, comes the need for a constant shift in tactics. A new age of strategy is emerging, with even the unlikeliest of Heroes making an impact.

Salvatore Argento has never seen a demon.
He has never aspired to become a Hero.
Yet his power might be the one to tip the odds in humanity's favor.

<u>Buy on Amazon</u>

WANDERING WARRIOR

By Michael Head

A divine quest to deliver justice.
One year to accomplish his mission.
After nineteen planets, there's something different about this one.

James Holden has reached the maximum level there is for a human. That's perfect, since he's the only one of his kind. A wandering warrior, without control of his destination, tossed between universes by gods who've failed to tell him why. James is the lone Judge on a new world in need of someone to balance the scales. He isn't afraid to do so with extreme prejudice. As the Chief Justice, he has to right the wrongs the innocent can't fix themselves.

As James quickly discovers, the roots of corruption run deep. Guilds choose to protect themselves rather than the people. Monsters roam the wilderness unchecked. Judgment is usually a decision between right and wrong, but nothing is ever that simple. This time, being the strongest human won't be enough to punish the guilty. James might have to recruit some new blood, even if he prefers to work alone.

On his twentieth world, he is going to win, no matter the cost. James will have to find a way to break past the limits of the system if he's going to have a chance at making a difference.

<u>Buy on Amazon</u>

KNIGHTS OF ETERNITY

By Rachel Ní Chuirc

When Zara awoke in chains she thought she'd gone mad.

She was Zara the Fury - mistress of flame and fear. Her name was whispered across the land, from ramshackle taverns to the royal court. Even the heroic Gilded Knights thought twice before crossing her path.
She was feared—*respected.*
Now she was curled up on a dirt floor on her fiancé's orders. Valerius, leader of the Gilded, mocks her cries for help. And the kingdom is on the brink of war over the missing Lady Eternity…
But that wasn't why Zara thought she had gone mad.
The reason why is that the last thing she remembered was blood, an arcade screen, and the gun that changed everything.

But no chains can hold the Fury, and when she gets out?
The world is going to *burn.*

<u>Buy on Amazon</u>

SCARLET CITADEL

By Jack Fields

Gormon Hughes is 19, thin as a broom, and has—not for the first time in his life—been swept into the path of trouble. Poor, recently heartbroken, and indebted to the sort of people who file their teeth into needle points and devour wriggling bloated spiders for fun, Hughes sets his sights on salvation.

That salvation is the Scarlet Citadel, a wealthy organization of pageant fighters, monster hunters, and secret keepers. With the aid of strange oracles, rare good fortune, and a unique power that bubbles like champagne in the core of Hughes' being, he must join the Citadel and advance himself.

But the ladder of progression is harsh and dark. The rungs are slippery.

And falling means disaster…

Buy on Amazon

<u>LITRPG!</u>

To learn more about LitRPG, talk to other authors including myself, and to just have an awesome time, please join the LitRPG Group

<u>www.facebook.com/groups/LitRPGGroup</u>

FACEBOOK

There's also a few really active Facebook groups I'd recommend you join, as you'll get to hear about great new books, new releases and interact with all your (new) favorite authors! (I may also be there, skulking at the back and enjoying the memes…)

https://www.facebook.com/groups/LitRPGlegion/

https://www.facebook.com/groups/GamelitSociety

https://www.facebook.com/groups/LitRPG.books

https://www.facebook.com/groups/LitRPGforum/

MALORY